MASEAH
MOUNTAIN

MASEAH
MOUNTAIN

JOHN THOMAS
EVERETT

Braveship
BOOKS

Aura Libertatis Spirat

MASEAH MOUNTAIN
Copyright © 2017 by John Thomas Everett

Braveship Books
www.braveshipbooks.com
Aura Libertatis Spirat

Cover Artwork & Design by Andrea Orlic

Book layout by Alexandru Diaconescu
www.steadfast-typesetting.eu

ISBN-13: 978-1-939398-88-8
Printed and bound in the United States of America

Acknowledgements

Writers of fiction are sponges. We beg, borrow and steal from anyone and anything we bump into in pursuit of creativity and entertainment, then wring ourselves out over a keyboard as required by the places and people that drive our stories. While this is relatively benign, transparent thievery, the shear amount of it I do has amassed a debt of gratitude to a wide range of family, friends, and acquaintances. My unwitting and generous contributors may never know their gifts to me, but that does not reduce my appreciation or diminish the value they have added.

Having taken the broad stroke, however, there are some very specific thanks that are also due. First, I'd like to acknowledge those of Loyola University Maryland's Sellinger School of Business and Management who recognized the need and took a chance on me in the development of my MBA elective, *Personal Effectiveness*. Preparation to teach this discipline forced me far beyond my previous conversational understanding of the topic. But, once I started in the classroom, I found that the learning had just begun. My students, going well below the surface in exploring their own lives during the course, became my real teacher. For that, I will always be grateful.

I would also offer thanks, once again, to my brother, J. Christopher Everett. In addition to his urging to keep writing, it was Chris who first introduced me to Steven Covey's *Seven Habits of Highly Successful People* years ago when we were both starting our business careers. While some may write-off Covey as "pop" social science, there is no denying the value of the emotional maturity concepts he has laid out in succinct, understandable and applicable ways. Dr. Covey was a threshold for me that sparked an interest that eventually led to other thinkers such as: Peter Drucker, W. Edwards Deming, Dale Carnegie,

Tom Peters, Tony Robbins, Deepak Chopra, Jim Collins, Steve Pavlina, John C. Maxwell, Daniel Goleman, and others.

As my writing has gained traction, I find myself continually going back to several mainstays for advice, counsel and encouragement. Foremost among these resources is my wife, Marge, who will always be my main go-to. Without priority, I must express appreciation as well to my sister Kate Warr, my smartest brother, Tim, my son John, my daughter Emily and my cousin Randy Everett. Friends who have given me regular support during the development of *Maseah Mountain* include: the Chesapeake artist Justin Woyowitz, Bill and Joanna Mammen, and my life-long cronies Mike Lent, Mike Roche and Tom Taneyhill.

Sincere thanks also goes to Lisa Cerasoli, my editor for the novel. Lisa's professionalism, skill and engaging manner proved to me the value of an excellent editor and the importance of the rules of punctuation that I obviously never learned in school.

Finally, I would be remiss in not thanking the coordinators and sponsors of the Clive Cussler Adventure Writers Competition, particularly Dirk Cussler and authors Jeff Edwards and Peter Greene of Braveship Books. Their support of *Maseah Mountain* was as satisfying as it was surprising to me and gave me, maybe for the first time, a real sense that maybe I am a writer.

We constantly seek shelter from the storm,
yet it is the storm that forms us.

Contents

PROLOGUE

The dogs were slowing. They were tired and hungry after coming so many miles, but they would have to wait for their rest, as would he. The sled was descending now, so the team should last.

They slid through a dreamlike, barren, black and white landscape under a sky of dead lead. The first blowing flakes of the oncoming storm had already begun to sting his cheeks and cover his goggles. He could also feel the wolves somewhere not far behind. They were starving and racing the weather as well.

Two miles above the Marmot Pass high country station, the huskies smelled their ravenous adversaries before they saw them. Big gray shadows ran parallel to the track, their desperation evident in the relentlessness of their pursuit. The sled's lead dog knew its business and pressed on, seemingly dragging the other dogs and the sled in its single-minded effort to move forward. The man trusted his lead, just as the dog trusted the man. The two had grown together in a lot of ways. But the other members of the team, especially the younger ones, began to lose focus, lifting their heads to watch the wolves narrowing in on them.

The mountain track took a sharp left turn around a cornice, and he was forced to a crawl to avoid the risk of losing the whole kit over a drop on his right. When he did slow, the pack was there. The alpha and three others, fire in their eyes and fangs bared, were spread across the run. He knew others would be coming up from behind for the kill. They had picked their spot well.

The lead dog knew what to do, however. It bared its own teeth and strained even harder against the harness to renew the team's speed. A less experienced, less aggressive dog might have stopped, resulting in a disastrous snarl of fur and snapping teeth as its mates plowed into its rear, and the sled into them.

The four hunters leapt aside, but only far enough to allow the team to pass. Then, with typical hobbling tactics, they attacked the hamstrings and flanks of the swing and team dogs. A snarling animal threw itself onto the man's back, nearly rocking the sled over onto its side. The wolf's fangs ripped into the heavy fur and thick leather collar of his parka, but failed to gain any real purchase. A second attacker missed the musher's leg, catching the sled's rail instead.

The man instinctively bent over sharply to his right while shifting most of his weight left, keeping the sled balanced. The mad, snarling gray mass flew off, skidded a few yards in the building snow and ice, then disappeared over the precipice. As the second ambusher attempted another dive at his calf, the man pulled a Winchester carbine and hammered the stock down on the wolf's skull.

Despite the team leader's effort, the sled slowed, as at least three of the huskies were injured and bleeding. The harness was dragging one of the swing dogs. The frantic noise of the attack, in the normally muted winter world, stood out harshly, raw and visceral.

The man braked and called to his leader to stop. The Winchester came up and barked once, and the largest of the wolves yelped in pain and began to bite at its stinging haunch. The man finished the wounded animal with a headshot. The gun's double report and the screaming of their alpha scattered the pack. They withdrew tactically to a nearby ridge, eyes riveted on the clamorous, chaotic scene below them.

The musher set the sled's snow hook and, talking quietly to his frenzied team, moved to the wounded and crying sled dogs. One had a torn throat and was bleeding out, leaving a wide crimson swathe in the white trail. The man quickly released the dead animal and dragged it away. He moved to a second dog that was bleeding heavily from a ragged gash along its left flank, its rear leg almost bitten in two. The dog was panicky and biting at everything around it. The man pulled his hunting knife, and in one deft motion, grabbed the dog's scruff and drew the blade deeply along its throat. It was a rough mercy to finish the job the wolves had started. The twitching animal was also released from the team.

The third dog was whining and favoring its right rear leg, but no blood could be seen. The man unharnessed the wounded animal and, holding the jaws, lifted it carefully. The dog was intent on the man, ready to squirm, bite, and bolt at the slightest increase in his pain. The man placed it gently in the cradle of the sled, covered it, secured it, and recovered the cargo tightly with the oilskin tarp. He moved the oldest of the team dogs to the swing and redistributed the remaining dogs in front of Butch, his powerful wheel dog. The man dragged the two dead dogs and the wolf in three bloody streaks well back behind the sled and left them. At least the remaining pack would be fed.

The musher regained the rear runners of the sled, retrieved the snow hook, and gave the order to his number one. The leader had already forgotten the attack; it was now deeply engaged in its favorite pursuit—finding out as fast as it could where the trail led. The huskies once again took up their signature call—not a bark, but somewhere between a yip and a howl. The sled slid off and continued its decent down the narrow trail, which was accumulating fresh snow rapidly. He wondered if he had stayed too long with the People this time.

The sled covered the last few miles to the remote mountain station, as the driving snow pelted the team and the temperature dropped. The peaks surrounding them had disappeared. The world was a howling, swirling box of white, and the sled had glided through it more on the instinct of dog and man than any clear path.

Finally, they slid down a sharp ridge, across a short snowfield, and up to the top of a long rise. Here, the man called a halt. He looked across the backs of the exhausted, panting, and anxious animals. He watched the breath and heat of the dogs rise into the frigid air, only to be snatched away by the swirling wind. A snippet of memory surfaced, and he recalled the steaming train that had left him on the platform those many years ago when he first arrived in this country.

Through the storm, he could just make out the straight edge of a low roofline below him. The refuge was less than a quarter of a mile away, all but invisible against the wall of a cliff. As expected, the place was unlit and well on its way to being buried in blowing snow. Still, it meant safety, warmth, food, and rest. The dogs knew it, too. He called again to his still willing leader. The team responded and the sled moved off with a lurch. The man felt his shoulder muscles begin to release some of the tension that had ridden with him since leaving the Shoshone village the day before.

He and his brother had built the Arcadian station years earlier from available stone and timber. They also had hauled a ton of rough lumber and a lot of other things up here by mule and dog. His brother knew what he was doing, so the building was sturdy, tight, and efficient. They had been smart enough to build over a spring, as well. Water flowing from a grotto in the cliff met any needs and provided enough cooling to keep food stock fresh for a while, even in the warmest summer weather.

The building was constructed in a long-bottomed "U." On one side was a small stable that could hold three horses or a dog team and enough fodder for a season. Half of the long base of the horseshoe was a sizeable work and storage room. The other half was the station's living quarters. This space held a rustic, beamed kitchen, the tamed spring, and a large wood-burning stove. A thick, braided rug covered most of a flagstone floor, and a wall of pine cabinets marched down one side of the room while a stone sink and a long granite counter ran down the opposite. A butcher's block, some worn fan-back chairs, and a heavy, scarred trestle table also were resident.

The kitchen gave way to sleeping quarters. This area, running parallel to the stable, completed the horseshoe and formed the final part of the station's three-sided paddock. A large river-stone fireplace, doubling as one of the kitchen's walls, heated the room. In front of the hearth were two overstuffed wing chairs and a sofa that had a long history of accommodating tired bodies. Here was where stories were told, a whiskey or two shared, and the fate of man pondered while staring deep into embers that shifted and tumbled into themselves below red and yellow flames.

Completing the room was a set of creaky, wooden bunks that faced a series of long windows, presently shuttered, that looked out onto a covered gallery. Beyond this porch, the view on a clear day offered towering mountain peaks that gave way to a high valley, stretching away into the distance.

The dogs brought the sled smoothly into the paddock and under the over-hang outside of the workroom. Tongue lolling, the lead turned and, with ice-blue eyes, looked at the man expectantly. The wind had grown steadily stronger, and whipped around the corners of the building, piling the snow up against walls and creating a whistling that rose and fell with its gusts.

With the sled's hook set, the man moved to the stable, unlocking and sliding open its heavy double doors. The doors moved easily on a mounted track, and again he was thankful for his brother's skills. Once the harness was detached from the sled, the man led the team into the stables. The dogs stood barking in harness while the man lit an oil lamp and filled the three roomy stalls with hay. Each animal was released into one of the two open stalls, where they milled expectantly, whining. The man hung the harness on a series of hooks along the wall in an attempt to avoid the inevitable tangle come time to run again. He placed the injured dog in a third stall by itself and closed the door. The animal was close enough to still be one of the team, but protected from the baser canine instincts when it came to weakened rivals, or even teammates.

The storm seemed to intensify its howling, and the snow, driven hard, assaulted the shutters of the stable. The interior of the shelter, while by no means warm, suited the dogs. They knew what it was like to sleep in the open cold. Once the man fed them from the dry stores kept in the stable, they began to let their fatigue take over. The dogs found tight, hay-filled corners or another husky to curl up against. It wasn't long before there was quiet.

Before his lead dog was quite asleep, the man called him to him. The team leader responded immediately, anxious to renew the unique bond between them. The man thanked his dog for its loyalty, bravery, and strength with a vigorous scratching behind furry ears and a few low, kind words. The animal's coal-black body swayed sideways with pleasure in an effort to create greater contact with its master's legs. The man straightened then, disappointing the huskie who had wanted the massage to last forever. With a chuck under the dog's chin, he grabbed the collar and led his leader back into the stall. The dog made room with a slight growl and flopped down amid three of its mates, then fell asleep.

The man retrieved his medical kit from the sled, now covered with a thick layer of snow. He reentered the stable and tended to the wounded dog. The damage, while undoubtedly painful and frightening, was not a hamstring, and would heal quickly. He unlocked the interior door that led to the workroom, then went out through the double doors, sliding them tightly closed and locking them. The animals were now safe from the coming brutality of the night.

He was cold, tired, and hungry, but there was work yet to do before he could share his team's rest. The weak evening light was rapidly fading to black. So, the man unloaded the sled, piling the snow-covered bundles under the overhang. He unlocked the wide door to the workroom and entered the dark, dry, cold, space smelling of lamp oil and wood shavings. After lighting lamps, he hefted the sled through the door and up onto two sawhorses near a substantial workbench. He would deal with it in the morning.

A well-used, wooden hand truck helped him move the contents of the sled inside. Then, he locked the workshop door securely against the now intense storm. Separating provisions from the rest, he carried them into the kitchen and closed off the workshop. His parka found a peg on the wall, as did his lined, deerskin overalls. Once he had the fire in the stove going, his boots and gloves were placed on its drying shelf. He removed a thick steak, a sizable potato, and a tub of butter from the store he brought; the rest went into the spring room.

Moving into the bunkroom, he was glad for the unwritten rule to prebuild a fire for the next user. He opened the damper and could hear the wind high up, ripping across the mouth of the chimney. With a single Lucifer match, he built a fire to a roar in the big fireplace.

The man smiled as he remembered the kindness of Joseph Bearclaw's wife, Maria, who had given him the butter he would use this evening. The thought of the rich spread melting into the potato made him very hungry. The steak was elk, which he had grown to enjoy almost as much as beefsteak. Hell, something as exotic as a well-marbled Delmonico was now just a distant memory. And for perhaps the thousandth time, he wished for a bottle of red. But that particular indulgence had been left far behind as well. There was no red wine in these mountains. He wondered why, among all that he had buried with little or no regret when he left the city, he still craved a simple glass of claret.

The place was cozy now and he was full and sleepy. He sat on one of the kitchen chairs with his stocking feet up on another. His oft-darned socks showed him yet another hole as he wiggled them at the warmth of the stove. He listened to the relentless wind and thought of his lost dogs, and the wolves, too. He was saddened by their deaths, and regretted having to do what he did. It was not just the work he had put into their training, nor was it the expense that would now be required to replace them. He had always respected life. After all, hadn't he spent much of his life practicing medicine? *"Do no harm"* had been his oath.

Many things had come clear during his time here in the high country. One of them was a certainty that the lives of animals were special—gifts, really. Each was unique and valuable, and had much to teach. Taking one of their lives was not to be treated lightly. He knew, too, that difficult choices had to be made sometimes, and that was okay, as long as there was principle and respect underlying the choice. For him, it was learning that lesson that had taken so much time.

He listened and imagined the insistent wind to be the mountains' haunting winter song. A very Shoshone sentiment, he realized, laughing at himself. Just the same, it was a melody he had learned to respect and appreciate. In his time up here, the Maseah Range and its soaring peaks had become a living force to him. Their power to create or destroy was pervasive and overwhelming. He also found them far from dispassionate, often cruel in their dispensing of life or death. Yet, there was a way that you could come to love the Maseah's peaks. The day he had begun to understand them as a much greater part of the whole than he was himself was the day he began to change.

The man pried his bones out of the chair and banked the fire in the kitchen stove. It would stay until the morning. He decided that the huskies would be asleep, and he would wait and check on them later that night. He padded across the now-warm stone floor to the sleeping area, added to the fire, and found a thick native blanket in a cedar chest. Wrapping it around himself, he settled into one of the soft, overstuffed chairs near the fire and lowered his feet onto the ledge of its raised hearth.

The storm continued its terrible rage, intensifying, then dropping off to nothing, only to pick up again to throw itself with renewed vigor against the walls of his sanctuary. The Maseah seemed to scream in frustration at its failure to tear down the sturdy, stone and timber walls, somehow knowing the man was inside and snug. Soon, he was asleep and dreaming.

CHAPTER 1

TRAGEDY AND DECISION

John Rocklan was visiting one of his patients in the University Hospital about midafternoon on the fifteenth of January, 1931, when he got the first of several requests to assist in the emergencies that found their way to the urban infirmary. A gunshot wound was bleeding all over Admitting. Before he knew it, the afternoon had become evening, evening had become night, and he was in trouble at home again. He and his wife, Helen, had just gotten past their argument over his missing their tenth anniversary two weeks ago. Now, he had done it again. This time, it was his daughter's birthday he had forgotten.

He and Helen never really argued. Rather, she did all of the talking and he pretended to listen. Usually, she went on about how he was so buried in his work that she and Lily had become just mere furniture in his tight little self-absorbed world. That wasn't quite true—he loved them both, wholeheartedly. But maybe she was right about his wanting to work all of the time. It was certainly true that he loved the hospital and the opportunity it gave him to practice what was starting to be called "emergency medicine." He couldn't find that at home, or in his staid, uptown office.

In fact, he was trying to make a point. He was trying to convince the hospital that it should take emergency medicine seriously by demonstrating the need for specialized facilities that are staffed and operated properly. He was trying to show the Board the future, but unfortunately, their accountants lived for today.

Rocklan had been practicing emergency medicine since he began. He had even written papers and a book on procedure. One of his JAMA articles offered an organizational and operational plan for an "emergency room." He had spoken on the subject frequently, was nationally recognized and was respected by his peers, although there weren't many of those in this field, even in this most medical of cities. His interest also had made him wealthy.

His father did it to him; there was no question of that. The old man, while not much of a father, was one hell of a doctor. He had come out of the trenches of Chateau Wood and the Somme in 1917 remote and selfish, but full of ideas, theories, and dreams about what could be done with severe trauma. The rest of his father's life was spent in an evangelical fervor to change the way it all worked in America.

So, his father's creed was a part of Rocklan long before he was even accepted at Maryland. He guessed that he was just carrying on the cause. That's why time got away from him so often. When he tried to explain this to Helen, she said that at some point, a son has to stop trying to gain approval from his father. Maybe that was true about him, but it was also true that he really enjoyed the steady flow of the type of down-and-dirty medicine that came through the big-city doors of University Hospital.

He had called Helen earlier to try explaining, but there wasn't anything to say except that he was sorry, and she had heard that many times before. When he asked to talk to Lily, he was told she was already in bed. The call ended in a long silence as he struggled for something to say. Eventually, all he heard was a soft click from the other end of the line.

Just before ten, things had finally quieted down and he decided that he would get a quick bite, then head home. As he scrubbed away his last patient, he thought about the gunshot victim who had died. He mentally ticked off his procedure and concluded that he had done all that was humanly possible.

Rocklan felt that he was quite good—no, great—and everyone who worked with or for him knew it. No one ever challenged him. Because of his skill, the interns anointed him with godlike status. The residents called him intimidating. The nurses were respectful and efficient, but never warm. It was his doing, he knew. He let none of them get close to him. Nor did he do anything to erode the pedestal they put him on. That took a conscious effort, given the interdependence demanded by the turmoil of emergencies. In truth, he had no idea whether anyone wanted to get close to him or not, but it mattered little. These things were not important, and he rather enjoyed the status he had achieved. He had earned some respect, he thought; it had been bought by his dedicated, groundbreaking work in a new field.

As he walked up a flight of steps on his way to the physicians' dining area of the general eatery, he thought of Helen and Lily again. She was right, of course. He hadn't been paying much attention lately to either of them. They were his life; he just didn't act that way sometimes. His work was important, damn it. His patients. This hospital. His career. It was all for them, as well. And those things demanded most of what he had to give.

Helen was not mollified by this argument, either. She called it selfish. During their last argument, she said she was living like a single mother. They were supposed to be married, she said. He was supposed to be a father and a parent, she said. She couldn't live like this anymore, she said. Then, she said she thought they should separate.

Nothing more had been mentioned over the last couple of weeks, and Rocklan hoped that the storm had blown over. He knew he needed to change, but it wasn't easy. He would do it, though, and she would feel differently. He would stop and buy flowers and a birthday cake. It wasn't much, but it was something. Maybe a start.

As he arrived at the cafeteria, he could see through its glass doors that the room was practically empty. He did spot Grace Solomon, however. She was sitting by herself, leafing through a magazine and slowly pushing something around on a plate. Rocklan considered Grace a peer, and he liked her. She was world-class talented and considered the top pediatrician in the city. It didn't hurt that she was smart, funny, and attractive, as well. She was also Helen's best friend.

"Sit down, John, you look hungry," she said, moving her things away. "I hear it's popping downstairs."

"It is. But when isn't it?" he asked, catching the eye of one of the volunteers and sitting down across from his colleague. "I've got it well under control, though."

"So says the famous, but humble doctor," she teased him.

Brushing off her jibe, he asked, "What's on the menu that's not going to kill me?"

"I suggest the meatloaf. I'm not sure what the little green things in it are, but they seem harmless enough."

"Must be the dietician's idea to cover more food groups in a single serving," he postulated. He ordered the meal with black coffee.

"The option was creamed chipped beef. Yesterday's headliner," Grace explained. "How'd the gunshot do?"

Without wondering how she knew about it, Rocklan briefed her fully, knowing that if he didn't, she would hound him until he did. Grace's medical interests and knowledge went well beyond her specialty. He didn't mind; there was probably no one better in the hospital to review procedure with, and it gave them something to talk about. Their only other common ground was Helen, and he didn't feel like talking about her. They gossiped lightly about the hospital's administration and shared some quick notes on the residents they had been assigned.

Then Grace asked, "You and Helen want to catch some dinner with Bill and me this weekend? I know where the Chincoteagues are fresh and plentiful. Maybe get back in Helen's good graces?"

Shit, he thought, *they've been talking.* It only made sense that Grace had Helen's side of his marriage. It was rare, though, that she ever said anything about it. Helen must be really angry this time.

Swallowing the last bit of meatloaf, and choosing to ignore the marital reference, Rocklan said, "You know how to set the hook, Grace. I'm in. But I have to talk to Helen." He was not going to make any social commitments for his wife, given their last conversation. "I've got to get home. I'll ask Helen to give you a call."

He stood with a small salute and headed out the door.

Rocklan almost got away when he was stopped by Mrs. Flannigan. One of the hospital's most experienced RN's, she had drawn the hospital's emergency duty and had been working with him all evening. She was someone he respected—efficient, tough, and talented. She knew, too, that he was the best around, and they worked well together.

Flannigan explained that they had gotten a call about a messy accident. The ambulance was on its way, and she could use his help. Rocklan hesitated, but only for a moment. He followed the nurse back into the hospital and into a scrub room. As he reached for a clean gown, he heard the sirens and listened to the technicians slam open the doors and the staff kick into action. Mrs. Flannigan was barking orders and people began to run. There were three patients, and it sounded bad.

He strode out into the hallway and Flannigan met him, matching his pace. She briefed him in an efficient staccato.

"Three arrivals. A man. A woman. And her daughter. Bad accident on the Old York Road. Cop said a cab and a drunk driver. The drunk died at the scene. The cabbie's banged up but okay, and the mother looks DOA. The little girl has lots of problems. She's in #2. Better start there. I'll verify the woman's status."

Rocklan nodded and swerved off into the area the hospital was using for emergency pre-op, as Flannigan continued down the hall to where the mother lay motionless on a gurney.

In Room #2, one of the better residents was quickly taking vitals while a nurse was trying to clean up the patient and prep the area around the girl's head. She was working around an intern who couldn't seem to stay out of the way.

Rocklan snapped on a pair of gloves and pointed to the intern. "You. Report to Flannigan. Now," he ordered, none too gently. "What do we have?"

The resident reported, "Head trauma, multiple fractures, arms and legs. Pulse failing rapidly."

Rocklan let his eyes run from the small figure's feet up to her battered face and blood-matted hair. As the nurse sponged the little girl's forehead, it began to sink in. The bloody, gray cloth coat. The torn yellow print dress. The blonde, almost white hair. And as the nurse swabbed the patient's brow, his daughter Lily's cornflower, blue eyes. The room spun. He reeled and lurched back against the emergency cart, which flew over, scattering metal instruments in a clatter all over the room.

The resident and nurse stared at him in shock. Then, recovering, they simultaneously refocused on the girl. The young doctor sprang into the chest massage procedure, and the nurse worked to keep the airway open. Rocklan stood catatonically, unable to fully process what he saw before him. After minutes of furious work, the eyes of the resident and the nurse met and they ceased their efforts.

They looked slowly up at Rocklan, who stared back. Then, he let out a sob and rushed to his dead daughter. Franticly, he began the chest message again, getting in three violent lurches before the resident and nurse could forcefully pull him from the girl. Rocklan struggled, letting out an animal cry, and then a simple "No, no, no!"

Together, they pulled him out into the hall, where Flannigan stood waiting for him, shaking her head. Then it hit him that there was another patient.

Helen.

He again attempted to break from the two supporting him, but Flannigan moved to him quickly and lent her strength to his restraint. He looked at her in desperation. She drew him in and held on tightly.

Rocklan didn't remember much from the ensuing days. There was a cursory investigation of the accident. There were arrangements, a funeral, and burials. In-laws arrived, cried and said things he couldn't process. There were lots of flowers and well-wishers that came with them. The hospital had granted him a leave that he never asked for or even thought about. His mother had called from California, but couldn't leave her latest man-friend, for reasons he couldn't remember. He felt like he was reading a trite novel that would have to end at some point.

Weeks after the accident, he sat alone in his study with nothing but the hollow independence that was once so cherished. Now, it was only acidic and condemning. He no longer thought of the hospital, his patients, his reputation, or anything that drove him prior to that night. He thought only of his loss and what could have been—what should have been.

Helen and Lily had been packed; their suitcases were in the cab. They were going to her parent's place. She was leaving him.

He had loved them, but he had done little to show them that. He felt now that he didn't deserve their devotion; yet, they both had given it to him. So, there was guilt, of course, and he let his self-flogging sustain him for a time. But even that eventually faded into the fabric of the life he was left with—the pain never leaving, always there, but now just part of who he was, rather than the focus of this new, pathetic existence.

After a few months, he was very alone. Grace had even stopped calling. When she sent her husband, Bill, to bang on his door, Rocklan left the man standing at the front door until he eventually went away. The hospital had run interference, so no one else sought him out or asked his advice. He recognized no responsibilities or obligations to anyone, even himself. He was content to drift in this self-centered sea. Sometimes, he would just sit, often not even bothering to get up to turn on the lights as evening and night came. Occasionally, he found something to eat. Sometimes, he would pour a hefty tumbler of scotch. But most times, the pre-Prohibition whiskey sat untouched. He wasn't interested in drowning his sorrows; he wasn't interested in wallowing in them, either. He was simply treading water.

At some point, he began to think about the flimsy life he had built. It never seemed to be gratuitous, but it did now. His skills, his contributions, his reputation, his family life, his friends, his money—all felt immaterial and gauzy, teetering, a stack of baby's blocks before the crash. He recalled the many patients he had put back together or whose pain he had eased, and he saw nothing but futility. He had been doing no more than pouring seawater into a hole on the beach.

As far as his marriage went, he had botched it utterly. There was no way to make amends. Even if he could, he doubted whether he now had the courage and resolve to do anything about it. So, his plan was to sit in his study until something happened.

It eventually did. It came in the form of an idea born of loss and guilt. The idea was to escape, to erase what was. He wouldn't rebuild; he would just be someone else. Not here—somewhere else. The thought was to obliterate the past as much as possible, to go somewhere unknown, to be someone no one knew. It would be a different model, one that would allow him to avoid investment in whatever he did and whomever he encountered.

It all began to take shape as he stared at the cover of a back issue of *National Geographic*, serving as a coaster for his barely-touched drink. Through sweat rings, he focused on the issue's main photo essay—"The Rockies." Inside, he found the new world he was seeking. It was a world of no boundaries—majestic, remote, forbidding, and foreign. It was not a place for most humans. It was crowded, however, with unnamed peaks, snaking, whitewater rivers, and hidden lakes. Bears, wolves, and mountain lions ruled this elevated realm. True, it was the domain of the Shoshone, the Nez Pierce, and the Paiute, according to the travel writer. But he saw its solitude as unchallenged. He envisioned that the white men who did tramp this alien universe had names like Jim Bridger, Kit

Carson, and Jedidiah Smith. It would require him to be someone he never was. It could allow him to forget the man he once was.

The idea served the growing imperative to flee the sad life he had built. He would not be the first seeking a new start in the American West. And it was 1931, after all. Why not? What could be lost that was of any value to him? Who was there to care one way or the other?

It took Rocklan some time to stir himself. Once moving, however, he launched into a frenzy of activity. He dealt with bankers, lawyers, accountants, real estate agents, executors, and hospital administrators. Documents received signatures and debts were paid, accounts consolidated, estates settled, and property bought and sold. By the time he was finished, a year had passed, and he was no longer a physician in an urban metropolis. Instead, he was an independently wealthy owner of a ranch in the high country of something called the Bitterroot Mountains in the great state of Idaho.

He talked to no one of his plans. He just didn't want to explain his logic, if there was any to it. He also feared that an explanation wouldn't pass the red face test. So, he would simply disappear to a three-thousand-acre mountain ranch that he bought from a realtor's photographs. He had hired hands and ordered supplies through a local agent. The help would run the place and teach him what he needed to know. His money would do the rest; at least there was plenty of that. He had always been in fair shape, and he was good with his hands. It wouldn't be easy physically, he knew, but he wasn't looking for easy—just a hiding place.

Chapter 2

Into Idaho

Rocklan stepped off the train in Idaho Falls in late October of 1932, amidst steam that hung in dry, cold air. He stood under a porcelain blue sky and stared across a ponderosa pine and scrub landscape to a distant, gray line of mountains. The station and its platform buzzed with activity. Beaver hats with flaps, dull, checked wool coats, and thick fur boots moved among others wearing long tan dusters and Stetsons. Bags, trunks, and crates were hefted onto steel-wheeled carts and pushed to the edge of the platform, where men with faces creased by the sun and wind loaded horse-drawn wagons and a few battered Ford and Chevy trucks. They worked silently and soberly.

Rocklan directed his bags to be stacked against the wall of the reception room. He entered the station house to verify that the majority of his effects, shipped weeks earlier, had arrived and had been forwarded. He also wanted to find the car and driver he had arranged to take him the three hundred miles north up into the mountains, to the town of Blackbird.

Heat and fumes from a large wood-burning stove hit him as he pushed through the doors. He scanned past the ticketing office, baggage claim, a lunch counter, and knots of travelers. Eventually, he spotted a man with a clipboard and a stationmaster's cap who seemed to be directing the flow of work. He made his way around and through the noisy activity to the man.

Without preamble, he interrupted the busy official. "My name is Rocklan, and I want to check on arrangements to get me and my things to Blackbird."

The master checked his clipboard and responded in an efficient and friendly way. "Ah, yes. Mr. Rocklan. We've been expecting you. All is as it should be.

Your trunks are waiting for you in Blackbird, being held by the real estate man up there. Hawkins is his name, I believe."

"Good," responded Rocklan without the same friendliness. "Transportation and a driver were also to be provided. I'd like to leave as soon as possible."

The stationmaster looked at him for a long moment, stroked a long drooping mustache, then said, "All arranged. Your driver came in on the same train as you did, but he had to go into town to get a truck. Should be about an hour or so. I'll find you when he gets back."

"An hour or so?" Rocklan asked. "I can see the town from the platform. What could take so long? And I ordered a car, not a truck."

"Mister, welcome to Idaho," said the master. "Better get used to a change. It'll be easier on you. There's a bar about twenty yards out that door." He pointed. The man's initial amiability was gone. He turned away to other business.

Rocklan stood, frustrated with the lack of deference from the busy stationmaster and unsure what to do next. He heard the conductor out on the platform calling "All aboard!" The train let out a scream from its whistle. A man leapt from a room marked "Gents" and bolted through the station doors, jostling Rocklan hard as he passed him. Through the windows, Rocklan watched the late passenger swing up onto the iron steps of the train as it began its slow roll away from Idaho Falls.

He turned back and decided he wasn't hungry. So, he looked for a place to sit, and found a long bench in front of the wood-burning stove. He made his way over to it, sat, and pulled out his itinerary. He was alone for a few minutes, until a family joined him, forcing him to the edge of the bench. Local Indians, he surmised, as he inched away from a very fat woman wrapped in a blanket and settling down beside him. The woman smelled of old wool and bacon grease. Other adults filled the remaining space on the bench.

Rocklan looked up from his papers and met the eyes of the family's two children, a boy and a girl, sitting on the floor, staring intently at him. He stared back, determined not to be intimated by these little savages. This game continued until he decided that, between the woman next to him and the stove, it was too hot in the station. He rose nonchalantly, and the children immediately pushed past him into the vacated spot next to their mother.

Eventually, his general dissatisfaction with his situation pointed him to the bar outside. Rocklan was surprised that there was a bar at all. Hadn't they heard of the 18th Amendment and the Volstead Act out here? He was used to knocking on doors with sliding peepholes to get a drink.

It wasn't much—a big, unmarked tent being used as a saloon. He threw back the flap and entered, sliding past three men dressed in dark, stained overalls over faded red Union Suits. They sat at the only table and chairs, a rickety set made by a carpenter of dubious skill. Beyond, he found six low stools lined up in front of a long sawhorse and plank table covered in a stained tarp. Rocklan took a seat. As he did, the three men quickly rose, stuffed their glasses into pockets, and left the bar, muttering. Four stools down from him, the bartender was setting a shot glass of clear liquid and a fat brown bottle of local beer down in front of a bent old man, the only other customer in the saloon. The old man snatched up the shot glass and threw its contents into the back of his throat. He grabbed the bottle and took a swig, then gave Rocklan a nasty, fuck-you kind of look. He too rose and left the bar, taking the beer with him.

"Bartender, I'd like a bottle of beer. What kind do you have?" Rocklan asked a thin rail of a man in a leather apron, now standing well behind the makeshift bar. His hand was on the edge of a flap in the rear of the tent. He looked leery of Rocklan, and watched him with some expectation.

"You are the bartender, aren't you?"

The man didn't move. "No, sir. I'm no bartender, and we don't have any kind of beer here. Idaho has been a Temperance state since 1916."

"What? I just saw you serve that old man," Rocklan said with some acid. He looked to where the customer had sat, but the shot glass was gone.

"No, sir. That was just Jim Longo. All the miners come in here to rest between shifts," explained the boney man. "I give them a drink of water and a soda pop, if I have one."

"That old geezer was no miner, and it wasn't soda pop he was drinking."

"Yes, sir, it sure was. The miners all look like that. I ain't lying. I got to go now, sorry."

With that, the former bartender was out the back flap.

Rocklan sat there and wondered what had just happened. He also wondered where his driver was. He rose and left the tent, only to be stopped by a couple of ugly specimens as he emerged.

"You a cop?" asked the larger and paunchier of the two.

"What?" asked Rocklan, not sure of the question.

"You heard me. You a cop?" repeated the man.

"No, I—"

"You a Temperance man?" interrupted the taller, stringier of the pair.

"I don't know what you're talking about," Rocklan replied.

"No?" asked the first man. "Then why'd you shut down our little business? You cost us some income."

With that, the heavier man slammed a fist into the bridge of Rocklan's nose. The traveler staggered back, tripping over a rope that secured the tent to a peg driven into the ground. He fell hard to the dirt, blood from his nose spattering in a broad arc.

Before he could rise, the two locals had him under the arms and up on his feet again.

"He ain't no cop. He's just some fool come out here from the East. I think he owes us the drink money from them chickens that beat it."

Again, the man swung at his face. This time, Rocklan slumped and turned his head away and down. The punch landed forcefully on the neck of the thinner man, who was driven into the side of the tent. The bigger thug quickly pinned Rocklan's arms from behind.

"Damn, Jeter, that hurt," whined the other man, picking himself up, then hammering his fist into Rocklan's solar plexus.

Rocklan was down again, and the two moved in to deliver a few well-placed kicks.

"That'll be all, boys," said a hard voice from behind them. "Leave the man alone."

The two bootleggers turned to see who dared to stop their amusement and stared at a big, bronze-skinned man wearing a sheepskin coat, a Winchester twelve gauge side-by-side dangling from his right arm.

The thugs moved away from Rocklan and separated. Slight smiles on their slack faces, they confronted the new man and began rocking on the balls of their feet.

"Rodney, we going to let some filthy Paiute tell us what to do?" asked the larger man.

"Shoshone," said the man with the gun.

"We don't care what kind of Indian you are. You're interrupting our business," said the wiry man. Ignoring the shotgun, the two bullies took a step toward the interloper.

With the bootleggers now close, without warning, the Shoshone took a hard grip on the fore end of his double with his left hand and jerked the stock upward with his right. The butt of the gun connected solidly with the chin of the taller man, driving his lower jaw forcefully into his upper molars and creating an audible clack, like a dog just missing a bone. The thug's eyes rolled up and away, and he crumpled in a heap in the dirt.

Before the bigger man could react, the toe of Rocklan's new mountain boot came up from the ground and connected with the soft material between the legs of the goon. The man bent over in pain, staggered away toward the tent, and began to vomit.

"Do you think that was fair?" asked Rocklan's defender, helping him up.

The Easterner was not amused by the man's humor. At this point, Rocklan thought of everyone in Idaho Falls as primitive and stupid. He was about to say so when the stationmaster walked up.

"Mr. Rocklan, I see you've met Eli, your driver. My men put your bags in the truck, and you're set to go. Sign here." Then he turned to the larger bootlegger. "Jeter, you need to move on. You've been providing a service, but you've worn out your welcome. Pick up your boy there. You've got twenty minutes before I call Sheriff Langley."

With that, he turned away, checking his clipboard.

The truck was actually a Willys Overland 91 touring car, only about ten years old, but its life had been hard. The original black paint could be seen in spots, but rust seemed to be the dominant color. It had both of its headlamps, but a stone had shattered one. The windshield sported a horizontal crack, and the wheels were missing the odd wooden spoke. The tires were round, but that's about all that could be said for them, or the spare hanging from the back. The ragtop was discolored, torn in several places, and pulling away from its framework. The front bench seat was covered in crazed leather, not quite holding in all of its springs and stuffing. The backseat was jammed with Rocklan's bags and a good deal of other cargo he didn't recognize. Boxes and bundles were also tied to both running boards, forcing the travelers to enter through the glassless windows. It was going to be a very cold ride—assuming the thing started.

The driver walked into the station house, then emerged with a spare five-gallon can of gasoline and a damp towel that he handed to Rocklan, who was dealing with his bloody nose. The Easterner took the cloth without thanks and turned away. The Shoshone strapped the can to the last available space on the running board. Then, with a sarcastically gracious bow and wave of his arm, Eli bade his passenger board their coach.

Rocklan was highly skeptical about this, and felt the man's mockery. He held his tongue, however, and climbed into the car. Eli reached into the cab, set the brake, and shifted into neutral. He lifted the lever to retard the spark, lowered the throttle lever, and adjusted the mixture. He asked Rocklan to hold the choke out while he moved to the front of the Willys and gave the crank two turns. Directing his passenger to release the choke and turn the ignition, he gave the crank another turn. The vehicle backfired loudly and began to shake violently. Rocklan's eyes bobbled in his head until the beast died. Eli repeated the procedure, and on the second try managed to get the touring car to settle down into a noisy idle. He climbed in, gave his traveling partner a broad grin, released the brake, and they were off. Rocklan said nothing, knowing he needed this man and glad to be leaving Idaho Falls under any means of transportation.

CHAPTER 3

INTO THE MOUNTAINS

Eli and Rocklan drove away from the train station, straight as an arrow for two hours, across the lowlands of scrub pine, spiny ground cover, and mottled earth to the foothills of the Bitterroot. As they closed on the mountains, the indistinct gray line morphed into a series of peaks with saddles between them. One of the indentations became a fold in the wall that earlier had seemed unbroken. There, they would find the road up into the mountains and the town of Blackbird.

The landscape was undergoing a dramatic change as the afternoon sun began to drop. October's reds, rusts, and yellows flamed from the oaks, maples, honey locusts, and black walnuts they rambled through. A river ran swift and cold on their right. The temperature was dropping, but the sky remained clear.

Neither of the men had spoken for the first two hours of the ride. Finally, Rocklan's interest in their direction and the time it would take to cover the three hundred miles got the better of him.

"How long to Blackbird?" he asked Eli over the engine noise.

"Oh, I'd say we should reach there sometime tomorrow evening," was the shouted reply.

Rocklan was more than surprised that it would take them twenty-four hours to cover the distance, and it showed in his face.

After a minute, Eli explained, "It's a steep climb. The road's not great, and driving this thing in the dark is dangerous."

"You mean we're not going all the way through tonight?" Rocklan bawled back, unhappy about the prospect of spending the night in the car.

The driver nodded. "That's right. We've got to stop."

The gathering of information in dribs and drabs from this taciturn Indian was annoying Rocklan. The noise wasn't helping, either. He wanted to know what lay ahead and what he could expect, and he didn't want to have to pull teeth to get answers.

"Look," he yelled, "I need to know what you have in mind. I have no idea who you are. Or what your agenda is. I want to know what's in front of me. So, I'd like a little more detail. Please." His last word had an edge.

Eli turned and considered Rocklan. "Well, since you said 'please,' I'll tell you."

The Shoshone watched his passenger get further annoyed and said in a half-bellow, "Blackbird sits atop a high ridge. It's not an easy drive, even in daylight. Too cold tonight to stay in the car. We'll stop at a friend of mine's place. He's expecting us. We'll go another two hours, following the Salmon River there. Once we get up into the foothills, we'll stop. In two hours, we won't be able to see anything anyway."

That much information constituted a speech from the man, and Rocklan was grateful for it, but the plan just served to raise additional questions.

"Okay, we're stopping. Tell me about this friend. And what's all this extra stuff we're carrying?"

Rocklan had never been a very trusting man. He was traveling up into unknown mountains; he was with a man he didn't know—an Indian at that; and they were going to make an unscheduled stop. All of this made the Easterner very uneasy.

"My friend is a Shoshone. A brother. Lives at a crossroads up here, where the middle fork of the Salmon comes in. Operates a Texaco. Lives there with his family. The gear is mine."

"Why am I hauling your gear?" hollered Rocklan, attempting to establish some sense of who was in charge.

Eli formed a small smile and shouted back, "You're not. I'm giving you a ride and hauling your gear. I'm on my way home. I was told you needed a ride."

This news kept Rocklan quiet.

"By the way, my name is Eli Whiteley," offered the driver. "I'm the son of the man you bought the ranch from." Then, he too fell silent.

Lying must be a way of life out here, thought Rocklan. While he had never actually seen the ranch, his attorney had done the background work necessary to be sure that it was a legal sale. The former owner, Pendleton E. Whiteley, a

Connecticut physician and businessman, was at one time the U.S. Ambassador to Australia. Dr. Whiteley was well known and well respected, amassing a sizable fortune, before retiring early and disappearing into these mountains. As far as anyone knew, he had never married and there was no record of children. And he was certainly no Shoshone.

Rocklan let the Indian's comment go, and chewed on what he knew about the ranch for the next few miles. It was a very large piece of property, but isolated. It was another twenty or thirty miles beyond Blackbird into the heart of the Bitterroots, and anyone who lived there had to be practically self-sustaining. Trips into the hamlet of Blackbird would be rare, and even then, the town could offer only the basic necessities if and when they were available. The property itself had little to recommend it. It was within a huge swath of protected national forest. For that reason, it was mostly undeveloped, except for a few Indian villages that had been there forever. How Whiteley got permission to buy the land and build a ranch was unclear, but the man had been well-connected in his day.

The land was home to soaring mountains, pristine meadows, and the occasional stream-fed lake. There was little wonder that it had been on the market for so long. Human habitation would be difficult, and further development unlikely. Summers were short; winters were long and unforgiving. Roads were either dirt or nonexistent, and the staples of modern life, like electricity, medical care, and sanitation, were abstract ideas.

Dr. Whiteley had spent a good portion of his fortune on the ranch itself. In one of the property's large, high meadows, nestled among the crags, he had built and maintained a large Western ranch house. An even larger barn held a workshop, stables, and ranch equipment, and provided plenty of storage. Fence and a series of smaller, functional outbuildings ran away from the barn to the fields and pastures that made up the rest of the lofty valley. It must have been hugely expensive to transport the materials needed to construct his lonely enclave. But it was all done with quality, and with the harshness of the environment in mind. The recluse seemed to have everything he needed. The fact that he had lived there for forty years was fair proof of it. The house did have some age, and supposedly, it had been vacant for a while, but Rocklan had been assured that the place was ready for immediate occupancy.

It certainly was more than he needed, and it was doubtful that he would use much more than the house. If there were animals, they would have to go. But he had set out on his chosen path, and he would see it through. It really made little difference anyway whether the place worked out or not. If it didn't, so what? He had nothing to lose, except for one thing—his memory. And he was hoping that this self-imposed, solitary confinement would help him to forget.

After a while, the Willys's laboring drew to a temporary end as they struggled over one more rise and the dim lights of a Texaco Service Station came into view. To call it a service station was a clear overstatement. A battered clapboard house and attached office with a single pump standing under a sagging overhang was their destination. In the fading light, Rocklan could see a dirt yard, populated with rusting automotive parts stacked against a tall, gray, plank fence. A number of fifty-gallon drums, several stacks of worn tires, the blowtorched bed of a Ford pickup truck, and an ancient Model T up on blocks completed the perfect vignette of the Great Depression in 1932.

A family of six—two adults and four kids—sprang from the house, calling and waving frantically as the travelers rolled into the yard and up to the pump under the station's overhang. The engine of the touring car died, punctuating its arrival with a deafening backfire. And because Eli thought the Willys's brakes were a bit soft, he stomped on them hard and got surprised by their efficiency. The result was a rather sudden stop that threw Rocklan against the windshield, giving his forehead a solid thump.

Their hosts ran to them, arms wide and voicing various greetings. As Eli climbed out of the contraption, he was swarmed under by the children, hugged by their mother, and clasped warmly by his friend.

The children climbed all over the Willys, and the woman leaned into the car with a big, welcoming smile, and said something to Rocklan. He didn't hear what she said, because the last four hours of engine noise had destroyed his ability to hear anything below a scream. He was watching a silent movie, and it gave him an otherworldly feeling that was both disconcerting and disorienting. He hadn't noticed his auditory handicap during the last two hours, because he and Eli hadn't spoken. But now, as he watched the moving lips of this woman and saw, but didn't hear, the boisterous kids, he felt incapacitated, rooted to the cracked leather seat, in need of assistance. The crack on his head and his sore nose didn't help matters, either.

The woman looked back at Eli, who said something into her ear. They both laughed heartily at whatever joke was told. Before Rocklan could protest, they were helping him to climb out of the Willys. Propping him up like an invalid,

Eli and his friend walked Rocklan past the station's office and into the adjacent house. The woman was gathering the children and hurriedly taking a flapping pair of overalls down from a sagging clothesline that was strung in the yard. The wind had come up, and it felt colder.

Rocklan's head and ears began to clear as they sat him on a big, comfortable sofa covered in a pattern that fit the West and its mountains. The interior of the home was quite a bit different from the impression left by the exterior. He was in a homey living room that someone clearly had taken pains to decorate with warmth and welcome in mind. Family pictures covered the walls, and a fine oil painting of a horseman, riding a high mountain meadow, hung over an old stone fireplace. The small fire crackled quietly, and hinted that the wood being burned was cedar. The last of the day's light could be seen through a set of broad windows that looked out over a trim, fenced-in backyard. Under the windows was an ancient oak sideboard that held tribal crafts made by young hands. Among these treasures, a framed photo of a proud chieftain was given a place of honor.

The children bounced on the sofa next to Rocklan, oblivious to his jangled state. They pelted him with whatever questions occurred to them, and even attempted to climb into his lap until their father chased them off the furniture. He could see their mother busying herself with setting a broad table for supper in a large, well-organized kitchen. The smell of stew and fresh-baked bread engulfed the house and made him realize how hungry he was.

"Bobby, this is the man who bought the ranch, John Rocklan. Mr. Rocklan, this is my good friend, Bobby St. Cloud."

St. Cloud picked up his guest's hand and shook it vigorously.

"Nice to meet you, John. Or is it Jack? In the kitchen is my wife Margarite. Her stew is a special treat," said the man, enjoying his rhyme.

The woman reacted with pain to her husband's humor, but gave Rocklan the same broad, sweet smile that she did outside. "And it's ready anytime you are," she called. Then to the kids, "Come on now, get in your seats. Remember what I told you about guests. Did you wash your hands?"

Rocklan stood. He was determined not to be cowed by the situation, but mostly he was drawn by the smell of the meal. They took places around a large, rectangular oak table with benches. Margarite began filling their bowls with a ladle that she dipped into a steaming yellow crock. The children were already rooting around in the covered basket of crusty bread and stabbing at two fat lumps of butter that stood on a flowered plate. Bobby poured glasses of cold apple cider.

Rocklan tested the hot stew in front of him, then dipped into his bowl, extracting a spoonful. He blew across the pieces of meat, potato, carrot, onion, and pea, then tasted it fully. It was a special treat, just as Bobby had promised. One of the children handed him the heel of a loaf.

"Louis, give Mr. Rocklan the soft part of the bread. He's our guest," chided the boy's mother.

Rocklan found his voice. "No, no, Mrs. St. Cloud, please call me John. This is wonderful. In fact, this stew is wonderful—the best I've ever tasted. The beef is so tender. Delicious! Thank you very much for having me tonight," he said, showing the first sign of simple grace since he arrived.

"It's elk," corrected one of the little girls.

"You are most welcome, of course, John," said the hostess. "Please, call me, Margarite. Any friend of Eli's is a friend of Bobby's and mine. Right, Bobby?"

That got a wry look out of Eli. Bobby was busy with the stew, but nodded vigorously.

One of the kids said, "And he's my friend, too."

The boy sharing the bench with Rocklan said, "Mister, you have a purple lump on your head. A big red nose, too."

"Thomas, that's rude!" scolded a sister, only a little older. She obviously had been assigned to keep an eye and ear on Thomas. "He can't help it if he's got a lump on his head."

That drew the entire table's attention to the angry mound between Rocklan's eyes. Bobby and Margarite simultaneously asked Rocklan if he had hit his head, if it hurt, was he alright, did he want some headache powders? Eli began talking to one of the children to hide a grin.

Rubbing the lump with his hand while chewing a tender piece of elk, Rocklan assured them that it was nothing.

The conversation swirled, as it does in families—Bobby and Eli exchanging news, Margarite needing to know how long Eli would stay, appreciation for the great dinner, more impertinent questions and observations from the children. Rocklan was content for the moment, occasionally keeping up his end of the conversation when he had to, but mostly focusing on the stew and the bread that made wonderful sopping. Eventually, he slid back on the bench and let it all wash over him. He was exhausted and began to nod. His drift into sleep was abruptly halted, however, as the children scrambled away from the table, excited after Eli had surprised them with gifts that he had brought.

"Margarite, Bobby, you'll have to excuse me," Rocklan said. "I'm beat. Can I trouble you for a flat place to lie down?"

"Oh, no. Please don't leave us. Not yet," pleaded his hostess. Margarite had been waiting for her chance. She had prepared her question carefully. She knew Bobby told her not to ask it and that he would be unhappy. But she had to know, so she asked.

"John, before you go, Eli said you bought the Whiteley ranch and he's taking you up there now. Tell me, what are you going to do with the place?" she asked innocently, ignoring the glare from her husband.

"Margarite, what he's going to do with the ranch is his business," suggested Eli. "Now, don't be quizzing him."

"No, it's okay, Eli," said Rocklan. "I don't really know what I'm going to do. I'll know better when I see the place. Right now, all I need is to be alone."

He watched a look pass between Bobby and Margarite.

"You want to be alone?" she asked with some concern.

Bobby stood and said, "Now, the man said he was tired, honey. Let's us give him a little bit of a break." He put his arm on Rocklan's shoulder. "You're in the second bedroom, and it's all ready for you. I'll show you." He steered him in that direction.

Margarite had already pressed it, so with a sigh, she let things drop and began to herd the children to their own beds. A young girl asked, "Mama, do I have to sleep with those boys tonight?" Her tone signaled a huge sacrifice.

Rocklan soon found himself stretched comfortably and seeking sleep. The kids had quieted and the room was dark. But sleep wasn't coming easily. And when he discovered that he could hear the conversation in the kitchen quite plainly, the opportunity for shuteye fled.

"Look, I'm sorry, baby. But I need to know," said the feminine voice among the sounds of dishes clattering.

"Honey, we all want to know. How do you think Eli feels?"

"I feel fine. It's not my ranch, never was. It's now his to do whatever he wants with it. It will be nice to see it one more time, but I'm going further up to spend some time with Red Cloud's people."

"I don't blame you," said Bobby. "Things are pretty rough down here. The crash has hurt everybody. Nobody has anything anymore, including us. What was it like in Chicago?"

"Real bad there, too. Did some interesting work on the Wrigley Building before I got let go. But there's no work for engineers. No work anywhere. Huge demonstrations in the city. People are angry and hungry. The Democrats nominated Franklin Roosevelt from New York over Al Smith. Rich and intellectual. Maybe he's got an answer," said Eli without conviction.

"Cubs won the pennant last year, though," offered Bobby with a weak smile. The clink of two whiskey glasses was heard.

"Eli, how can you be so offhand about this? What about Susan and all of the People?" asked Margarite.

"That might be all over now, my friend. Nothing stays the same. How are you all doing?" Eli knew that his friends had sacrificed to treat their guests well.

"We're fine. We're fine," answered Bobby, passing the question off.

"Well," said Margarite, standing and making signs of her own retirement to bed. "You better work this out, Eli. It's important. I'll leave you two to talk." She kissed them both and disappeared.

Rocklan listened a little while longer to their talk of old friends and days in the mountains together. Eventually, the drone of the men's voices allowed him to nod off.

Chapter 4

Blackbird

When they finally said goodbye to the St. Clouds, it was raining and cold. A thin sheet of ice had formed on the auto parts and other casual decorations in the front yard. Margarite's hot breakfast was a distant memory when Eli managed to restart the touring car after three tries. A set of tire chains was borrowed, in case they were needed higher up. Then, Eli fished a heavy blanket and two rubber ponchos out of the baggage. He even found the car's near-useless window flaps and mounted them as best he could in the roof's rusted and bent track intended for that purpose. Not all of the weather would come in on them—just most of it.

Eli doubled back to give Bobby one last thump on the back and Margarite a hug, while slipping an envelope into her apron pocket. Rocklan wondered whether he too should have left something.

They lurched out of the yard and splashed onto the macadam road, taking the fork that led up. What followed were ten hours of freezing, white knuckled motoring. The noise of the Willys and the chattering of their teeth made conversation nearly impossible. When they eventually had to mount the tire chains, conversation was precluded altogether. Twice, they skidded off the road. Once, a man with an ancient tractor assisted them. The second time, a tree stopped their slide, doing damage to the right front fender and knocking off the broken headlamp. Rocklan's pushing was enough to get them back on the track that time. But an hour from Blackbird, they skewed sideways in an attempt to avoid hitting a fallen limb. This time, the running board was bent upward, forcing the baggage tied to it to block Rocklan's window exit. Eli used an axe on the limb to get them on the way again.

The late day had little left when they honed in on the lights of Blackbird. Their timing was good, since they had poured the last of the gas into the tank some miles back. The weather had turned from freezing rain into light snow as they climbed the mountain road to the town on the ridge. Eli found a covered garage behind the *Edgar Allan Poe Motor Lodge and Lounge* and pulled the Willys to a stop. Hunched over and shaking, they made their way through the backdoor of the lodge.

A fire, a whiskey, and a room were needed. But the lobby's hearth was cold, and it was no surprise to either man that the bar was closed permanently. Damn Prohibition. There were rooms available, however—again, no surprise, since the burg looked deserted. Before long, Rocklan was in a room by himself, buried under every sheet and blanket he could scrounge.

By morning, the snow had stopped, but fog had settled in. Warmer air had made the world gray and claustrophobic. The sun was only a smear. As he stared out of the window of a diner he and Eli had found, Rocklan saw Blackbird as the negative of an old photograph. Snow bled down the street, black-stained and melting. Everything was slowly dripping—trees, buildings, street signs. If they were in the mountains, Rocklan couldn't tell it. The town's dour appearance made him wonder why anyone would choose to live there.

"I've got to see a man named Hawkins," he explained to Eli. "He's got the rest of my stuff, and I've got some final papers to sign. He's arranged for supplies and their transport. Supposed to have hired some temporary help for the ranch, too. Should be finished around ten. What are your plans?"

Eli had completed his mission in getting the traveler to Blackbird, and Rocklan expected them to part ways once they arrived. The Indian seemed to be a competent sort—more than he expected. But Rocklan didn't like the man much, and didn't really care what his plans were.

"I'm taking you up to the ranch," said Eli. "It's on my way, and I'm getting paid for it."

"On your way? I understand that there's nothing up there but the ranch."

Eli ignored the observation and added, "If you're not finished here until ten, we'll be waiting until the morning to go."

"What? Are you saying we have to waste the day and another night here?"

"Help yourself finding another guide," answered the Shoshone. Eli was just as tired of this man as Rocklan was of him.

"Wait a minute," said the Easterner, realizing that finding another ride might be difficult. "Why do we have to wait until morning?"

It was Eli's turn to look out of the window at the dirty snow forming puddles in the rutted road of the sad town. Then he turned and gave Rocklan a hard eye.

"Look, I understand that it's not easy being dependent upon another man. But you're a babe in these woods, and you're just going to have to get used to that fact."

He knew he had hit the white man where it hurt. It was time for a dose of reality. So Eli continued, "You need to realize that our little trip has just started. That Willys stays. We go by wagon from here. Twenty-three miles, most of it up. You capable of doing that yourself?"

Rocklan just stared.

"If we leave at ten, we won't get there by dark," lectured Eli. "We'd be caught in the mountains with no shelter. It's supposed to snow, and the wolves are active this time of year. You do want to make it in one piece, don't you?"

The Indian's question stunned him. John Rocklan had depended on no one for a very long time. It was precisely this sense of helplessness that made him so edgy. The mention of wolves scared him. He knew that wild animals would be a part of this world, but he never thought about them being a part of his personal world. The realization that they would now play a role in his decisions was startling.

"Why don't you go see your man?" Eli continued. "He'll fill you in on a number of particulars. Get your papers signed. I'll take care of the gear, the wagon, and the horses and meet you back at the lodge around dinner. I've got some people to see."

The Indian rose, threw some small bills on the table, and pulled on his heavy sheepskin coat. "By the way, if all you've got is that thing you're wearing, you might want to visit the general store down the street. If they have heavy parkas, get one of those. Better gloves, too."

With that, the man walked out of the diner.

Clyde Hawkins was a grinning, weasely sort. Again, Rocklan was forced to rely upon someone he didn't trust. The real estate broker was fiftyish, yet he was spotted with acne that spread from his weak chin up into his thinning hair. It was difficult to assess the man's roots, given his olive complexion in this world of tanned and red men. "Hawkins" couldn't be the name he started out with in life. This too was disconcerting to Rocklan, who thought he had begun to figure out the people he had encountered in Idaho.

They sat together in a small office of mismatched furniture. A framed picture of Herbert Hoover in his stiff collar hung on the wall. Next to it was a high school diploma. Hawkins was generously offering his political opinions.

"And Roosevelt will lose. Hoover is too entrenched, and has spent to be sure he serves another term. As I think about it, Roosevelt is pretty rich, too. Well, like I always say: Politics has become so expensive that it takes a lot of money even to be defeated."

"Will Rogers," said Rocklan.

"Huh?"

"Will Rogers. It was Will Rogers who said that," corrected Rocklan. "Look, Mr. Hawkins, can we get to why I'm here? I understand you have some documents I have to sign."

"Yes, yes, of course, Mr. Rocklan," said Hawkins as he began pulling files from his desk drawer. "In this town, I'm the chief cook and bottle-washer. I do some real estate, I do some legal work, and I usually can get most things folks need. Got to do what you can in these times. Yes, indeed. By the way, you sure have gotten a bargain on the Whiteley place. Yes, sir. Prettiest spread around."

"Have you seen the property?" asked Rocklan.

"Well, no, I haven't, but lots of folks say—"

"Look, can we get to the papers I have to sign? There are some other things I need to know, as well." Rocklan was impatient with the agent, despite the fact he now had a whole day to kill.

Hawkins stopped grinning and said, "It's all here, ready for signature. But before we go any further, you owe me for the supplies and the other arrangements I made." As long as this guy was going to be a shit, Hawkins was going to make sure he got paid first.

Rocklan set his checkbook on the desk between them. "You'll get yours, but not before you fill in a few blanks," he said.

"Those checks good? No offense, but like I said, these are hard times," said Hawkins.

"Same bank that cleared the advance I sent you," answered Rocklan. Another time, he might have taken offense. But now, all he wanted to do was get on with it and get away from this parasitic man.

Hawkins put an array of documents in front of his client. Rocklan signed them faster than the real estate broker could explain what they were.

"You told me the place was ready to move into," started Rocklan. It was his disrespect for the agent that formed his questions into statements.

"It is. Fully furnished. Old Dr. Whiteley left everything. As we all do." Hawkins grinned at his worn joke.

"The name on the ownership transfer document didn't say 'Whiteley,' it said 'State of Idaho.'"

"Well, when Dr. Whiteley died, he had no will that anyone could find and no record of surviving blood relatives. The state conducted its own investigation and came up dry. So, ownership fell to the People of Idaho and the place was put up for sale. That's where I came in. Since the ranch sat on the market for a year without a nibble, Boise gave me an auction date. I was setting that up when you bought the place."

"You were arranging for some hired help I could rely on until I can get settled," Rocklan stated.

"Yes, sir. The help is there, waiting for you. I asked Eli to take care of it for me."

"You know Eli Whiteley." Another statement.

"Of course. Everyone in these parts knows Eli. He's been away, but I contacted him when I knew you were buying the ranch. I set up your ride with Eli. As it turns out, he was coming home anyway."

"Home?" Rocklan finally asked a question.

"Yes, sir, Eli is Dr. Whiteley's adopted son. He was born in one of the high villages. The story goes that the old man found Eli's mother way up beyond the ranch, on the trail, starving and in trouble. She was carrying a young boy and pregnant with another. It seems he plucked them out of the snow and brought them home with him. They say that Whiteley eventually adopted the boy and a younger sister, although it must not have been recognized by the State of Idaho, given the problems with the estate. Eli was raised on the ranch, lived there his whole life until about ten or twelve years ago."

"What happened ten years ago?"

Hawkins started to warm to the conversation now that he had Rocklan's interest.

"The old doctor sent him away to school in Chicago. First to Loyola, then to Illinois. Came out with an engineering degree. He worked in the city for a while, too. I guess he was building things. I couldn't tell you where or what. Came home every now and again. And Lindy down at the post office told me that he wrote the old man regularly over the years. I don't know much more than that. But I do know that Eli's one smart cookie, even for a Shoshone. And I don't just mean educated."

This explained some of what Rocklan had overheard at the St. Clouds'.

"He told me that taking me up there was on his way. What do you think he meant by that?"

The question got a guarded look from Hawkins. There was something he wasn't telling Rocklan.

"Can't say for sure. Maybe he's visiting some of the high country bands. There's still a lot of them up there."

This answer solidified Rocklan's mistrust of the real estate agent. There was something going on, and he would get a straight answer out of Eli one way or another.

At dawn the next morning, Rocklan met Eli in the lot behind the *Edgar Allan Poe*. The Shoshone obviously had been up for a while and was waiting for him. There was a sturdy, tarp-covered freight wagon packed with baggage, supplies, and other bundles and boxes. An alert, paint cow pony was tied to a lead on the back of the wagon. Two of the most ungainly horses Rocklan had ever seen were in the traces.

"Did I pay for those horses?" asked Rocklan with an edge, in no better mood than when he first arrived in Idaho.

"No, you didn't, Mr. Rocklan. You paid for these two mules," answered Eli with no little sarcasm. "These ladies will get you there, don't fret yourself."

Stung, Rocklan climbed up onto the wide spring seat without another word. He tried to get comfortable on a threadbare cushion, all that there was between his rear end and the wooden bench. It was going to be a long, sore ride.

The early air was misty, but the promise of warmer weather and a stronger sun bode well for a clear trip. Eli threw a carpetbag into the well at Rocklan's feet, added his Winchester shotgun and two canteens of water. He handed the Easterner a brown paper sack of donuts and a thermos of coffee.

"You all set?" Eli asked as he climbed onto the seat and took the reins.

"Look, before we leave, I've got to get a few things straight," said Rocklan. "I'm paying for all of this, so I need to know what I'm getting into. You're the adopted son of the man I bought the ranch from. The ranch is where you grew up, and somehow you lost ownership of it. Now, as the new owner, I'm going back up there with you? Doesn't that sound a little odd? What are your intentions? Why is my ranch on your way?"

Eli shrugged. "I'm getting paid. The trail up into the back bowls of the Maseah Range runs right by your property. I'm visiting some of my people up there."

"Maseah what? I thought we were in the Bitterroots," said Rocklan, distracted by the new information.

"We are in the Bitterroots. The Maseah is one of its ranges. It's a Shoshone word, meaning 'to grow.' My people believe that these mountains are a source of growth, both physical and spiritual. The ranch is called 'Maseah Mountain,' after the range."

But Rocklan wasn't in the mood for a discussion of Indian beliefs. He was going to get some answers. "What's all of this cargo we're hauling? There's more than my stuff and supplies back there. It looks like this time, I am paying to carry your bags."

"Not really," said Eli. "There are a few things for the Shoshone, but I also bought two shortwave radios. Thought you might like some contact with the outside world, and I'll set them up for you. Gratis."

"I didn't ask you to do that. Maybe I want to be alone. Maybe I don't want to contact the outside world." Rocklan was angry that this man made a decision for him, but he was getting sidetracked from his main point. "I hope you're not thinking that you're going home to the ranch," he said bluntly.

"It's not safe without a radio," said Eli. "And I told you once where I was going. If you don't want me to bunk at the ranch for the night, okay, I'll make out."

Rocklan glared at the Indian, but soon realized that he had gotten all that he was going to get—for now. He would come back to this subject later. So, all he said was, "Let's go."

Eli again shrugged, then whistled shrilly, slapped the reins, and yelled, "Ho, mule! Giddap!" The wagon began its trek into the mountains.

Chapter 5

Maseah Mountain

Blackbird's ridge ran for ten miles, paralleling the range of the Bitterroots that Eli had called the Maseah. At the end of it, they descended into a broad valley and pointed toward a pass rising up on the other side. The road had been good on the ridge, but as they dropped down, they followed a raised track that wove its way through half-frozen wetlands. At times, the marshy ground swamped the road, creating patches of mud and ice. The mules didn't like this muck, and neither did the men dragging them through it.

During one particularly stubborn ordeal, Rocklan peevishly made a suggestion that Eli let the pony help them pull. The situation and the man made Eli ornery, so he refused, telling his traveling partner that the horse was a present and that he wanted it in good condition. They both knew it was the right thing to do, but Rocklan let it go.

The small caravan also came across an occasional rockslide. It was mostly minor stuff that could be kicked or rolled away. Twice, however, they were forced to lever sizable boulders off the road.

The uneven, rocky track often made hanging onto the wagon seat an essential skill. Many times, Rocklan found it easier just to walk. It was a primitive way to travel, without a doubt, but it had its rewards. The beauty of the place was not lost on him. In fact, he was stunned by the majesty and power of it all. The peaks above him were humbling in their dominance. Like a slap in the back of the head, he felt the idea of mountains become a reality. A large chunk of his resolve calved away as he realized the enormity of his decision. This was a world that Rocklan could not control in any way. This environment was going to be more than just a factor in his future; it was *the* factor. It was *the* future. For the first time, he was glad that Eli was with him.

They stopped a mile or so through the pass, at a crossroads that offered a flat-panned area just off the road. The mountain meadow still had thin grass, but it was more gold than green. It also offered a spring, so travelers used the place regularly. Rocklan was mesmerized by the view back down the road and across the valley to Blackbird's ridge and the dark lowlands beyond. Behind him rose the Maseah, the sun full on its peaks. He could not escape the feeling that he was looking at his own history in geological form. He was leaving those low, dark days behind and traveling up to his rest and retreat. It was a little like dying, he thought.

The men gave the animals an hour, then they took the road that led further into the mountains. The alternative route ran away from them, tracing the length of the valley.

Not far along, the climbing road used a wide track cut by foresters for fire prevention reasons. The travelers' route wound through dense pockets of pine and larch holding on in the small dales they moved through. Eventually, as they rose, they left the last trees behind and made progress across gravel fields, bushes clinging to mountainsides, hemlocks, bear grass, and low sedge.

Rocklan had not pursued Eli about his plans, as he had intended. The Indian was right—Rocklan was dependent upon the Shoshone, for now. He also had just spent the morning laboring alongside him. While he wouldn't call it a bond, he at least felt they had struck a truce. He still wanted to drive the issue to ground, but ultimately, he decided it best to let Eli come to him. If the man wanted something, he would eventually ask for it.

The travelers established a routine that allowed steady progress on a road with only gravity and the recurring switchback as hazards. The men rotated tasks, sometimes walking, other times riding or driving. They found that taking the lead of the mules was necessary to get them over some of the longer or steeper rises. A chill breeze, blowing steadily down the mountain pass, didn't help the animals' desire to pull against it. The wind also signaled a change in the weather.

At one point, Rocklan led the jennies up a short rise and around a bend. As he did, the mules fidgeted, then screamed and stopped dead. Immediately, they began to strain at their traces and pull away from the man holding them. They had first smelled and then saw the black bear in the road, long before

Rocklan did. But the bear's nose was even keener than the mules'. It already was interested and moving toward the scent.

This abrupt rendezvous with nature forced a loud "Whoa!" out of the startled man. The noise slowed the bear, but it immediately roared back at Rocklan.

Through that heart-stopping sound, Eli commanded, "Don't run! Don't move!"

This froze Rocklan long enough for Eli to say, "Female, probably pregnant, foraging prior to hibernation. Don't hurt her."

Rocklan was incredulous that Eli thought he might hurt this monster. Just as that thought surfaced, the black bear snarled and took a powerful shuffle forward. Rocklan's survival instinct was on hair-trigger when Eli again ordered, "Stop!"

"Then shoot the bastard, quick, shoot it!" yelled Rocklan.

"She—it's a female," said Eli. With that, he struck the flint of a road flair he had stashed in the carpetbag. He tossed the flair between Rocklan and his antagonist. The bear sat back, snorted at the flair's smoke, shook its big head, then continued its walk across the road and disappeared down a berry-covered slope. Rocklan wobbled over to the mules and grabbed the halter, steadying both the mules and himself. He looked at Eli.

"What's the matter?" asked the Shoshone. "Happens a lot this time of year. This place is full of huckleberries. The ladies need to store fat now."

"You knew an encounter was a possibility?"

"An encounter? That's what you call it?" Eli laughed as he climbed down to trade places with Rocklan, who was thoroughly agitated.

"For Christ's sake, Eli. I could have been mauled. Scared the shit out of me."

"It's good to have a healthy respect for nature," offered Eli.

"That's all you have to say? Some smart comment? I thought you were supposed to be my guide up here."

"Guide, yes; babysitter no." Eli knew that was cold, so he quickly added, "But don't worry, I'll keep an eye on you."

Rocklan slapped the reins and fell into a fume as they resumed the trip. His secret pride at surviving the scare and the spectacular scenery they were moving through worked him out of it quickly though, and the routine resumed. As compelling as the peaks were, he was now far more alert to his immediate surroundings. He began to notice the life around them—marmots whistling warnings to their colonies as the invaders approached; wary, white-tailed deer standing stock-still on a slope; distant mountain goats, clinging to sheer cliffs; something fat and furry diving under a rock. If animals counted, he wasn't going to be alone up here at all.

As the last sun lingered on the high crests, they left the road and followed a grassy track. In a quarter mile, they rolled into a broad, lush bowl among the peaks. At one end, Rocklan could see a big house on a rise. It looked like it was balanced on the edge of a precipice. Below it were other buildings. Fences began to emerge, as well. Then, he saw two horsemen riding furiously right at them.

Grinning, Eli pulled the mules to a halt, stood, and waved at the horsemen. The ponies were upon the caravan in a rush. As the young riders skidded to a stop, they whooped happy greetings. Their mounts, panting hot breath in the cool air, danced and skittered around the newcomers. As they did, the two teenage boys turned this way and that in their saddles, trying to face Eli. They were dressed in flannel shirts, flapping, red wool jackets, and grimy, well-worn jeans. They wore straw cowboy hats, turned up sharply and sporting brass conchos around the brims.

"Eli, Eli! What took you so long? We've been waiting for you for two days!" cried one of the boys. The other gave a low whistle and yelled, "Who's the pretty pony for?" as he eyed Eli's privileged guest, tied to the back of the wagon. Then, together they shouted, "That the new owner?"

"My God, you two have grown," said Eli. "It's a shame neither of you have gotten better looking," teased the man. That brought hoots and youthful retorts from the two.

"Boys, this is Mr. Rocklan. The place is his now. These two wild men are Matthew and James Bearclaw," he said to Rocklan.

"I'm Matt," said the older boy, extending a hand that was jerked away by his pony's desire to run again.

Rocklan dropped a half-extended hand and offered the young teens a weak smile and a nod, but nothing more. Handshakes aside, the boys still made sure that Rocklan knew they were very glad to meet him.

"Let's get up to the house, mi amigos. Is Susan around today?" asked Eli.

"She's here. She's been waiting with the rest of us. What took you so long?" repeated Matthew.

Eli noticed the look on Rocklan's face and said to the boys, "You two go ahead and tell them we're here. Which one of you has the faster pony?"

"I do," claimed James, spurring the animal around and taking off like a shot back toward the ranch buildings.

"Blackie may be faster, but I'm a better rider," shouted Matthew, kicking his own lively pony into a sprint, determined to make a race of it.

"Susan? Others?" asked Rocklan, looking hard at Eli.

"Susan is my younger sister," responded Eli. "Dr. Whiteley, my father, took my mother and me in when we needed help many years ago. Susan was born not long after. We both grew up here."

"How many others are there, Eli? I knew I should have gotten this clear before we left. You know my intent is to spend time alone." Rocklan was furious at the subversion of his plans.

"You wanted help, didn't you?" asked Eli innocently.

"Don't give me that! It looks to me like your whole tribe has moved in."

Eli's eyebrows shot up, but said nothing at first. Then he said, "Nothing has changed. We'll be gone once you have your feet on the ground, just as agreed."

"How many, Eli?" demanded Rocklan.

"Well… there's those two." Eli indicated the racing teenagers. "Their mother, Maria, manages the house and cooks the meals. Their father, Joseph, is Maseah Mountain's foreman. My sister, Susan, is here of course, and she usually has one or two young girls or boys to help her. This year, it's probably the Blue sisters, Patty and Carly. "

"Help her do what?" shot in Rocklan.

"Oh, things," answered Eli. "And then there's Daniel. Daniel Bilbao, the ranch's wrangler. He also has the other animals and the barn. That's it."

"That's all?" asked Rocklan sarcastically. "Including you, that's nine people! Wasn't it clear to you what my plans are?"

"Don't flip your wig, Rocklan. Like I said, we'll be gone when you get settled," answered Eli calmly.

He called to the jennies and aimed the wagon for the broad front of the ranch house. He was home. No cranky white man was going to spoil what he had looked forward to for so long. The population issue would work itself out, he knew. This was the Maseah and it always had a say.

As the wagon entered the paddock created by the house and the large barn, it gathered the people Eli had listed for Rocklan. Their greetings and shouts back and forth with Eli were happy and affectionate, and the Shoshone took it all in with a broad smile. The entourage arrived together at the big house, where a young woman stood on a wide, covered porch that ran level with the sides of the wagon. Two young girls next to her bounced and clapped, then followed along the gallery as Eli pulled smoothly past the double front doors of the ranch house. A hand-painted banner over the entryway read: "Welcome, Mr. Rock-land!"

The wagon continued to the entrance to the mudroom and the kitchen. The woman followed, laughing and mocking Eli's overall appearance. When the mules were pulled to a halt, Eli set the brake, leapt over Rocklan onto the gallery, and picked his sister up in the air. Setting her back down, he held her for a moment. Then he gave the two younger girls warm hugs and whistled at their beauty, embarrassing them no end. The girls were a sweet pair, at least until they responded with pure acid to the insults hurled at them by the two boys, still on horseback.

As the reunion went on, Rocklan too climbed from his seat onto the porch, as much as to get away from the greeters in the road as to relieve his sore bottom.

"Susan, I want you to meet John Rocklan, the new owner of Maseah Mountain." As she extended her hand with a smile, Eli continued frankly, "Mr. Rocklan is unhappy about us being here. He wants to be alone, it seems."

Susan Whiteley dropped her hand and the smile, straightened, and asked, "He wants to be alone in the Maseah?" She reinforced her skepticism with an appraising look at Rocklan that assessed his mettle. Her face said she came away unimpressed.

"Look, I hate to be so direct, but that was the deal," said Rocklan. "That was why I bought this remote place. I have no idea why you and your brother are still here. I can't get him to explain his intentions. But I do know that you have no legal claim on the property, and at this point, I consider you to be trespassers.

If the rest want to stay and work for me until I get settled, fine. But the job isn't permanent."

Susan looked at Eli, then at the Bearclaws and Daniel, all of whom heard Rocklan's statement quite clearly.

"Eli, you should never have brought this fool up here." She turned, gathered the two girls, and strode into the house.

"Mister," began Maria Bearclaw as she climbed the steps to the gallery. "None of us want a job from you. You need to understand that this ranch is our home, regardless of who bought it. If we leave, we leave you to die. If we stay, we stay together and you might survive the winter. You'd better think about it."

Then she turned and joined Susan in the house, as if Rocklan's comments were too outlandish to consider seriously.

"Now you've got the women angry," observed Eli. He joined Joseph and the two teens, who had ignored Rocklan and were unloading the wagon onto the porch.

"Wait, a minute. Didn't you hear me? You can't just pretend that things are the same as they always were. I want anyone who doesn't want the temporary work I'm offering off the ranch by tomorrow night. Do you understand?" Rocklan said to the group.

"He doesn't get it," said James to his brother.

"He will," said Matthew.

Joseph indicated to Daniel that everything for the house had been offloaded. The wrangler climbed aboard and drove the rig across the yard and through the big doors of the barn. The boys began carrying bundles and bags into the mudroom and kitchen.

Rocklan stood there in frustration while the ranch's incumbents went about their tasks as if nothing had changed. As Joseph and Eli walked away, Rocklan heard the foreman mention that they could expect a bit of weather that night.

Chapter 6

Where the Heart Is

Rocklan was at a loss. He sat silently, chewing on a last hunk of cornbread, considering his options. They were damn few. He didn't understand these people. They were carrying on with their lives as if he didn't exist. Well, that wasn't exactly true—he was invited with the rest of Maseah Mountain's squatters to eat the supper that Maria had prepared. He accepted because he was quite hungry, but he tried in various ways to convey that his sharing of the meal in no way meant acquiescence to their tacit demands. So, he sat at the end of a massive oak table in the ranch house's huge country kitchen, trying to create a disdainful aloofness.

Despite his churlish pantomime, he found himself in the midst of an animated family affair. Not at all like the sedate dinners Helen, Lily, and he used to have. It was obvious that these people thought and acted as if they were family. There was genuine concern for welfare, fascinated interest in stories told, gusts of laughter, and constant teasing. When someone spoke of the passing of friends, all showed reverence and regret. When someone else spoke of a successful hunt or a major milestone achieved, there was support and appreciation. Jokes were tolerated, even encouraged, and the relater more often than not became the object of the humor. It was not quiet, nor was it settled, as people were up and down constantly. The two women, Maria and Susan, barely sat at all, choosing to eat a spoon of this or a fork of that as they served the table. Yet, they never missed a word of the conversation or an opportunity to contribute. It seemed a true tribe, bound together not through blood maybe, but through shared experience, respect, and something else. Love?

45

Rocklan was not part of it, though. Except for the regular filling of his plate, he was ignored.

His alienation gave him a chance to observe each of Maseah Mountain's denizens, but his attention kept returning to Susan Whiteley. She clearly was one of the most beautiful women Rocklan had ever seen. Not only that, she was a real force in the family. Strong in her opinions, yet loving in her touch, Rocklan could see the bonds she maintained with each person at the table. A tousled head, a whisper in an ear, a brief kiss on the cheek, a little extra on a plate—these were the devices she employed without contrivance.

He also wondered about her roots. She didn't look like Eli or any of the other Shoshones he had seen. In fact, in appearance, she was more like his Helen than the Native American he knew she was. He regretted the tenor of his introduction to her.

As the meal wound down, the teenage boys began balancing spoons on the end of their noses in an effort to impress Patty and Carly. The girls obviously found the behavior amusing, but they were not about to admit it. With that, Rocklan rose and moved away from the table, across the kitchen to a set of long windows facing the back of the house. What he had seen of the place impressed him. The building was situated on a rise, at one end of the mountain bowl. That meant it probably had stunning views from every angle. Their arrival at dusk prevented seeing anything now, so he stared through his reflection at snow swirling in the light of the kitchen.

"Joseph tells me it shouldn't amount to much." Eli had walked up behind him. The supper was over, the cleanup well underway, and the Bearclaws were moving toward the door and their family quarters in the barn. Daniel was already gone.

When Rocklan said nothing, Eli asked, "Would you like to see your house?"

"Yes, I would," the Easterner managed. He looked over Eli's shoulder to Susan, who was watching them as she washed a dish in a large, stone sink with a pump that hovered over the basin like a vulture on a branch. She turned away as he looked at her.

"Well, you came through the mudroom and storage area. Lots of room for supplies there. Attached to it are a root cellar, a big cedar storeroom, and a sweat lodge. We keep cold and wet weather gear, guns, and ammunition in the cedar room. Snow equipment, boots, skis, poles, and the like are in another large closet. Obviously, this is our kitchen. It's set apart from the main house, of course. We have to watch out for fires."

Eli indicated the large cast iron stove. Nearby, logs and kindling were stacked neatly alongside a well-used ash bucket. There was a walk-in pantry and a great march of tall cabinets made of some light-toned wood. Through the glass of the upper units, Rocklan could see a good supply of kitchen equipment and dinnerware. The counters were smooth, gray stone, and a worn butcher's block held a number of knives and cutting tools hanging from slots on the side. A Gibson electric icebox stood in the corner, but as far as Rocklan could tell, there was no electricity. Grooved wainscoting ran up the walls, and nowhere was there blank space above the paneling. If the walls weren't covered with utensils, cookware, and drying herbs, they held a worthy series of miniature landscape paintings done in smoky oils that Rocklan made a note to look at more closely another time.

The room was lit by numerous oil lamps, which gave it a sepia glow. In the daylight, the windows surrounding the room would turn the kitchen bright. In one direction, Eli explained, the glass provided a spectacular mountain scene; in another, an unobstructed view of the working part of the ranch and the mountains beyond.

The men moved out of the kitchen through a wide, paned atrium that connected the kitchen to the main part of the house. As they did, they felt the chill of the November night and saw the snow accumulating on the tiny ledges of the atrium's squares of glass. The short passage also contained a side door. Eli ignored it and opened a second door at the end. They stepped into a huge, western-style living room with a high, beamed ceiling and an immense river stone fireplace. Susan followed them into the passageway, but then entered the first door in the atrium and disappeared.

"Where's that door go?" asked Rocklan, stepping back into the passageway.

Eli hesitated, then said, "Well, I guess you should know it all. You will before long anyway."

This got Rocklan's attention, and he braced for more interesting news.

"That goes to the clinic," said the Shoshone in his typically terse way.

"The clinic?" parroted Rocklin, not expecting Eli's answer.

"Yeah, Dr. Whiteley ran a clinic for the people of the high villages for years. Anyone who needed it, really. Susan runs it now."

"Susan?" Rocklan continued with his confused echo. "That's illegal, even in Idaho."

"What's illegal?" asked Eli.

Exasperated, Rocklan said. "Running a clinic without a license. Practicing medicine without sanction—or worse, without training. What do you people think you are doing?"

"Would you leave the People without medical care?" asked Eli with a small smile.

"The who? Yes, whoever they are, I'd leave them without *bad* medical care," replied Rocklan heatedly. He was again furious. It had been building from the start of Eli's tour. To hear the man talk about the house as if he still owned it was galling. It also didn't bode well for getting Eli out of there. Now this—an illegal clinic!

The door in the atrium opened and Susan stepped through it. She obviously had heard the best part of the conversation.

"Eli, this man you brought to us, he's not just a naïve fool—he's an arrogant, naïve fool. A dangerous thing to be up here. Old Billy Whiteshoe is with us. He's dying, but he said he might try a little of Maria's soup first."

Susan gave her brother the same small smile he often used and pushed past them back into the kitchen.

Susan's hit-and-run comments stung. Rocklan should not have even cared about her opinion. Yet, her shots were unsettling, and not just because he hadn't been quick enough to respond.

Eli returned to the living room with the new owner behind him.

"Why would you assume it's bad medicine?" he asked the white man, referring to the clinic. "Susan knows what she's doing. She should, by now. Her smoke therapy, huckleberry rubs, and all-night spirit chanting are the best in Idaho," he laughed at his sister's expense.

"She shouldn't be using primitive medical mumbo jumbo at all," replied Rocklan, missing the sarcasm.

"Look, my pompous friend, I know you're a big-city doctor." Then, to Rocklan's surprise, Eli said, "You're not the only one who does research. Do you think I'd bring you up here without knowing whom I was traveling with? Only an idiot would do that."

Rocklan ignored the jab, but still he was caught unawares. How much more did this man know about him? And what did the woman mean earlier when she said that Eli had brought him to them? He bought the ranch from real estate photos! He was coming here whether Eli brought him or not. Rocklan again felt like the ground was moving under his feet.

"You probably should know something about Susan. As long as I can remember, she worked with my father treating the Shoshone. She carried his bag when he visited the villages. She assisted him in everything from headaches to surgery. By the time she was twelve, she was setting broken legs and stitching open wounds."

Noticing Rocklan's doubt, Eli sighed and continued, "Our father trained her, sure, but then he sent her to medical school at the Johns Hopkins University in Baltimore. She interned, did her residency, and was on the Hopkins hospital staff for over six years. That enough training for you?"

Once again, Eli had spent as much time with Rocklan as he could stand. He pointed to a large, curving staircase whose risers led to a balcony overlooking the common room.

"The tour is over. The master bedroom is up those stairs. Your bags are in the room. Find your own way."

With that, the man walked away and down a hallway to the right of the big stone fireplace.

Rocklan lay under a quilt in an enormous sleigh bed, listening to the wind and blowing snow. The room's fireplace cast a reflection in a set of large windows that must have commanded a striking view of the Maseah. He was as tired as he had ever been. He told himself it was the altitude, but it had been a day of hard labor and unwelcome surprises.

He realized that he was powerless. The isolation of the place assured that. They held all of the cards, and he held none, for now. He understood what they were doing—they would stay as long as he needed them, and they were going to make sure he always needed them.

This business of running a free clinic was another complication. Okay, maybe the medicine she practiced was good. So what? He wasn't about to run it, and they would be gone.

Whatever their intentions, Rocklan didn't like being conned, and he let himself play the offended party for a while. But at some point in his reflections, he once again realized how utterly vulnerable he was. Not that he felt threatened in any tangible way; it was just that his total dependence upon Eli and the others rankled and frustrated him. The only way he was going to be able to take back control was to tolerate the situation long enough to learn the things he needed to learn. Then, once he was self-reliant, he would set things right. For now, he needed them and would play their game.

At least he was where he wanted to be. Rocklan had fallen in love with the mountains and their soaring beauty immediately. He was also taken by the ranch, the house, and its setting, all of which offered the potential to cleanse him of his past.

He sensed, too, that the people living here were good people. Even Eli, as annoying as he was, had impressive nobility about him. Imagine him, a Shoshone Indian, a professional, an engineer, trained in the best schools! Speaking of training, Susan was a Hopkins physician—the best in the world. What was she doing here, of all places?

Susan. Whew! And with that thought, he fell asleep.

CHAPTER 7

THE LAY OF THE LAND

Rocklan woke to sunshine, but the hearth had gone cold hours before, and the room was icy. Staying on the braided rug, he moved to the window to check the snow and found a white world spread at the feet of the Maseah's towering pinnacles. It looked like about six inches had fallen. He used the cold water in a basin next to the bed, dressed, made his way down the stairs, through the house, and into the warm kitchen. There, he found Maria and Joseph sitting at the table, drinking coffee.

"Good morning, Mr. Rocklan. Coffee? Some breakfast?" asked Maria.

Maseah Mountain's new owner nodded to both offers, thanked her, and sat down. Maria set a steaming mug in front of him, then began frying bacon and pouring batter onto a griddle.

"Where is everyone this morning?" he asked over the rim of his mug.

"You're the last to wake, Mr. Rocklan," answered Maria. Eli's gone, and Susan's with a patient—the Brothers boy, Tommy. He's got a broken leg and is running a fever. His father and his uncle brought him in early this morning on a travois. Poor kid. They're in the mudroom, keeping warm and waiting to talk to Susan."

Ignoring most of Maria's Morning Report, Rocklan focused on Eli's absence. "Eli's gone? Where did he go in this snow?"

"Mr. Rocklan, this isn't much of a snow," commented Joseph. "Certainly wouldn't stop Eli from doing what he's doing."

"Now, Joseph, it's Eli's business. Just leave him to it," chided Maria.

"What's his business?" Rocklan asked the foreman.

"It's a long story," answered Maria for Joseph. "One that maybe he should tell you, if he wants to. If Joseph told you, it would be gossiping, and one thing Joseph does not do is gossip. Right, Joseph?"

"No, Maria," answered Joseph, knowing from experience that it was only wise to contradict his wife in private, if then.

Maria put the pancakes and bacon in front of Rocklan, gave him a knife, a fork, and a napkin, and slid a plate of butter and a crock of syrup in his direction. As he took his first bite, Susan blew into the room from the atrium passageway.

"Well, I see Mr. Rock-land has finally rolled out!" was her welcome to the Easterner. She walked to the pot of coffee, poured a cup, then sat down across from Rocklan.

"How's Tommy's leg?" asked Maria.

"His leg will be fine in a few weeks, but he is one sick little boy. Had to ice him to get the fever down to a manageable level. Not sure what it is. Maybe just the break. I set his leg, gave him something. He's more comfortable now. Resting. The girls are with him. That must have been one hell of a ride down here for him."

Rocklan listened with interest and concern. They were administering drugs as well? But he said nothing; he wasn't sure he could have spoken anyway. Between a mouthful of pancakes and the presence of Susan Whiteley, coherence would have been a crapshoot.

"Joseph, it looks like we'll have to put Tommy Sr. and Uncle Crow up for a day or so. Okay?" asked Susan. "When's Eli getting back?" Then, realizing anew that Rocklan was there, she said quickly, "Never, mind."

She rose, took a sip of the coffee, and moved to the mudroom door. "I'll tell the Brothers clan the situation and let them know they can have the barn loft." At Joseph's nod, she stepped into the mudroom.

Rocklan was biting back his anger at not being consulted on the latest guests to Maseah Mountain, but he kept his peace. Just as he was swallowing the last of the breakfast, Susan returned.

Rocklan's pique eventually cut through his earlier reticence, and he finally said to Susan, "Not to be too naïve or arrogant for you, but don't you think I might have some say in who stays here and who doesn't?"

Susan looked at Maria and Joseph looked into his coffee cup. Maria began to respond by waving a ladle, but Susan raised a palm to her.

"Yes, you're right, Mr. Rocklan. I should have asked you. Please accept my apologies," said Susan.

Joseph waited for the other shoe to drop, but it never came. All Susan did was nod back when Rocklan nodded his slow acceptance.

Maria's ladle found the stone sink with a clatter.

Susan smiled, and without changing her decision to put up the two visitors, said, "Eli thought you might want to see some of the property today. Joseph said he would take you around, and the horses could stand some exercise. That sound good to you?"

Rocklan's reaction was not expected. "Horseback? In this snow? What's the temperature out there?" He knew it sounded whiny as soon as he said it.

Some other utensil found the stone sink.

"Oh, you'll be just fine. The horses like the snow, if they can run in it. And if you keep going, you and the horse will stay warm," said Susan cheerily.

"If I go anywhere, it won't be before someone tells me where Eli went and what he's doing." Rocklan's tone was brittle.

"Susan, I told him..." began an agitated Maria.

Joseph rose, interrupting Maria with a kiss, and said, "I'll check on the horses. It's Saturday, so I think the boys will be coming as well." Then he fled.

Rocklan's question hung in the air until Susan said, "Eli left for one of the high villages early this morning. He's courting Red Cloud's adopted granddaughter, Ayasah. That pony you traveled with is Eli's way of breaking down Red Cloud's resistance to the match. And if I know that old man, it should do the trick."

"Eli has plans to marry?" asked Rocklan, once again surprised.

"It's about time, I'd say," threw in Maria.

"He has plenty of time, Maria," responded Susan in a way that said this was a well-worn topic between them. Then to Rocklan, she said, "There's something else."

She had Rocklan's attention in more ways than she realized.

"My father started a tradition here at Maseah Mountain that has continued for as long as I can remember. It began one bad winter, when there was famine in the high villages. While he couldn't feed all of the People, he did what he could and invited one of the villages down here for the worst part of the winter. They took over the barn, and they have been doing it ever since. Some years ago, the mountain bands began to rotate which one would stay at Maseah Mountain for a few weeks each winter. It is both a treat and an honor for them."

Rocklan couldn't believe what he was hearing. He had decided to play their game, but this was too much.

"Let me get this straight. Every winter, you invite a tribe of Indians to sleep in my barn."

"That's close, Mr. Rocklan. But get it correct. The tribe is Shoshone. There are bands spread out all over the Maseah. It is a single village or band that joins us," explained Susan.

"Okay, a band, then. How many people are you talking about?"

"Oh, never more than twenty-five, thirty-five tops. The bands are smaller these days."

"So, we're expecting thirty-five Indians to freeload in my barn this winter," Rocklan summed up sourly.

Susan's temper was a lot closer to the surface than Eli's typically was. "Look, you..." she stormed. Then she paused, took a breath, and started again.

"We are Shoshone. Not 'Indians.' They are us—Eli and me, the Bearclaws, Daniel too, indirectly. Show us a modicum of respect, please. It's a privilege to have the People and their elders here. And if it keeps the old ones with us a little longer, then it's worth it. Hell, it's no inconvenience anyway. The barn gets a complete overhaul every winter. They bring their own things, including food. They make it their home. That's why we have never had to make one damn repair on the old place since it was built. That goes for all of the buildings on the ranch. The bands do their part. And their stay is a sort of homecoming. In many ways, they are my father's children, just as Eli and I are."

The storm hadn't quite blown out, so Rocklan kept quiet in the face of this angry, beautiful woman. Susan's face was still pink, but her tone fell a few notches.

"Let me see if I can make you understand. The Shoshone loved my father. He was thought of as their spiritual father, their guardian, as white as he was."

"A saint," interjected Maria.

"When he found my pregnant mother and Eli near death, he saved them by bringing them down here to live," Susan continued. "When I was born, he married my mother. That made him Shoshone. When he got too old to ride from village to village to care for the sick and injured, he opened the clinic.

After he died, the winter stay on the ranch became a revered pilgrimage—a special event that is a very big part of the honoring of Shoshone ancestors."

Rocklan had begun to sense the depth of feeling and history surrounding this place he had bought. The photographs that spurred his initial interest captured none of it, nor did the real estate agents explain the ranch's ties to the Shoshone. Unknowingly, he had bought the equivalent of a religious shrine.

"To answer your question fully," said Susan, "Eli has gone to bring the Wolf Clan, Red Cloud's band, down to Maseah Mountain. It is a happy coincidence for Eli that it is also Ayasah's band."

"We just might have a winter wedding," Maria said.

"Maria is a romantic," explained Susan. "Now, I've got to check on the boy." She stood and moved toward the atrium and the clinic door.

"Wait, Miss Whiteley. Dr. Whiteley. I have some other questions…" started Rocklan.

"Later. We'll talk later," she said and kept walking.

At that point, Joseph returned with two enthusiastic teenage boys.

"We're all set, Mr. Rock-land. You can ride Hawk. He's not as fast as Blackie, but he can get along. Won't throw you, either," said James, being helpful.

"The snow's perfect. It's great out there. And the ponies are full of themselves this morning," said Matthew.

Great, thought Rocklan. He had not been on a horse in several years. But the boys' spirit was infectious, and Maria was holding his parka open. As he pulled it on, she handed Joseph a thermos of coffee and a sack of sandwiches for the afternoon. The Easterner had much to think about, distracted by all of the things that he had been told. So, he went along without further argument.

The four riders rode the edges of the remote valley on the cold, clear day. The high sky was a brilliant blue without a cloud to interrupt it. The air was thin and only partially warmed by the bright, but weak sun. When they stopped, the breath of both man and horse hung suspended in the windless day. Visibility was superb, and the sense of size and distance was almost overwhelming. The mountains stood out around them, proud and indomitable, in their greatest glory. Susan had been right about the snow—it caused no difficulty for the horses, and painted the landscape with its purity.

Rocklan's riding was a bit rusty, and his pony often showed his impatience, but the owner's skills were coming back quickly. His ability wasn't returning fast enough for the Bearclaw boys, however, who amused themselves by sprinting ahead out of sight, then pelting back just as fast, only to circle and tease the adults, who were pacing themselves and their mounts. Joseph kept even with Rocklan the whole time and, without being conspicuous, watched him carefully as they rode.

It turned out that not only was Joseph a good guide, he was also a knowledge-able teacher who loved his subject. When they came across tracks in the fresh snow, he pointed them out, identified the animal that made them, explained their owner's habits, and speculated on their intentions. In this way, the city man began his first lessons on the Maseah. Soon, Rocklan could distinguish between the imprints of rabbit, skunk, deer, elk, fox and squirrel. They even spotted rare evidence of a bobcat.

Maseah Mountain's foreman talked about the peaks around them, offering history and naming each to help his charge remember and recognize them. He told stories and pointed out unique features of the crests, almost suggesting sep-arate personalities for each. As a result, the summits began their first emergence in Rocklan's consciousness as individuals within the Maseah Range. Joseph's fascinating monologue placed each peak east, west, north, or south of the ranch, using the house as the center of a compass. He also showed Rocklan each of the passes out of the bowl, offering direction and eventual destination for the various tracks.

Joseph talked of the weather and what could be expected from the impending winter. He was poetic in his description of the green, flowered spring, the short, intense summer, and the golden fall. He spoke as if there were little difference between the elements and the mountains themselves. For him, they were, in fact, one and the same. He urged reverence and respect, explaining that people of the high country needed to understand the climate in ways that those living below did not. The foreman made it clear that the need went far beyond just understanding. It included prudent, vigilant action that, even then, never guaranteed survival. The foreman reinforced this message with harrowing stories of the trials of man and animal.

At one point, Rocklan commented on this struggle, referring to living in the mountains as a "battle." At that, Joseph shook his head.

"My father told me one time never to fight the mountains. He said we must find a way to live with them, to accommodate their demands, to become a part of who they are. To do that, you must know yourself first, he told me. Then you will see that you are an important, but lesser part of the whole. The mountains require honor and respect, and do not tolerate pride."

Rocklan immediately thought this quaint, native lore. Picturesque, childlike, and complete bull. But during the stretches of silence on the ride, he thought about Joseph's words. He didn't quite get them, but he couldn't forget them, either.

The leisurely tour took most of the day, and the boys had ridden back to the barn long before the two men. It was late afternoon, the sun was resident only in the Maseah's highest elevations, and it was decidedly colder than when they started. Joseph was talking about the trees, shrubs, and other plants that could be found in each of the seasons. He explained that the growing season was short and the soil poor, only yielding a little wheat—just enough grass and hay and only the heartiest of vegetables, some of which Rocklan had never heard.

The property's new owner was tired and a bit saddle-sore, and only half-listening. It had been a long, absorbing day. As the house and barn came into view, he was struck again how its situation on a rise within one end of the mountain valley gave the impression that it was perched on the edge of a drop. He knew that there was at least a hundred yards between the house's back door and any cliff, but it still stood out against the sky and mountains. He could see smoke rising from its chimneys and warm light from its windows. For the first time, he had a sense of homecoming, and perhaps he began to understand a little of Eli's joy and relief in seeing the place.

It had been a day like no other, eye-opening and humbling. Rocklan wanted to thank the foreman for his powerful lessons and to appreciate the easy way he delivered them. But as he began, the Shoshone interrupted, telling him that the horses needed rubbing down, and that dinner was an hour away. The foreman would see him then. Joseph left him on the porch of the ranch house at the mudroom door and led the horses away to the barn. Rocklan wondered if he had somehow embarrassed the man.

Leaving his wet boots and hanging the parka in the mudroom, Rocklan found Maria and the two Blue sisters in the kitchen.

"Oh, you're back," said Maria. "Did Joseph show you the ranch? Wonderful, isn't it? Are you hungry? Supper in an hour. Carly, don't burn yourself on that skillet."

Her conversation was disjointed, but her movements around the stove and its oven, and her directions to the girls, were closer to ballet.

"I probably should know this, but is there a place I can wash up? Perhaps a little hot water?" Odd that he had not even considered the subject of hot water until now.

"The hot water's in the big kettle on the back of the stove. Use that rag to lift it. There's a bucket you can use. The door next to your bedroom is a washroom. You'll find everything you need there. Commode, too. Don't slop the water in the living room. Patty, those potatoes need more mashing." Maria spoke in a rat-a-tat way as she stirred something in a pot and eyed the table that Carly was setting.

Rocklan stood for a moment, then obeyed Maria's direction. On his trip upstairs, he stopped twice to wipe sloshed water away with his stocking feet. He was surprised at the backache produced by hauling the bucket up to the second floor, but decided that the day's ride must have had something to do with it.

He felt better after a wash, and lay down on the bed for a few minutes before dinner. The next thing he knew, he was being shaken insistently and a young voice was saying, "Mr. Rock-land, wake up, wake up. Momma sent me to get you. Dinner's getting cold, and she means it!"

Rocklan bolted up and watched James run out of the room, slide out into the hall on the polished oak floor, and scramble down the stairs.

A few minutes later, he joined the Maseah Mountain residents, who had already started the meal. They were discussing Eli and his love life in ways that they probably wouldn't have had he been there. Patty and Carly were particularly interested in the speculation of something permanent between Eli and Ayasah.

Rocklan's arrival gave the boys the opportunity they were looking for to change the subject.

"How'd you like the ride, Mr. Rock-land? It's beautiful up here, isn't it? Wait until you see it in the spring," gushed Matthew.

"Rocklan. The man's name is Rocklan, not 'Rock-land,'" corrected the boy's mother.

"Your riding was better than I thought it would be, Mr. Rocklan" said James, pronouncing the name slowly. He was trying for a compliment, yet delivering an unintentional backhand.

Rocklan took it well and even tried for a little humor. "Won't be much longer and I'll be riding around you two."

That brought gales of laughter from the boys, who believed themselves to be the best who ever sat a horse. Joseph chuckled a little himself.

"That's enough, you two," said Maria. "Leave Mr. Rocklan alone. He'll get the hang of it one day." She passed him a bowl of rich, brown gravy.

Rocklan, who thought he quite had the hang of it already, couldn't keep a look of heartburn from his face at the cook's attempt at defending him. This brought an amused Susan into the conversation.

"Maybe Mr. Rocklan just doesn't like horses," she wondered, looking to keep him discomfited.

"Hey, I like horses just fine. Believe it or not, I used to ride quite a bit. Before I was married, I used to do some jumping."

He was sorry he said it even as it was being said. He had had no intention of giving these people any insight into his former life, and hoped they would ignore the reference to his marriage.

"What kind of jumping?" shot James, who was immediately interested in anything done on horseback.

"You were married?" asked Carly simultaneously, expressing surprise that some woman wanted to spend a great deal of time with him.

Susan saw the impact of the girl's question and quickly changed the subject. "Now that you've seen a little bit of the property, perhaps tomorrow, Daniel can introduce you to the animals, and show you the other buildings here at Maseah Mountain. Patty, please pass Mr. Rocklan the fiddle greens."

"Yes, I'd like that," said Rocklan, quickly filling his mouth with Maria's meatloaf.

Daniel too was focused on the dinner, but stopped chewing long enough to say, "Anytime. You'll find me in the barn whenever you're ready." Then, addressing the table, "By the way, the mare's definitely pregnant. We should see a nice new foal this spring."

"Woo hoo!" yelled James amid general approval. "Can he be mine?"

"No, he certainly cannot be yours," said his disgusted brother. "He belongs to Mr. Rock-land—ah, Rocklan—now."

"I said that's enough, boys," said Maria. "Now, finish up. Don't you have some chores to do before bed?" She looked at Daniel, who nodded while making a shovel motion, like mucking out stalls.

With groans, the boys bolted their last bites, stood, glared at the girls—who were offering them teasing grins—and went out through the mudroom noisily.

As the rest were finishing and Maria and the girls began to clear the table, Susan asked Rocklan if he had a few minutes. She wanted to show him her father's study and library. He probably rose from the table a little too fast to indicate nonchalance about her suggestion.

Rocklan followed Susan through the living room to a set of red oak double doors. Through them was a large, paneled room that continued the theme of dark wood. The walls of the study were lined with shelves, only interrupted by a white marble mantle and a lit fireplace, adding even more warmth to the space. The shelves were laden with books of all shapes, sizes, and subject. There was art, literature, science, and business. Rocklan recognized a number of prominent medical works. A rolling ladder, offering easy access, leaned against the ledges holding the volumes. The room truly was a library, and a well-used one at that.

In one corner stood a massive, rotating globe on a stand. Next to it was a broad table covered in maps, some furled, others weighted down with smooth stones. On the opposite side of the room, a huge, carved mahogany desk and red leather swivel chair rested in front a large set of paned windows. The desk was obviously in full use, being spread with letters, stacks of folders, loose documents, reference tomes, a large oil lamp, and the tools of office work, including an ancient Remington "noiseless" typewriter. A pair of tufted leather wingback chairs fronted the desk, matching the swivel behind it.

The middle of the room was covered in an immense, colorful Persian carpet that displayed an amazing array of mountain animals, romping among geometric patterns and stylized flora, painstakingly woven into a work of considerable size and art. On the rug were arranged four ladder back chairs. Each chair held a student's lapboard.

With a hand on one of the chairs and making a broad sweep with the other, Susan said, "Mr. Rocklan, welcome to Maseah Mountain's library."

Then she paused. "Wait, I can't keep calling you Mr. Rocklan like you were one of my touchier Baltimore patients. How about I call you John?"

"By all means," answered Rocklan a little stiffly.

"Good," she said. "And I'm Susan, okay." It wasn't a question.

"This room used to be Dr. Whiteley's study. He spent more hours in here than he ever wanted to, especially as he got older. He used to hate the idea that the room would ever be thought of as his 'sanctuary.' My father was very fond of saying that the Maseah was his sanctuary.

"When Maseah Mountain drew the People, it drew their children as well. The doctor saw this as a great opportunity. He also saw a way to address a number of things on his mind with one stroke, as he often did. So, his answer to aging, to getting trapped in a room, to rampant Shoshone ignorance, and to the need for childcare was to turn the room into a schoolhouse.

"Now, every day, with the exception of Saturdays and Sundays, I play schoolmarm to the two boys and my girls. Sometimes Joseph is here, teaching them the natural world and how to best live within it. Off and on, we have guests that instruct the kids in the Shoshone ways. When the children of the bands join us, the classroom moves over to the barn loft for the greater space. We do some adult education then, as well—helps to pass the days when the snow keeps us inside."

"So you are both doctor and teacher. What subjects do you teach? Is there a program you're following?" asked Rocklan with real interest.

"Oh, I teach them all. That forces me to do a lot of reading myself. As they say, keep one lesson ahead of the students and you'll be just fine," she said with a smile. "The girls are a little different, though. I have them in a sort of pre-med course, like my father did with me."

"Just the girls?" he asked. "Why not Matthew and James?"

"It's simply a matter of interest, really. If those two wanted a life of medicine, they could have it. But, they're too much like their father, Joseph, and would rather be outside in the mountains."

"It seems a life of medicine up here means you would be in the mountains," Rocklan observed.

Susan laughed. "That's certainly the truth, thanks to my father."

"What's the endgame here?"

"Well, that goes back to my father, as well. His idea was to do a little succession planning. I was his first student, and he thought that worked out just fine. So, in his travels to the high villages, he was always on the lookout for boys and girls who might have the aptitude for medicine and the desire for doctoring. Once he found a likely candidate, the boy or girl was invited to join us down here."

"And now, Patty and Carly are the next generation?"

"That's right. Those two will be our tenth and eleventh graduates. But they're a little different. When I found them, they had the smarts and they had the drive, but they also had the need. Their parents died a year ago in an avalanche, so now they're not only students, they're a part of the family."

"That's quite remarkable," Rocklan said, impressed.

"There's another piece to my father's plan," Susan added. "Up until his death, we had the financial wherewithal to send our students to medical school after they left us. Now, that's a real question. We've been lucky with scholarships so far, but they're hard to rely on. We also hope that the Bearclaw boys will leave for more formal schooling someday."

Rocklan felt like he had been hit with a two-by-four. Now that he had a few more pieces, it dawned on him. *She has sprung the trap*, he thought. Now, he understood all of the comments about "Eli bringing him up here." Now he saw more fully what they had in mind. Not only were they hoping to continue to live and work Maseah Mountain as they always had, they thought that perhaps they could get him to fund the education of their progeny, as well.

She had set it up nicely. A full day on this stunning ranch, a good meal, a warm fire, a beautiful room, a heartwarming story—all part of the plan. Her persuasiveness was formidable. Add to that her intoxicating allure, a fact that he was sure she was well aware of, and she had woven the web expertly. But he was having none of it.

Instead of reacting to what he saw as the truth, he remained quiet and unchanged. He was not going to give this smart woman an opportunity for further persuasion, or a chance to use that sharp tongue of hers, if persuasion failed. He feigned reflection and said nothing, taking a stroll around the room, looking at the available reading.

Inside, he was once again fuming. His male ego had taken another beating—this one done expertly, and with kid gloves.

Finally, Susan said, "Well, I'll leave you to look at your books. I've got to check on my patients."

With that, she turned and left Rocklan to himself.

Chapter 8

The Barn

The next day, Rocklan woke early, thinking he would be the first up. The view from his windows revealed a pewter-colored day, but the sun was just up, and maybe it eventually would burn off the morning gray.

Arriving in the kitchen, he found Maria filling the percolator basket with fresh-ground coffee. *It's tough to beat these people out of bed*, he thought. She greeted him and put the sugar bowl and an empty mug with a spoon in it on the table. Daniel Bilbao came in just as the smell of the fresh java began to fill the room. He had a pail of milk in one hand and a wire basket of brown eggs in the other.

Maria took both from him and said, "Joseph tells me there's a lot of snow coming. Maybe late tonight. The first big one of the year. Scrambled eggs, Mr. Rocklan?"

As Rocklan nodded, the wrangler replied, "Yeah, I talked to him earlier. That man knows the mountains. So, we'd better plan on it."

"I hope Eli was able to get Red Cloud and the People moving. It's going to be close if it's coming in tonight," Maria fretted.

"Oh, I think Eli knows it. They may have to deal with a little bit of the front end, but they'll be here," observed the barn man. "At any rate, the barn's about ready for them, and by tomorrow, they'll be snug and out of the storm."

Maria grunted her understanding, but preferred to fret a bit more as she beat the eggs with a whisk. "Well, if they're getting here tonight, you'd better show Mr. Rocklan the place before they take it over."

Daniel looked at Rocklan with the question.

"Sure," he responded. "I'm ready whenever you are."

64

"I hope you're going to eat these eggs first, now that I've beaten them," said Maria.

"I'll meet you in the stables in a few minutes, Mr. Rocklan. I want to check on Hawk. I think he picked up a stone bruise yesterday," said Daniel as he rose and went out through the mudroom.

"The stables are on the lower level, John. I'll take you over there when you're ready," said Susan, coming into the kitchen. Behind her were the Blue girls, looking fresh-scrubbed and crisp.

The use of the familiar 'John' from Susan got an eyebrow raise from Maria, but she said nothing.

Susan reported, "Tommy's much better this morning. Fever's gone and he wants to try out his new crutches. He can travel and I want to get his father and Uncle Crow out of the barn in enough time to get them home before the storm hits. Also, before Red Cloud arrives. It wouldn't do to have another band in there when the old mountain goat shows up. Maybe we can loan them one of the small wagons."

"Then looking at Rocklan, she said, "Oh, I'm sorry. That's okay with you?"

Rocklan was listening, of course, but he didn't realize Susan was talking to him. There was an awkward pause, then he peered up to see her looking at him.

"Oh, sure, sure," he finally said.

Susan spent the next few minutes directing Patty and Carly in their duties for the day. Billy Whiteshoe needed a bath and some skin cream to avoid bedsores. The other single room and the bigger dorm room needed to be readied, just in case Red Cloud brought some sick or hurt with him. And there was some scouring of the common lavatory that was required.

"Do Joseph and Daniel have the barn ready?" she asked Maria. "Blankets? Food? Everything else?"

"They've got it under control, Susan, you know that. The People will be bringing most of what they eat, as they always do. And I pulled the extra blankets out last night."

The doctor gave the table a quick drum solo, rose, gave the cook a kiss, and asked Rocklan if he was ready.

Rocklan stood and nodded as he jammed the last bite of toast in his mouth.

The barn, like all of Maseah Mountain's structures, fit the land quite well. While the house sat on a rise in the mountain bowl, the barn was built just below it, taking advantage of the hill as it continued to slope. The weathered, white building rose two stories above its lowest level, which was created as the hill fell away. On either side of the main building were two wings, made of gray-brown stone.

The architect had built the barn across from the ranch house, but on an angle, so as to avoid blocking the view from Dr. Whiteley's porch. He could sit in his rocker and still see across the fields of the high valley to the mountains beyond.

Susan and Rocklan crossed the road between the house and barn, using a low bridge that spanned a swift stream. The masons had used the same river stone to build the arch that they had used on the barn's wings. The stream came from the Maseah, and manmade tributaries served both house and barn.

As they walked, Susan explained that the left wing of the structure held a ranch office, living quarters, and a kitchen. The right wing provided storage rooms and a large workshop. She and Rocklan ducked through a smaller door in the wide, center doors of the barn and onto the main floor. He was immediately blinded by the change in light. He was also assaulted by the smell of horses, cows, hay, and machine oil. One other distinct odor muscled its way in among the others.

They stopped to let their eyes adjust to the light and their noses to the ambiance of the barn.

"One may wonder how the smell of chili can survive in this earthy and pungent atmosphere." Susan was perhaps trying to warm a little of the chill that arose between them the previous evening.

When he didn't say anything, she pointed to a doorway into the barn's living area. "Through there is a good-sized kitchen. It smells like Maria's going to give Red Cloud the gift of heartburn with her chili tonight. My guess is that he'll prefer the gift Eli gave him—to ride, not to eat, of course."

Susan knew the impending guests were a sore subject with Rocklan, and by his lack of reaction to her little joke, she knew it would continue to be. She didn't care; he needed to get over it.

"Okay. Well. I'll leave you in Daniel's good hands. You can find him down there." She pointed to a break in the floor that was a broad, hay-strewn ramp leading to the lower level. The main floor of the barn was roomy enough and the ramp sufficiently wide to turn a wagon and horses, then drive the rig down the decline and into the stables. It was an ambitious construction, and practical.

Rocklan thanked Susan's back as she strode away. Then, he walked to the ramp as directed. A lean, black barn cat with white mittens began to rub itself against his ankles as he descended to the other animals and Daniel.

He found the wrangler re-shoeing Hawk outside of one of the numerous stalls in a long row. Lying next to him was a mottled sheepherding dog. As Rocklan approached, the dog jumped up and ran to the newcomer, tail wagging rapidly. Rocklan extended his hand to allow the dog to get his scent, then bent and began a thorough ear scratching, making a permanent friend.

"That's Matilda. She's the one who really runs this place. She comes from a long line of Australians. Dr. Whiteley brought her grandparents back with him," explained Daniel. "Her mate, Job, is around here somewhere."

As he stooped to the dog, Rocklan could see down the long shed row, and through several stone arches that supported the floors above. At the end, he could see Matthew doing something with tack in a workshop.

When Rocklan straightened, James came up behind him. The boy was carrying a full bucket of water, both hands on the rope handle and waddling with the weight between his legs.

"Mornin' Mr. Rock-land," he said. "Git. Git outta my way, you!"

The boy nudged the cat out of his intended path with his foot. The dog ignored the lesser being.

"Don't be kicking, Roscoe, James. He's got work to do. I saw a hole in one of the sacks of cornmeal. Don't give him a reason to hide out and sleep all day."

"That mangy cat doesn't need a reason to sleep all day," growled the boy.

"Well, that's done," said the barn man, tossing a hammer into a wooden toolbox. I didn't notice you having any trouble with him yesterday, Mr. Rocklan. Must have stepped on something at the very end of the day. A little bruising, but he'll be fine now. Not going anywhere for a couple of days, anyway."

"Joseph says we'll get about two feet, starting tonight," offered James. "I sure hope Eli gets back."

"He'll be here, don't worry. What you need to worry about is all of that hay you dropped on the ramp. There's wood to be stacked, too. Get a move on, now. There's lots to do before tonight," said Daniel.

These poor boys get plenty of direction in this place, thought Rocklan.

"Daniel, I can find my way around. Looks like you're pretty busy," observed the owner.

"No, no, no, Mr. Rocklan. The work will get done. These are good boys. They don't really even need me to tell them what to do. It'd be a pleasure to show you around. Why don't we start down here?"

For the next couple of hours, Rocklan got the grand tour. The men and the dog worked their way through the lower level, starting with the impressive, two-story woodworking and mechanical workshop on one end, to a sizeable chicken coop and rabbit hutch on the other. In between were a dozen stalls holding six horses and two mules. There were three pens for Flower, Hope, and Gerty, the ranch's dairy cows, and assorted enclosures containing other animals, including three pigs, two goats, and five sheep.

The level opened to the outside through a wide set of sliding doors, flanked by runs of windows that provided light along the shed row and pens. On the other side of the doors were a large corral, the loading ramp, a chicken yard, additional animal enclosures, and access to the fields in the valley.

It was obvious that Daniel was in his element and very serious about his responsibilities. When Rocklan asked why a ranch of this size didn't have more stock, the wrangler wished out loud that he had more, like it was when he was growing up in Mexico. But he then explained that while the valley was certainly big enough to run a real ranch, the grasses, and the short summer couldn't support herds of animals. So, they had always kept just enough stock to serve the needs of Maseah Mountain's residents and their occasional visitors.

They climbed the ramp to the main floor, Daniel noticing that James had done as he was told in picking up the loose hay. As the men stood about where Rocklan and Susan had earlier, Maria came from the house to check on her chili. Matilda left them then and followed the cook into the barn's kitchen.

"Maria swears she never gives the dogs anything," laughed Daniel. "But, whenever she's around, both Job and Matilda, follow her like she was the second coming."

The barn man then pointed out the ranch's store of farming equipment, tools, wagons, dog sleds, spare parts, tack, lumber, feed, firewood, kindling, and innumerable other necessities for sustaining life at Maseah Mountain. All were well-organized and stored for access according to the season and the timing of their use. Hand tools hung in neat rows from the walls and rafters. The machinery looked well-used, but in good repair. A potbellied stove stood in the middle of the huge room on a wide bed of firebrick. A two-foot wall made of the same brick also ringed the heater.

The men then moved into the adjoining wing that housed the ranch office, the kitchen, and a decent area reserved as living quarters. Here, Joseph and his family had taken several of the rooms, but there were other rooms still vacant. The kitchen could only be called "functional," but it clearly had Maria's stamp on it. At the moment, that stamp was a huge pot of venison chili slowly boiling on a black iron stove. The office was Joseph's workshop, and there the men found him sitting at a battered desk, doing paperwork. The work area looked out into the corral through a long set of jalousie windows.

"I hope you're impressed with Daniel's operation, Mr. Rocklan. He runs this place like a well-oiled machine," said Joseph. Then seeing Rocklan's interest in the various piles of paperwork, he explained with a wry look, "The State of Idaho gets its due, even up here. So does the Forest Service. They also like to know what we're doing, just in case we're harming the environment or the 'minorities' in the Maseah. At the moment, I'm ordering a few things that we need air-lifted in here this winter."

"Air-lifted?" asked Rocklan.

"We've found over the years that once we build up enough snow, we can get a bush pilot to drop in what we need in a fly over. We've thought about building an airstrip. But in the meantime, a guy out of Boise will fly his Bellanca C-27A up here for us. Once Eli gets the shortwave set up, it'll be a lot easier to arrange."

Rocklan had forgotten about the radio, and his face made Joseph wonder whether he had said too much.

"What are you having dropped in here?" the owner asked.

"Oh, some of this and some of that—additional grain, some sugar, beans, coffee and the like, fuel, a few machine parts, Susan's medical supplies. Things like that."

"May I ask who's paying for all of that?" Rocklan pressed.

"Well, I think that's a topic you need to discuss with Eli and Susan, Mr. Rocklan." The foreman had a set look on his face; he said no more and was not likely to.

"You can bet I will," said Rocklan, reverting to the sourness he first brought with him to the ranch.

Daniel and Rocklan left Joseph and went to explore the loft. They were again joined by Matilda, and now the other Australian shepherd, Job, made an appearance. Maria had chased the animals out of the kitchen.

The troupe climbed a broad set of stairs in one corner of the building. The steps led up and through a sizable pile of staples, organized and stacked in burlap sacks. Their location around the stairs gave the impression of emerging from a bunker, but the floor was primarily used for storage of hay. Bales were stacked high and deep with daily use, creating varying levels. The floor was also covered with a couple inches of the stuff. A wide aisle, however, was maintained down through the center of the fodder. There, the potbellied stove from the first floor was replicated. Access to the two floors below was through a wide trap, hung with a block and tackle.

Rocklan expressed concern over the fire hazard that the stove presented. He imagined the ease with which all of it could be ash. The barn man nodded as Rocklan spoke.

"You're right to be concerned, Mr. Rocklan. We all need to be. The moment we're not is when things burn down. This stove is not used, nor is the one below, unless the Shoshone are here. When they are, in the dead of winter, the heat is needed on these upper floors. So, someone attends the two stoves around the clock.

"The People know how critical that is, and not just for the heat or because of the risk of a fire. This ranch is a very important place to them. Dr. Whiteley's kindness and their belief that he was their guardian make Maseah Mountain a place to revere. That respect became part of their traditional honoring of ancestors. As a tribute to those that came before, the fire is tended faithfully while they are here. That's something you may not understand, but you can be confident that the barn will not burn down while the Shoshone are here."

Rocklan was not convinced, of course, because Daniel was right—he did not understand. There it was again. Shoshone beliefs. Tending of fire to honor ancestors? What kind of primitive culture was going to live in his barn for two months?

Daniel continued to talk about how the barn loft was used when the People were in residence. Overnight, it would turn into a community constructed of hay bales. Families would live together, and there would be a central council area where most of the band would gather at night to talk, share stories, and decide those things needing decision.

The men and dogs made their way back to the main floor and continued down to the stables. When Matthew whistled for Matilda, she responded immediately. Job thought about it a moment, then followed her at his own pace.

Daniel took the owner out into the corral and through a gate held with a looped chain. He spoke of a typical day when the People were there. He mentioned several projects he wanted done and was looking forward to getting some help. He talked of the frigid, windy nights and the warmth of the Shoshone council. He fondly recounted evenings spent listening to their stories, some ancient, some new. Finally, Daniel remarked on the relationship between the adults and their children. Here again, he spoke of respect, explaining that it was rooted in the Shoshone reverence for the Maseah itself.

"The People venerate their old; they honor experience," he said to sum it up.

The men walked along a fence line that reached to several outbuildings. There was a springhouse, a pigsty, a butchering shed, a large, covered woodpile, and two open enclosures used during warmer weather for various harvesting tasks.

The last stop was the sled dog compound. As the men approached, the animals set up a steady barking. There was a larger shed and maybe a dozen doghouses scattered throughout a large, chain-link enclosure. Many of the animals had been sleeping, curled up in the snow. With the presence of humans, the dogs leapt up onto the flat roofs of their small shelters and increased their appeal for attention.

"They are a noisy bunch," commented Daniel unnecessarily. "They hope we're here to take them for a run. That's what they live for."

"I've never driven a dogsled before," admitted Rocklan.

"Oh, you will before long, I'm sure," answered the wrangler. "It's the only way to travel, once you get the hang of it. It's a bit like skiing—easy to learn, more difficult to get good at it."

Rocklan didn't bother to mention that he had never been on skis before, either.

"Are they huskies?" he asked.

"Yeah, Siberians, all of them. We've tried malamutes in the past, but we keep coming back to these guys for their stamina and their smarts. This bunch needs some work, though. A lot of youngsters here. Unfortunately, we lost a couple of dogs to a grizzly this past summer. That's a story you'll need to get Joseph to tell," said the barn man, offering no more.

The dogs kept up their noise until the men were out of sight, then they returned to sleeping and waiting for the next chance to run. Daniel and Rocklan made their way back to the barn, where the wrangler left him to join Matthew, hammering something in the big workshop.

Again, Rocklan was impressed with Maseah Mountain. Its structures were tight, well-maintained, and efficient. He was also struck by the amount of work required to run such an operation on a day-to-day basis, even a small one such as this. It was quite obvious that he was not going to be able to do it all by himself. Not without letting it fall into disrepair. Even then, there would be the animals to manage. He wondered about the expense of the operation, and how Eli and Susan had kept it going. It wouldn't be easy to run the place—or pay for it, for that matter. Perhaps he could keep the Bearclaws and Daniel on. But even that was no given, especially if Maria was serious about her threat to leave. Another large chunk of Rocklan's resolve to execute his plan of isolation fell away. Of one thing he was sure, however, and that was his growing infatuation with Maseah Mountain itself. He could think of no other place he wanted to be, and he was very glad that he was its owner.

CHAPTER 9

A CHANGE IN THE WIND

Supper on the evening of the Shoshones' arrival was catch as catch can. A pot of chili and a loaf of bread were available on the stove for whoever wanted it, but Rocklan saw no one other than Matthew. The boy was sitting at the kitchen table, swabbing an empty bowl with the heel of the loaf. Rocklan sat with him for a few minutes, then the teen was off to do something else.

Eventually, Maseah Mountain's owner made his way into the library, where he spent the better part of the evening perusing his choices of reading material. It seemed that Dr. Whiteley was a man of varied, but excellent taste and a bit of a collector. The classic novels were well represented, as were biographies and history, especially the American Civil War. An entire section was dedicated to the Native American Indian, with a concentration on the Crows, the Blackfoot, the Paiutes, and the Shoshone. The medical reference was also extensive, probably because both father and daughter had contributed to it. There were engineering texts and compendiums of architectural drawings. Writing on the lively arts was joined by a number of bound photographic essays on ballet and theater. Music, too, was present; the library's shelves held both sheet music and histories of the composers. Leaning against a stand in one corner, unnoticed during his first visit, were a pair of concert violins, accompanied by their bows.

Without thinking, Rocklan gravitated to the medical books. Idly, he wondered what they were teaching at Hopkins these days. He reached for a well-worn copy of *Gray's Anatomy* that must have been Susan's school copy, given the edition and the notes written in a feminine hand. As he riffled the pages of the reference, his eye caught the title of another, older tome. The title startled him—*Anatomy: Descriptive and Surgical.* Pulling it carefully from the shelf, he realized he was holding a very valuable, first English release of Henry Gray's masterwork. Published by J.W. Parker in 1858, this book was the root source for what by 1932 had become the ubiquitous *Gray's Anatomy*.

He placed the book reverently on the desk, lit another lamp, and sat down to study it more closely. The snow outside the windows behind him had started to come down furiously, and he could hear the wind stiffening. He read an inscription on the overleaf that identified the book as a gift from father to son upon graduation from Harvard Medical School. The note read: *To my son Pendleton whom I love dearly and of whom I am very proud, may this work guide you to do great things. Dad.*

In addition to being an extremely rare book, it really was a record of Dr. Whiteley's medical life. It had been his working copy as he plied his trade for over fifty years. Rocklan was fascinated by the book itself, but he was particularly taken by the loose notes, articles, and letters jammed in among the pages. He recognized only a few of the names he read, but he could easily see that a collection of these papers could be source documents for some future biography of the mountain doctor.

The letters were not only postmarked from around the world, they also came from a parade of national and local officials, Shoshone chiefs, village elders, and others. One was a note of thanks and recognition for service to the nation from President Theodore Roosevelt, dated 1909; another came from James Henry Hawley, the ninth governor of the State of Idaho, thanking the doctor for his work among the Shoshone.

Perhaps this book did lead Dr. Whiteley to do great things, thought Rocklan. He carefully returned everything to the book the way he had found it. As he did so, he noticed that several pages of the text had been inadvertently stuck together, probably by a spill of candle wax. To his surprise, when he separated the pages, several leaves of loose paper fell from the book.

In a brief read of the first page, Rocklan quickly realized that he had found what could be the missing last will and testament of Dr. Pendleton E. Whiteley. He learned, as he read, that if this document was authentic, it changed everything.

Among other things, it was the doctor's intent to leave Maseah Mountain equally to Eli and Susan. The condition for the ownership transfer was that the ranch and its property would never be sold to someone outside of the Shoshone nation, and never for commercial purposes. It was his wish that

Maseah Mountain would always be a source of medical care, education, refuge, and solace for the People. The handwritten document was signed and dated. It looked to be the same signature he saw on other papers in the old textbook.

Rocklan was at a loss of what to do. If the will was real, he stood to lose the ranch. Or, he could be caught in a lengthy legal battle with an uncertain outcome. That was if he brought it to light. If he allowed the papers to remain missing, nothing would change for him. As he began to struggle with this dilemma, Susan appeared in the doorway. Without her noticing, he slipped the will under the leather blotter that covered the desk.

"Doing a little light reading, John? Oh, I see you've found my father's first edition *Gray's*," she said, coming into the room. "Have an interest in medicine, do you?"

Rocklan suspected that if Eli knew of his background, it was likely that Susan did as well. He was not going to rise to her bait, however. So, he ignored the question and said, "You have a special book here. And the note from Roosevelt is very impressive."

"They were great friends, he and Teddy. The president would come up here to hunt and fish on occasion."

"I can easily see why this place would attract presidents," commented Rocklan.

"Speaking of visitors," she said. "Red Cloud and the Wolf Clan have arrived. A bit snow-covered, but none the worse for wear. Eli's getting them settled."

Rocklan stood quickly. "Great, I'd like to meet my newest guests." He wondered if he was a bit too anxious to move away from the desk.

"Well, that's not going to happen until tomorrow evening, I'm afraid," said Susan.

"Tomorrow evening?" Rocklan was confused.

"Yes. See, tradition holds that the band has a day to order their new home—to make it their own. Once that's done, Red Cloud will be ready to receive you."

"What? Receive me?" he asked incredulously.

Susan laughed at Rocklan's annoyance. "Yes, he has this idea that meeting the new owner of Maseah Mountain, the venerated Dr. Whiteley's replacement, should be a formal affair." She was enjoying his discomfort.

"Replacement?" Rocklan was reduced to one-sentence questions as Susan fed him information in bits. This was the exact thing that peeved him most about her brother, Eli.

"Oh, just go with it until tomorrow evening. It's no big deal, and it will make for a much smoother next couple of months. Let's go out to the kitchen. Eli will be in shortly."

Wanting to vacate the library anyway, Rocklan followed her through the house, grousing about his barn and they were his guests and it should be his to say when they would meet, all of which Susan ignored.

In the kitchen, they found the boys, Daniel, Maria, and the Blue sisters all buzzing about the arrivals. Eli, at present, was passing the baton to Joseph, who would have the honor of turning the barn over to the People.

Maria was saying, "That old humbug better keep his butterfly out of my kitchen over there." For two months, the Bearclaws would have to share living quarters with Red Cloud and his second wife, Kimama. The name in Shoshone means "butterfly," and there was a lot of history between the two women, especially since Red Cloud was Maria's older brother.

"Did you see what that girl, Haiwee, was wearing?" said Carly to her sister. "Those are boys' jeans, and they don't fit her!"

Patty was just as appalled.

"I wonder why Eli came back leading the pony," asked Daniel.

"Yeah, I saw that," said James. "Red Cloud was riding ole Cactus."

At that, Eli came in from the mudroom. He looked tired, cold, and depressed. The gathered knew immediately that something was wrong. When he hung his wet sheepskin coat on a peg, Susan threw a blanket around him and sat him down at the table. Maria poured something out of a stone jug into a coffee cup, filled a bowl with chili, and set both in front of him. Eli ignored the food, but picked up the cup and took a long pull. Both teenage boys watched him drink with interest and wouldn't have minded a taste themselves. That was not going to happen with Maria there.

Eli shook his head, either from the drink or the situation, and said, "Red Cloud will not accept me as a match for Ayasah. He wouldn't take the pony, either, although he wanted to. Ayasah is furious. She's ready to write him and the whole band off."

"What!" shrieked the women and the two girls.

"Wait'll I get my hands around that old man's neck," raged Maria.

"Now hold on, let's hear it all from Eli, then we'll string that old phony up," suggested Susan.

"Phony Shoshone! I like it," laughed Matthew.

"You be quiet, boy," threatened his mother. "This is serious."

Eli took another drink and explained. It seemed that Red Cloud had something personal against Dr. Whiteley that caused a falling out between the two men. It wasn't that he didn't appreciate what Eli's father had done for the People for all those years. In fact, it was only that kindness and his clan's respect for the doctor that allowed Red Cloud to come to Maseah Mountain this winter at all. The elder said he couldn't deny his clan their turn; otherwise, he would not have come.

"I am going to strangle him," said Maria again, pouring Eli a little more.

"If that's the case, why the hell didn't he stay in his village by himself and freeze—just send the rest of the clan?" asked Susan.

"Because he'd miss those warm, cozy nights in our loft, drinking shine and telling lies," answered Maria with vehemence.

This got a big laugh from both boys and the girls too, except that the Blue sisters cut off their mirth when they saw Maria's face.

Eli continued with his tale of stymied love. "He would not talk to me about the problem he had with my father. All he would say is that no stepson of Dr. Whiteley's would marry a daughter of his."

"The senile old crow! Ayasah is his adopted granddaughter. Eli, you are his grandson. Where does he get off so high and mighty?" asked Susan, keeping the barrage going and looking at Maria. But her partner in outrage had fallen silent and moved over to the stove.

"What did Dr. Whiteley do to Red Cloud?" asked Patty.

"Eli, you're his grandson?" asked a confused Rocklan.

But before the Shoshone could reply, a hopeful James interjected, "What are you going to do with that pony, Eli?" The whole marriage thing was lost on the boy.

"James!" barked Matthew, disgusted with his brother's greed, but interested in the answer himself.

Susan picked up on Maria's abrupt change in demeanor and was baffled by it. She didn't know what it meant. She would find out, but she couldn't do that with everyone here. So, she cut off the questions from the others, citing Eli's need to get some sleep. Then she steered him out of the kitchen and away to his bed.

Rocklan was semi-amused by the stir, but not all that interested. So, when Susan and Eli left, he made his way back to the library, shutting the door.

By the time Susan returned to Maria and the kitchen, the cook had returned to the Bearclaws' quarters in the barn.

Chapter 10

The People

The next morning, Rocklan sat on the big, soft sofa in the living room, enjoying a fire and drinking a second cup of coffee. Overnight, the storm had dumped over a foot of snow on the ranch, and was showing no signs of relenting. Oil lamps lit the room, their light falling on Rocklan's lap, which held a detailed map of the Bitterroot Mountains.

He wanted to understand the mountains, and the Maseah Range particularly. It seemed a daunting task, due to its sheer size. He realized too that looking at maps was not going to be sufficient. He would have to get out there to explore and experience this world.

That thought brought him up short. Had he already forgotten his plans to hide himself away from the world? No. And anyway, he might find solitude in the mountains, away from Maseah Mountain sometimes. He wouldn't have to be alone, not all of the time.

He rose and walked to the windows facing the barn and the fields. There wasn't much beyond the barn that he could see except blowing snow and white mounds as it covered the ranch's buildings and fences. Light escaped from the window blinds of the Bearclaws' rooms, and he could see a bit of smoke arising from at least three chimneys before it was snatched away by the wind. He watched Eli emerge through the small door. The Shoshone pulled his collar tighter, hunched against the wind, and plodded through about a foot and a half of snow on his way to the house.

Rocklan had been trying to avoid thinking any more about the will he had discovered the previous night, but it was the first thing that surfaced in his consciousness when he awoke. It also destroyed any attempt to concentrate on the maps he had pulled from the library. This was not going to be easy, and he wanted some time to let the situation perk a bit. There was no rush; no one could do anything about it at the moment. By keeping it to himself temporarily, no one was harmed and he could be sure that whatever he decided, it was well thought through.

When Eli came into the kitchen, Rocklan joined him. Maria was there, but Joseph and Daniel were in the barn. Susan was in the library with Patty, Carly, and the boys. It was the last school day before the classroom moved over to an area of the loft that would be reserved for the purpose.

"The loft has been rearranged, and Red Cloud is approving work assignments this morning," Eli was explaining. "By noon, Daniel will have more help than he knows what to do with. Those animals won't know what hit them."

"Speaking of that," said Maria. "I need Daniel to butcher a sheep and pluck four chickens. I still have some of that elk left, but not enough. Maybe take one of the pigs tomorrow. The People brought food, but I'd like some fresh meat for tonight and later." Then she looked at Rocklan, who shrugged. He had given up his need to be consulted.

"What's going on tonight?" he asked.

"Once the People have the place the way they want it, they'll send word, inviting you and everyone else over there," said Eli. "After introductions, it's a party. Food. Cider. Hard cider for the adults who want it. Then, later, Red Cloud will hold council and break out that abysmal bathtub gin he makes."

Maria, showing disapproval of her brother, shook her head at the mention of gin, despite the fact that she herself kept a jug of "medicinal" spirits for special occasions. "It's not just about drinking," she clarified. "There's a lot more—the dinner, the kid's games, stories, the show. James is even going to read something he wrote."

"But it's likely to be a late night for us," continued Eli. "There's a whole year of stories to be told."

"You mean there's five hundred years of stories to be told. That old man loves hearing the same moldy tales over and over again," observed the cook.

"Well, since this whole thing has been totally out of my control, and I'm involved whether I want to be or not, is there any other protocol I should be aware of?" Rocklan asked.

"Not really. It will be pretty formal between you and Red Cloud at first, but all you have to do is taste his booze and listen to his stories. You may have guessed already that he's a proud man, full of self-importance. Out of these mountains, he probably wouldn't be given the time of day. But up here, given his knowledge of the Maseah and his experience, he is respected and honored."

"Not by me," Maria clarified.

Eli stood and looked out of the big windows in the rear of the kitchen. It was still snowing hard, and the wind was creating drifts against anything that would stop it.

"If this keeps up the way Joseph thinks it will, the snow will be deep enough for the airdrop," Eli thought out loud. Turning to Rocklan, he said, "By the way, Joseph told me that you were concerned about the lift and the cost of the supplies we've ordered."

"I'm just interested in expenses that I had not anticipated," answered Rocklan a little defensively.

Maria laughed. "What is it about Maseah Mountain you did anticipate, Mr. Rocklan?"

"Well, that's a good question, Maria. It's certainly true that I've had a few surprises," he said, not completely with rancor.

"At any rate, you need not worry; Susan will cover it," said Eli.

He then walked over to a large cupboard and drew out two of the cartons that had traveled with him and Rocklan from Blackbird. Placing one of them on the big kitchen table, he opened it and began placing kit parts for a shortwave radio in neat rows.

"I realize that this thing threatens the isolation you're looking for, Rocklan. And if you want, I'll take it with me when I leave. In the meantime, I think it's wise to have some contact with the outside world, especially in this weather, with all of these people with us. We might even enjoy a little music in the process."

Rocklan's brief stay at Maseah Mountain had begun to change a lot of his previous plans. In the back of his mind, he knew this. But still he hadn't quite come to terms with the fact. There was one inescapable truth he couldn't avoid, though—his ideas about living up here by himself seemed impractical, if not ridiculous. With some embarrassment, he recalled his arrival, his comments to Susan, and her reaction to him.

Caught between a decision on what to do about the will and realizing the truth of what Eli said, Rocklin responded, "This place has a way of changing one's plans. What you say is, of course, the right thing to do. I don't know what

I was thinking when I said I didn't want a radio up here. But I do know now that I would enjoy a little music."

Maria moved to close the cupboard Eli had left open. She had a smile on her face that Rocklan didn't see.

"Doesn't that radio need power?" Rocklan asked as he watched Eli unload the box.

"Indeed it does," answered Eli.

"Eli's got an idea how to solve that," said Maria. "Magic!"

"You're absolutely right, young lady, I do have an idea. And it'll work, too," said the engineer.

"Will it work on that squatting monster over there, as well?" asked Maria, pointing to the refrigerator in the corner.

"It should, at least for a while," he answered.

"What's your idea?" asked Rocklan, interested.

"Magic," Eli said with a grin. "Just like Maria said."

Susan and Rocklan met in the mudroom, agreeing earlier to support each other in the dash across the road and into the barn. He had put on a rep tie and a tweed jacket and vest. Susan was in a long, thin, stylish dress. She complimented it with a few fine pieces of deco jewelry. Her hair was pure Myrna Loy, one of Rocklan's favorite actresses. He thought she looked terrific, and paid her a small compliment.

"You think so?" she asked modestly in response. "They say that during hard economic times, the dresses get longer. I guess I like it well enough, though. At least it covers up most of these." She held up one of her practical leather and sheepskin boots.

Once bundled in parkas, they plunged together out onto the porch, down snow-clogged steps, through drifts, over the bridge and up to the center door. As they leaned into the biting wind, Susan took his arm and pressed in close to him. It felt good and he was glad for it.

The door of the barn was pulled open as they arrived. A young man in a dark blue, knit sweater bid them welcome and asked for their parkas.

"Thank you ..." Susan started.

"Rick, Dr. Whiteley. Rick. You sewed up my leg one time. Remember?" said the twenty-something. "You were just a kid."

"Rick, I want you to remember that I'm still a kid," she said with the Whiteley smile. "John, this is Rick Eagleson, evidently, a former patient of mine. Rick, meet John Rocklan, Maseah Mountain's new owner."

The men shook hands, and the temporary doorman told them that they were the last to arrive. The Shoshone had been hard at work on the main floor of the barn. It was well-lit and the potbellied stove was doing its job. Farm equipment had been moved out and three long tables moved in. A fourth table sat at the head of the others. They were covered in multicolored cloth and in the process of being filled with a variety of interesting foods issuing from the kitchen. The smells were alternately wonderful and agricultural—after all, it was still a barn. Wolf Clan women and girls moved around them with purpose, smiling at Rocklan and greeting Susan familiarly.

Rick led them up the stairs and into the warm loft. This floor had been transformed, as well. A broad public space had been created, centered on the twin stove. Off the area were several side "rooms" that led to sleeping quarters and space for other uses. One of the side areas was bright and crowded with older people, including Joseph, who was standing in the bale-constructed doorway. They were laughing and enjoying the company.

As the latest arrivals emerged from below, they were quickly surrounded and welcomed by a mob of Shoshone. Men reached for Rocklan's hand, and the women alternately complimented and teased Susan, as friends do. Children called her name and peered at Rocklan. Everyone had been waiting for them, and the party could start now.

As Rocklan and Susan gained some breathing room, Eli and Ayasah joined them. Rocklan was introduced to Eli's pretty intended, and the two women hugged warmly and looked truly happy to see each other.

"Ready for the meeting of two great personages?" Eli asked of the group.

"I feel a little like I'm attending the Treaty of Versailles," Rocklan joked.

"Well, here comes Von Bismarck now," said Ayasah.

Susan's laugh was unladylike, and she bent with a hand to her mouth to stifle it. As she did, Red Cloud emerged with an entourage from the anteroom of straw.

Rocklan didn't know what he had been expecting. Somehow, he imagined that the Wolf Clan's leader would be dressed in feathers and braids, like the head on a buffalo nickel. In fact, while most Shoshone seemed to dress like everyone else in Idaho, Red Cloud was an exception. He wasn't wearing feathers, but he was decked out. The elder looked like what they used to call back in the city a "Hep Cat," or at least the Shoshone version of the same. He wore an oversized, greenish, sharkskin suit with a white shirt and an open-neck, spread collar. A medallion made from a rock of some sort hung down his front on a leather thong, between wide lapels. And because he really was a bent old man under the packaging, the talisman swung like a pendulum, well away from his sunken chest. He wore a white fedora with a black band on his head, and a pair of L.L. Bean duckboots on his feet.

"He should never wear white this time of year," said Susan in her friend's ear.

Ayasah, who was trying to maintain a defiant front, in light of her grandfather's recent infuriating pronouncement, spit out a short, sharp bark of a laugh. But she quickly resumed the chin-out attitude she wanted to project.

These two are dangerous together, thought Rocklan.

Joseph did the introductions formally. Red Cloud took up the tone and shook Rocklan's hand in three short chops, then let go abruptly. Not knowing what to do next, Rocklan bowed from the waist, like he was meeting the Emperor of Japan. The two women fell against each other trying not to laugh. But Red Cloud clearly appreciated the deference Rocklan paid him. It earned him another three quick handshakes, and in response, Rocklan bowed again.

That was it for Susan and Ayasah. Joseph frowned at them both, and Eli led them away to say hello to some friends that he suddenly had spotted.

The introduction had gone well, and the newest denizens of Maseah Mountain cheered and began to mill around and move toward the stairs and the dinner downstairs. Red Cloud put his arm around Rocklan's shoulder, reaching upward in an awkward embrace and forcing the taller man to crouch. The shoulder pads in the Shoshone's suit jutted at odd angles. This was an obvious attempt to signal dominance to the rest of the clan, but the old man's teetering walk and natty appearance produced more comedy than dominance.

As they made their way with the crowd, the elder's medallion swung forcefully into Rocklan's ribcage several times. It surprised him how heavy the thing was. The stairs didn't come quickly enough for Rocklan, but once there, the attempt at dominance ended and Rocklan became a crutch to help the old man down the flight and into the banquet.

All in all, the dinner was a huge success. The tables were filled with chattering people passing dishes, dealing with impatient kids, and laughing with friends and family. The head table held Red Cloud and Rocklan, of course, but also Susan, Joseph, and a few other elders of the Wolf Clan. Maria had a place there as well, but was too busy marshaling the kitchen to sit for long. Eli also had a seat at the table of honor, but chose to sit with Ayasah and her friends.

Everyone enjoyed the dishes, both meat and vegetable, that the women had prepared in abundance. Both types of cider flowed, and the raillery was as plentiful as the food. The dinner started out sedately enough, as Red Cloud thanked the Maseah, his host, and everyone else for being there. He hoped that the clan would take full advantage of the opportunity to pay respect to the past and prayed that the future held good things for all. As soon as he was finished, the gathered plunged into all that had been prepared for them and the noise level soared.

Because conversation was limited to those nearby, Rocklan was Red Cloud's captive. The Easterner was getting along famously with the old Shoshone; at least, he thought he was, with the possible exception of one exchange. It came when he was telling Red Cloud about Eli's plans to set up the shortwave radio. Evidently, Rocklan must have sounded condescending when talking about the wave technology, or Red Cloud was just looking for an opportunity to deliver a message. Whichever it was, the Wolf Clan's leader went off a bit in an effort to educate the new owner of Maseah Mountain.

"I think lots of people in the lowlands think we are savages, squatting in caves up here," he began. "In fact, we are happy and well satisfied with what the Maseah gives us. It is a beautiful, simple way to live and raise families. We live in houses like everyone else, and when we want to, we live under the stars. We are principled, artistic, and spiritual. Some of us are even well-educated." He pointed generally in the direction of Susan and Eli.

"We choose to live up here. Many who leave come back. If you visit us, you will see how we live. We live in harmony with the mountains. In fact, the

Shoshone are a living part of the mountains. This ranch is also a living part of the mountains. The rewards for this are many. The changing beauty of the Maseah is just one of the rewards. Look how it paints itself tonight." The old man raised his arms to the sound of the wind and snow outside the barn.

Red Cloud's message was similar to the one Joseph delivered to him during their ride. It was also clear that the elder thought of Rocklan as a caretaker, not an owner of Maseah Mountain. To Red Cloud, he may be important, but not as important as the annual pilgrimage from the backcountry and the associated Shoshone rituals. It was obvious that no one had spoken to him about Rocklan's plans.

As Rocklan was realizing this, he heard Red Cloud conclude "…and you will always be welcome."

In response, the Easterner heard himself simply saying, "Thank you."

Shortly after, Red Cloud stood, and his entourage of elders stood with him. In leaving the dinner, the Shoshone turned to Rocklan and invited him to join them in the council later, after some Wolf Clan business had been concluded.

"What was Red Cloud bending your ear about?" asked Susan, moving over to talk to him as the dinner party began to break up.

"He really doesn't have any idea of what my plans are," said Rocklan with some guilt. "He talks as if this will go on forever. I don't own Maseah Mountain; I'm just the innkeeper."

"That's because he believes it all belongs to the Maseah," Susan said. "Even when my father was here."

"Well, I'm not looking forward to the day he realizes that the Maseah doesn't have the deed."

Susan looked at him with a bit of mocking in her eyes, but she said no more, and her look was not quite as disapproving as it once was.

"So what's next?" asked Rocklan.

"Well, the Wolf Clan families will gather in the common room for singing, storytelling, a little music, and some cute plays. You might call this the Children's Hour."

Seeing his face, she continued, "You might find you enjoy it. The kids are really good, and they've been practicing hard for some time. This is a big night for them. James has a story to tell. I might even play a tune or two, if I feel like it."

"You? Was that your violin I saw in the library?"

"Yeah. I don't play nearly as much as I did when my father and I did duets, but I keep my hand in. Tonight, you might hear something new. I call it my 'Mountain Bach'—part baroque, part hillbilly."

"I would like to hear that," he said with sincerity. "But Red Cloud invited me to join him."

"Oh, you won't get in there for another hour or so. Come sit with Eli, Ayasah, and me."

She led him over to Ayasah, who was sitting comfortably on a couch of bales and loose hay covered in a blanket. She was watching Eli hold court with some of the boys. He was telling them about meeting Rogers Hornsby in 1930 when he was in Chicago. "The Rajah" was hitting .325 when he broke his ankle playing against the Cardinals. Eli was introduced to the great man in the dugout at the end of the season, after he had taken over for Joe McCarthy as the Cubs' manager.

Ayasah made room for the two, and they settled in as various mothers readied their young stars. What ensued over the next hour was one of the best times Rocklan had had in years. Susan had been right about the skill of the performers and the effort they put into the various routines and vignettes. The presence of Rocklan and Susan seemed to spur them to great heights.

When James stood and shuffled a handful of papers from a yellow legal pad, the audience clapped and stirred in anticipation. He drew himself up and began with an explanation.

"This is a story of Sacagawea of the Lemhi Shoshone. She was fifteen in 1804, and about to have a baby when she was captured by a Hidatsa raiding party. She was then sold to the Mandan, who gave her to a Frenchman as his wife. Unknown to her was a Northern Shoshone warrior who loved her and was searching for her. Arriving at the Mandan village, the warrior was heartbroken to learn that Sacagawea and the Frenchman had left with the white men, Lewis and Clark. So, he followed the expedition in hopes of winning her away from the Frenchman. It is a tale of hardship and triumph."

James entitled it "The Corps of Discovery and Hope." Rocklan was taken with the characters in the story and the emotions the boy was able to produce in his listeners. The work was raw, but powerful. When James got a standing ovation from the Wolf Clan, especially the children, he blushed and sat down quickly. Rocklan could see, though, that his embarrassment was balanced with a sense of satisfaction and pride.

When Susan was prevailed upon to play, she feigned reluctance, then commenced to bring the house down. Rocklan laughed hard at her animated, booted footwork that was coordinated with the violin-turned-fiddle. In truth, both her dancing and her playing had more hillbilly in it than Bach. Regardless, it was wonderful. The loft's audience was clapping and stomping with such enthusiasm that it drew the old men from their council.

At her concluding flurry, the clan exploded with applause, cheering and calling for an encore. Finally, after way too many theatrical bows, she flopped down beside Rocklan and chuckled with delight at her modest success. It was perhaps at that moment he began to fall in love with her.

When Joseph came to bring him into Red Cloud's council, Rocklan was reluctant to leave Susan. But it became very clear that, as host, he had no choice. Eli begged off with a sly look at Ayasah. And even though women were welcome at this point, Susan bid Rocklan goodnight and made her way down out of the loft.

Rocklan was quite comfortable. He sat in a chair of straw he had built in the rear of the council room. His feet were up, his tie was off, and his vest unbuttoned. To his surprise, Maria and Joseph had come into the council room together, just after he did. Maria tossed him a blanket, and then she and her husband built their own nest in another corner. Although the place was fairly warm, he immediately put the wool cover to good use. He pulled it tight around him as the weather outside continued to howl.

The council space was full, but not crowded. Several lamps had been placed on a low table in the center of the room. They lit the area dimly, and the only faces Rocklan could see clearly were those closest to the lamps. These were the Shoshone storytellers, their words magnified and given an otherworldly aura as the light from the lamps played on their faces.

He listened to old stories of the Great Snake, the Eagle, and the Hare. In between these mythic parables, the People were told tales of great heroes, seekers of truth, and the greedy. They were reminded of the Bear River Massacre in Utah. They heard again of Chief Pocatello and Chief Washakie. They told of Jim Thorpe, the great Sac warrior-athlete—how he won Olympic pentathlon and decathlon gold in 1912, and how it was taken away from him later.

At the moment, Rocklan was listening to an animated speaker tell the story of Coyote and Fox traveling in the Bitterroot Valley. Their purpose was to warn the residents of the coming of humans. In the process, it seems Coyote—being the fool and trickster he was—ran afoul of Bighorn Sheep. Bighorn Sheep was so angry that he charged Coyote, missed, and embedded his horns into the trunk of a ponderosa pine. While the incident is ancient, the story goes that Bighorn Sheep's horns are still lodged in the tree. And for this reason, the tree is believed to have special power to grant blessings, drawing the People from miles around.

As the storyteller brought his tale to a conclusion, Rocklan took one last pull from the jug that was being passed. He had to admit, as bad as that first taste was, the stuff had a way of growing on you. He then noticed Red Cloud hunch closer to the table of lamps. Evidently, he had saved his narrative for last.

"Good," said a whispered voice in the dark, "we can go to bed after this."

Red Cloud began by telling his listeners of a proud family of wolves. The male was very satisfied with the litter of pups that his mate had just produced. Tragically, only two survived the harsh winter, one male and one female. Just the same, they were an honor to him, and he spent many days teaching them the mountain ways. His pups grew to be strong hunters and important members of the pack. He watched them as they took their own mates and produced their own children, and again he was satisfied. As the days passed, the wolf grew to love his children more than even the Maseah itself.

This insulted the great range, and it vowed to punish the wolf for his infidelity. One day, his son, instead of hunting with the pack, decided to try eating berries, as his cousin the Bear did. This wolf grew so fond of the fruit and the ease of acquiring it that he stopped hunting altogether. Eventually, he followed the berries all the way down the mountain to the flatland, and was never heard from again.

Before long, the wolf's daughter-in-law became impatient waiting for her mate's return, and she took another mate. This infuriated the elder wolf, who loved his son and hoped that one day he would return. In his anger and righteousness, he cast the unfaithful wife out of the pack, telling her to take her progeny with her. This is how the Maseah—and the Shoshone, who are a part of it—deal with betrayal, he concluded forcefully.

As Red Cloud was finishing his lesson, there was a disturbance in the corner of the council room. Joseph was struggling to hold Maria down, who was determined to stand.

"Joseph, let me go," she hissed. "I will stay here no longer with that man."

As she tore away, she grabbed handfuls of hay, throwing them away from her in frustration and anger. She strode to Red Cloud and looked down at him from out of the shadows.

"You are dead wrong, brother," she spat at him. "You cannot see your foolishness, even now. Think about your actions. He is your blood grandson!"

Maria glared at Red Cloud for a moment longer, then stalked away to join the storm outside. Joseph's face was hard-set as he followed her.

An embarrassed silence hung in the room for way too long. Then people started to rise, stretch, and make their way out. Rocklan was among them, shuffling through the straw and baffled by was he just saw and heard. A little trouble in paradise? Just the same, he had enjoyed the stories and recognized them for what they were—the propagation of Shoshone tradition, for better or worse.

Chapter 11

Cabin Fever

The snowstorm eventually blew itself out the next day and the skies became a high, hard blue. Over the next week, it felt a bit warmer, but with each nightfall, the wind and the bitter cold returned to the Maseah. These fluctuations formed an icy crust over the deep, soft powder. Rocklan amused himself one morning by watching Wolf Clan kids attempt to walk on the hard shell, then unexpectedly break through to their screaming delight. It looked like fun.

He had not ventured far since the People's arrival. Yet, he rarely saw Susan. After the first night, she had launched into a round of full physicals for all of the visitors. This effort produced some new residents in the clinic. She found a couple of fevers of unknown origin that bore close watching for possible spread. One man came to her with a broken arm that he had been suffering for a week until he could see her in the clinic. She delivered a young woman's first son three days after the clan took over the barn. There were assorted stitchings, edemas, and muscle strains as a result of the work on the ranch, and at least one or two suspected bad hangovers. Through all of this, she taught Patty and Carly medical technique while increasing their responsibility for patient care.

Susan also was constructing a clinical record of her experiences treating the Shoshone, building on notes that her father had started years ago. Her submissions of articles to various journals on what she called "mountain medicine" were beginning to generate interest, even outside of the States.

She continued her teaching, but was just one of several instructors, including Joseph and others from the clan. Meanwhile, she kept Patty, Carly, and the boys at their own pace, holding informal sessions with them in the library whenever Rocklan was not there.

Finally, Rocklan noticed from a distance that Susan also maintained a busy social life with the women of the band. She engaged in a wide range of clan activity, including spiritual sessions, crafts, and a regular program of exercise that looked like a cross between yoga and tai chi. One afternoon, he watched Ayasah and Susan strike out together on cross-country skis, disappearing quickly into the thin pine woods surrounding Maseah Mountain.

In the seams of all of this, he looked for opportunities to talk to her, but she seemed little interested in finding the time to talk to him.

Regular "family" dinners continued, but it was rare that all were there at one time. Even when Susan and Rocklan were together, the opportunity to talk privately never seemed to materialize. Absence was, in fact, making his heart grow fonder, but it seemed pretty plain that his feelings were not shared.

It had been nearly two years since his wife had died. And these days, despite sincere attempts, he was having difficulty bringing her face to mind clearly. Once, to help his recall, he dug deep into his bags to retrieve a photo of Helen and Lily. He immediately regretted doing it, or even keeping the picture, for that matter. All of the old blame came flooding back, and with it, new waves of self-reproach. His attraction to Susan was eating at him in more ways than one.

As the winter started to take real hold, Rocklan spent most of his days in the barn with Joseph, Daniel, or the men of the Wolf Clan. Nights, he generally spent in the library. His objective was to keep himself occupied, and that is exactly what he did.

Rocklan worked alongside of the Shoshones assigned to the care of various animals. He cut wood, split, stacked, and hauled it. He joined the crew painting the inside of the barn and helped others in overhauling the farm machinery. He forked hay, mucked stalls, milked cows, and fed chickens. He even got filthy working with the men who had the disgusting task of tearing down and rebuilding the henhouse.

The Easterner never missed an opportunity to learn. He established regular sessions with Joseph and Daniel, and sometimes with Eli. Daniel taught him the messy art of butchering, and while he did, Joseph lectured on the nuances associated with preparing game as opposed to livestock. There were shooting lessons, including rifle, shotgun, and bow. Use of a knife and tying of knots were also part of the curriculum. He learned the planting cycle and the operation of the machinery. He used hand tools and repaired anything he could find to repair. Joseph showed him his system of books and the ledgers, which Rocklan picked up quickly, even making suggestions for improvement along the way. Once, he cadged Maria into showing him a few of her secrets to preparing a stew.

When the weather was particularly brutal and his eyes burned from reading, Rocklan could be found with Joseph in the barn, practicing the four-beat rhythm of casting a fly. Time and time again, he would focus on wrist, elbow, and shoulder, until the rod became part of his anatomy. He would sense the delicate parabolas of line forming behind him, then watch as the loop sang past and unfolded in perfect flight. It took him all winter, but eventually, he was able to gently drop the fly into the bucket of water Joseph had set out fifty feet in front of him. Then and only then did the Shoshone foreman begin his lessons on the mind of the trout.

On days that the weather permitted, Rocklan was out in the snow. Mathew and James pushed him hard in introducing him to cross-country skiing. Joseph made sure he could imitate the apelike rhythm required for moving in snowshoes. Eli taught him how to read and use a compass, twice taking him on long snowshoe hikes for orienteering practice. The three men also spent time teaching him survival techniques, impressing upon him their importance, especially in winter.

But within this curriculum, there was one class that had Rocklan's fullest attention. His fascination with the huskies and the sleds they pulled was fast turning into preoccupation.

He could not get enough of the dogs and their single-minded passion for running. He felt their drive and imagined himself part of it, one of the team. This was a new, but powerful feeling for Rocklan. So, after a few spills—some more harrowing than others—he began to pick up mushing easily. He became familiar with harness, rigging, and tug lines. He learned commands and studied each husky, their strengths and their weaknesses. He learned the difference between lead, swing, team, and wheel animals, and how to best use each.

Rocklan's training started with Joseph following him on trails around the ranch. Soon, they were venturing out of the bowl. The exhilaration of speed and teamwork was only matched by the soaring royalty of the Maseah itself. The men tore along the great range's mountain trails, dipped into its high valleys, and glided past its frozen lakes. It was on these runs that the mountains opened up for Rocklan.

He no sooner strung the harness and got the dogs settled from one run when he started thinking about the next one. He recognized the potential for both freedom and isolation in the dogsleds. And most nights, he would fall asleep with the sound of the dogs still in his head.

Those evenings that he wasn't totally exhausted, he spent in the library. He had always read, so he lit into the trove in the library with some enthusiasm. While it occupied him, his reading didn't always keep his mind off either Susan or the will. Those two distractions remained relentless in their pursuit of his consciousness.

The winter rhythm of Maseah Mountain kicked in and powered the enclave through the snow and stinging cold of the end of 1932 and the start of the New Year. Routine and ritual replaced the excitement of the visitors' arrival. Because of the weather, if they weren't working, the ranch's denizens were often tucked away not far from the nearest source of heat. But one bright, clear day, the sound of a twin-engine plane could be heard climbing toward the valley. This mobilized all at Maseah Mountain, because it signaled the advent of the much-anticipated airdrop.

Three times the plane flew low over the bowl, each time dropping several large, heavily wrapped bundles that buried themselves harmlessly in the deep snow. The event became a game to find the treasures and haul them back to the barn and house. The pilot dipped his wings on his last flyby, and soon the engine noise faded, leaving only his dropped cargo as proof that he was ever there.

Eventually, weeks turned into months and the cold began to lose its fiercest bite. The Wolf Clan was beginning to mobilize for the return to their village, and the rhythms of Maseah Mountain began to change yet again.

One morning, Rocklan found himself alone in the kitchen with Maria. In his time on the ranch, he had come to realize that the woman was the heartbeat of Maseah Mountain. There was little that went on that she didn't have a hand in or wasn't directly orchestrating. And her motives were always obvious—she watched over those she loved.

Rocklan liked her and her crustiness. In many ways, she reminded him of Mrs. Flannigan from University Hospital, a person whom, in retrospect, he would have liked to have known better. With that in mind, he made an effort to cultivate Maria. She saw it, of course, but didn't seem to mind.

The cook was looking out of the window toward the barn. A thaw had arrived, and there was a steady sound of draining water in the spouting as the snow on the roof began to melt.

"Well, it won't be too many more days before Red Cloud and the clan pack up and head north," she observed, making conversation.

"Susan was right," he said. "They have been no problem at all. In fact, Maseah Mountain is much better for their visit. I met some very decent folks this winter."

"Is that to say you've also met some indecent folks among the Shoshone?"

"Now Maria, don't be baiting me. You know what I mean."

"I know what you mean. There's only one I would classify as indecent," she said.

This brought to Rocklan's mind the night of the clan's arrival. He had wondered about Red Cloud's little tale and the angry words it brought forth from his sister. Rocklan hadn't been able to gather any insight from the general conversation around the ranch, and he had been afraid to open a sore subject with her. He thought he would try now.

"Mind if I ask you a question?" he started.

The cook's antenna went up, but she said, "Sure, what's on your mind?"

"Remember the first night, when Red Cloud told the story of the proud wolf?"

"I do," she said, now looking at him.

"Well, I know it's prying, but I've been wondering what made you so angry that night."

"It is prying," she said, turning away.

"My apologies. I just thought that maybe there's something I could do."

"That old idiot has to do it," she said, still sore just thinking about it.

"What?"

Maria was silent as she threw away the morning's coffee grounds. She remained that way as she filled the ash bucket from the stove. Rocklan stayed patient. Finally, Maria sat down at the table across from him and sighed.

"What I'm going to tell you is not talked about. In one way, I'm hoping Red Cloud's story is his feeble attempt to clear the air. On the other hand, if it is, it doesn't explain his treatment of Eli."

"What? I don't understand," Rocklan said.

"We have to back up a little bit," she explained. "You know that Red Cloud is my oldest brother, right? Well, his tale of wolf families is really the story of Maseah Mountain. And you are aware that Dr. Whiteley married a Shoshone woman?"

"Yes, Susan or Eli mentioned it."

"Well, Petah, his wife, was married to another. In fact, she was married to Red Cloud's favorite son, Anoki, my nephew."

"Dr. Whiteley's wife was already married?"

"Yes, but there's more to it than that," Maria said. "Anoki was never a strong person. He was alcoholic, and never accepted the responsibilities that were his. His father expected him to lead the clan. Petah expected him to be a husband. And when Eli was born, she expected him to be a father. He was none of those things. What's worse, he used to beat her."

"But still, she was married to someone else," Rocklan reminded her.

"Yes, yes, of course. But listen to me. "Dr. Whiteley used to make regular rounds of the villages. That's how Petah met him. I brought her to him when he reached us. She was pretty battered when he treated her. Periodically, he would come back and find not much had changed. He took an interest in her because she was bright and had ambition. He was always looking for help with his practice. But he knew she was married, and so he said nothing to her. In time, it became obvious to me that something existed between them."

"So, what happened?"

"Well, when Eli was about five, Anoki left. He just left. And no one has seen him since. I believe he left the Maseah for good."

"What did Petah do?" Rocklan was caught in Maria's story.

"For a few years, Petah was alone, supported by Red Cloud because Eli was his grandson. That was a bad time for her, living under his roof. In some way, I think my brother blamed her for Anoki's disappearance."

Rocklan nodded, so Maria continued, "After a time, on one of Dr. Whiteley's regular visits, their attraction to each other caught fire. And the doctor began to make more frequent trips to the Wolf Clan's village."

She stopped to watch Rocklan's reaction. When he shrugged, she went on, "Well, at some point, it started to become obvious that Petah was pregnant. These things happen even with the greatest of caution. When it came to Red Cloud's attention, he was furious. It was a betrayal. It was a betrayal of his missing son, and it was a betrayal of his generous hospitality. The old fool."

"So, your brother expelled her from the village? And Eli too?" Rocklan asked with disbelief. Then, seeing Maria's surprise that he knew, he quickly mentioned the story related by Hawkins in Blackbird.

"Well, the story you've been told is surprisingly accurate," commented Maria. "There was no way anyone was going to separate Petah and Eli. So, she took him with her. Her distraught and dangerous plan was to walk to Maseah Mountain and Pendleton Whiteley. The village was higher up in those days, and the trip longer than it is today. There was snow coming, as well."

Maria stood and walked over to the stone jug of medicine she kept for special needs. She lifted it, then put it back down. Instead, she drew a glass of water from the pump and sat back down.

"Dr. Whiteley arrived in the village on horseback with one of his herding dogs a day after Petah had left with Eli. When he found out what had happened, there were hard, irrevocable words said between the men. In the process, Red Cloud made some outrageous accusations. The doctor immediately set out in search of the mother and child, and found them late that day near death, as you already know."

"What were Red Cloud's accusations?" asked Rocklan.

"My brother accused Dr. Whiteley of murdering his son, Anoki. It was not said directly, but the implication was there. The old man had no reason to think that other than through his warped sense of reality, or just pure malice.

"Anyway, while Dr. Whiteley never talked about it, Petah would say later that she didn't remember much about how she and Eli survived that winter night, alone in the Maseah. She does remember sheltering under a pine tree. That's where Dr. Whiteley found her, and that's where they rode out the storm together. Eli remembers being tucked in a blanket and sleeping with the dog. I guess the warmth of the horse, the dog, and the doctor was lifesaving."

Rocklan could not imagine sheltering under a tree in a snowstorm. The cold must have been horrific.

Maria began to wind her story down. "The doctor brought Petah and Eli down to the ranch, and that spring, Susan was born. Petah never left Maseah Mountain after that. She and the doctor had a lot of happy years together, raising those two and caring for the Shoshone. Petah was his wife under any reasonable rules. She was also his right arm and his best friend. I know, because it wasn't long after Susan was born that Joseph and I joined them here at the doctor's request."

"So, Susan is…" started Rocklan.

"That's right," interrupted Maria.

That night, Rocklan lay in his bed, thinking about Maria's narrative. He listened to the occasional sound of melting snow sliding off the roof. These people, who he was going to dismiss so easily when he first arrived, were human beings of depth, feelings, and courage. It occurred to him that this simple realization was one that he had not had with his own family. Helen had been right—he never did really see her or Lily for who or what they were. The thought made him feel worse than the self-centered guilt he had been nurturing.

He stared at the pale shaft of moonlight that intersected the bed. He thought about the ranch, he thought about the dogs, he thought about Susan. Then, he thought once again about the will.

He would do the right thing; he knew that now. Maseah Mountain was Eli's and Susan's legacy. And as much as he had fallen in love with the place, he could not take it away from its rightful owners. It may be true that the Whiteleys ultimately couldn't afford to keep it, but that was beside the point, for now. Just the same, he was not quite ready to tell them what he had found. He was still driven to find the solitude that he hoped would purge him of his ghosts. And so, he decided to hold onto the will. Come warmer weather, he would take off for a while by himself. Maybe visit some of the high villages. Explore the range. Get to understand it, as Joseph and the others suggested. Be by himself for a time. While he was gone, nothing would change; he would pay the bills, and Maseah Mountain would continue as always. When he returned, he would set things right, even if it meant he would have to leave.

Chapter 12

Flying Solo

The Maseah surprised its residents with a powerful snowstorm in late March, and the mountains seemed to hold their snow well into April. While this might have shifted some habits of the range's hunters and their prey, to Rocklan, it was a godsend. It meant that he had more time with his dogs.

Early that spring, he had left his dependency on Joseph far behind at the ranch while he and the huskies explored the elevated world in which they lived. He took with him all of the lessons the foreman taught him, and those of Eli and Daniel as well. Twice, this instruction was responsible for saving his life. Other times, he found that his own resourcefulness made the difference. Regardless of the difficulties he faced, Rocklan pressed on in pursuit of living his life through experience and independence.

The first stop in his travels was Red Cloud's village, some weeks after the clan had returned from Maseah Mountain. He brought with him the letters and gifts given to him by Susan. Some were for the Wolf Clan, and others for villages and clans scattered throughout the region. He also had with him a letter of introduction from Eli, and he secured another from Red Cloud. These notes, along with his deliveries, assured the white man's welcome around every hearth he encountered.

Rocklan enjoyed the pause in each village and the people he met there. It was not just for their food and warmth, but also for the stories, the directions, and the advice on everything from wildlife to weather. He came to look forward to these periodic social contacts after spending a few days on the trail. Still, most of the time, he was alone with his dogs.

When he was between villages and out in the open with night coming on, sometimes he would construct a tent from a tarp, using the sled as a supporting structure. Other times, he would find what natural shelter he could and huddle over a fire for warmth, or to roast a rabbit or some other small game. Often, shelter meant a rock outcropping to cut the wind and the late snow that seemed to hang on forever. It was not an easy way to live, but it was what he had been looking for.

Sometimes, under cover, surrounded by the huskies, he would think of Susan and their last conversation before he left. He remembered every detail of the evening she found him in the library with his maps. She had come to him with letters for friends in some of the remote bands.

Susan sat comfortably in one of the leather chairs in front of the desk. Rocklan was in the other one.

"Maria tells me you are going up to the villages," she started.

"Yes. I want to take the dogs and see as much of the Maseah as I can."

"Well, one thing for sure," she observed. "You'll have the opportunity to find the solitude that's so important to you."

This sounded a lot like a criticism to him, so he said nothing in response. With his silence, she plunged into her request of him to deliver some mail. She, Eli, and Maria had correspondence they wanted sent with Rocklan, and even had presents for various people, honoring birthdays, weddings, and anniversaries.

"Thank you for doing this," she said. "Some of these people I haven't seen or talked to in a while. Oh, and I have a few prescriptions. Would it be too much to ask you to deliver them as well?"

"Yes, of course, it's no trouble at all—assuming I arrive at each of these villages," he said with a smile, acknowledging his inexperience.

"Just remember what my brother and the others have taught you," Susan said, showing a trace of concern, but knowing that nothing she said would stop him. Nor did she want to try to do so.

Very sensitive to her every tone, and taking the opportunity, Rocklan said, "Look Susan, I know I haven't been the most pleasant of people up to now. But

I've come to understand a lot of things since I arrived. There are some things I've said that I regret, especially things I've said to you. I wish I could start over with you."

Susan knew immediately where he was going with this. For some time, she had sensed his feelings toward her, and that was the very reason she had been avoiding him. She was a bit tired of it, and she wanted to set the record straight. Susan was not one to live without clarity in her relationships.

"John, I think I need to let you know where I stand. You're a smart man—certainly a quick study. And your time here has done you a world of good in many ways. But I find you introspective and secretive. You seem to be carrying a lot of baggage that I don't understand. For reasons I am not interested in exploring, you have hidden who you really are, and have made certain decisions that I find odd at the very least. This is not the kind of man I could with live with for very long. I'm telling you this not to offend you, just to be sure that there is no misunderstanding and that there are no, ah, expectations between us."

Rocklan was, of course, stunned by her candor. As always, he had been looking at her and a possible relationship from his perspective alone. There was no arguing the points she made, and apparently, there was little opportunity to change her mind.

"I appreciate you being so direct with me. I see what you are saying, and I hope I haven't caused you any discomfort," was his response. It was not what he wanted to say, and normally he was not one to give up on something so easily. But Susan was not someone to be pushed, either. If something were ever to work out between them, she would come to it on her own. So, he had his answer to the question he never asked.

Like many of their conversations, this one concluded awkwardly. His silence and his embarrassment signaled an end to the matter. So, she thanked him for delivering the correspondence and medicines, and left him to his travel planning.

Rocklan was gone for almost two months with the dogs. He returned in the mud and melting snow, only to sleep, eat, saddle a horse, and pack a mule in order to continue his exploration. However, the use of the mule—despite the fact that he owned it—was conditional. It came with a load of correspondence, assorted bundles, and medical supplies. He, in fact, had become the Maseah Mountain mailman.

There were a few things Rocklan wanted to do before he left again, however. The dogs needed putting up for the coming spring and summer. He and Daniel talked as they kenneled the animals. They both watched Buster, Rocklan's heroic lead dog, closely. Buster had been everything to the Easterner. The animal probably taught his master more than Joseph did. But the gallant old dog, as deep-hearted as he was, had begun to show his age. And the rest of the team knew it.

Rocklan did not hesitate in his decision to retire his fearless friend. It was either that or watch the team deal with it in their own way. He would not let that happen.

Daniel understood immediately, and assured Rocklan that Buster would live out his life in peace. There was room for him in the barn.

Soon after, Rocklan was back deep in the mountains. Red Cloud had been right when he spoke of the rewards of beauty that the Maseah bestowed. Late spring in its remote valleys or atop its bare rock crests was a changing world of color and shape. There was a newness and life that he had never before experienced. In many ways, his travels during this time overwhelmed him. His frame of reference for experience itself had changed. He had no model for guidance—everything was new. There was a distinct freedom in that, but not a lot of comfort, for he rarely knew what was going to happen next.

The third week he was on horseback, wolves attacked him. Normally shy of humans, the small pack's recklessness was driven by hunger. The mule bolted, and his horse threw him while kicking at the hunters. Rocklan managed to stun one and wing another with a shot from a Winchester rifle before the group scattered. In tumbling off of the horse, he had gotten kicked. Now, his shoulder hurt and he had to find the pack animal.

The mule, being a creature that remembers its experiences, backtracked the way it came. Rocklan found it standing, fully loaded, next to other mules at a hitch in the Shoshone village he had left just the day before.

It was getting late and he was hungry. He also needed to get some ice on his shoulder, and wouldn't mind sleeping in a bed one more time before moving on. Fortunately, Rocklan had met some people in his earlier stop, and they had an extra room.

The next morning, he woke, collected his gear and the animals, said goodbye to his friends, and went looking for breakfast. He was feeling stiff, but better, especially after he cracked open one of Susan's deliveries of aspirin.

He bought two bean tortillas from a woman he passed and ate them as he noticed a loud group at the end of the street. A moving crowd had formed a ring, like they were watching a bareknuckle fight, shifting as the combatants battered each other this way and that. Rocklan's curiosity drew him in.

To his surprise, the fight was not between boxers, but two violent and aggressive dogs. As Rocklan reached the human ring, the circle of bodies shifted toward him and he found himself on the inner edge of the mobile arena. Suddenly, they were there, right in front of him, snapping and snarling, fangs bared, going for the throat. He leapt back unharmed, but now stayed two bodies deep in the crowd. He stared in disgusted fascination and shuffled with the crowd's atavistic dance.

Both dogs were big for the breed, one even bigger than the other. They were Siberian huskies, but maybe there was some other breed mixed in as well. The larger animal was coal black, the other with the standard white markings. He had seen dogs fight, of course; it was part of the territory. But he had not seen ferocity like this. One time, Buster took on a bear, and Rocklan saw what fear an angry dog can generate. But to see two such enraged temperaments in direct opposition was unique and horrible.

Rocklan saw no betting or side-taking among the yelling crowd. But there was a big Shoshone man with a long club, tracking the pair and bellowing about the devil killing his lead dog. Periodically, the man would catch up to the combatants and take a hard swing at the black dog, but miss.

In a lightening rush of crazed fury, the bigger dog lunged and clamped down on its adversary's throat. That's when the Shoshone connected with the club. The first blow was solid and stunned the animal. The second had to break some ribs. The third swing never got started, because Rocklan stepped in front of the furious man.

"What d'you think you're doing?" the man roared, drawing back the club.

The big, black dog was hurt badly, and it lay still at Rocklan's feet.

"Wait, wait. I'll give you fifty bucks for the dog," said Rocklan with his hands out toward the man. "I'll take him as he is."

A fifty-dollar offer in 1933 would have stopped a train.

"You know anything about this animal?" asked the man, astonished at the offer. "I don't want to take your money without you knowing what you're getting."

Rocklan had found an angry, but honest man. "Tell me."

"This Siberian mix is a big, strong son of a bitch, nearly eighty pounds, but he's untrainable. I've been running dogs my whole life, and I've never seen one like this. He's killed one of my swing animals, and he was about to kill that one, my lead," said the man, moving to grab his sizable husky, still quivering from the fight.

"I got this black devil from a Canadian man," he said, prodding the prone dog with the club. "I think he used to beat the beast pretty good."

"Have you run him on the lead?" asked Rocklan.

"No, I haven't. I don't trust him. He's got the bearing, intelligence, and the muscle, but I won't put him on the lead of my sled. I'll take the fifty, Mister, if you're serious."

"I'm serious. It's in my pack. Help me get the dog down the street, and it's yours," said Rocklan.

So, he found himself back with his friends. During his first visit, Rocklan had established that he would pay room, board, and stabling whenever he stayed. As a result, they were very glad to see him yet again.

The husky had sustained a severe blow to the head and, as suspected, three broken or cracked ribs. The ribs would heal, but the ex-big city surgeon was concerned about the head trauma. The dog lay in a warm, hay-strewn barn stall for two days, semiconscious. There wasn't much Rocklan could do other than wrap him and make him as comfortable as possible. Again, he dug into Susan's supplies.

On the morning of the third day, Rocklan brought a little grain soaked in beef broth, hoping the dog would take some. When he opened the stall door, the dog leapt past him, shoving him hard against the wall. Because the barn door was closed, the dog had nowhere to go. He turned and bared its teeth at Rocklan. A low, dangerous growl came from deep in its throat.

The man slowly put the bowl of food down, backed away, and showed the dog his open palms. The dog feigned a charge at him, snarling and barking, but Rocklan stood his ground. Soon, the food overpowered the dog's fear of the man. The husky edged up to the bowl, watching the man through his brow. While he wolfed the food hungrily, Rocklan found a pump and filled another bowl with water, placing that within the dog's reach. Once it finished, the animal backed away quickly and again looked for an escape. Rocklan held a piece of dried elk out to the Siberian. The dog came to it, snatched it away from him, ran away about twenty feet, and hunkered over it until it was gone.

Rocklan held another piece out, and again the Siberian came to him. This time, the dog didn't snatch the meat, but simply took it in his mouth. Rocklan held it tighter and gently extended his hand to the dog's scruff. The animal immediately ducked and hopped away. When Rocklan showed him the elk again, the dog returned and this time, Rocklan let him have the meat. The third time, the dog stayed and allowed himself to be scratched behind the ears.

"I'm told your name is Black Jack," Rocklan said to the big dog. "Well, Jack, I have plans for you."

In another day, they were ready to travel again. Rocklan rode slowly out of the village, trailing the mule, followed stiffly by the big, black sled dog.

Man and dog bonded quickly, and Black Jack was rarely very far from Rocklan. The animal seemed to revel in his freedom, at times bounding away after a squirrel or deer, only to return panting, with what Rocklan could only describe as a silly grin on his face. After a long day of climbing mountain tracts, the dog seemed reluctant to rest, as if the next day wouldn't bring more of the exquisite same.

As the weeks passed and spring moved toward summer, Rocklan made the rounds of the high villages and investigated remote areas, teeming with game, fed by swift streams, and dotted with hidden lakes. He watched the habits of moose, elk, deer, mountain goats, and sheep. He even saw the occasional black bear and once, a mountain lion. The big cat was far off and high up; it was Black Jack who spotted it first. Luckily, his encounters—as he once called them—were at a distance. Herd animals and smaller game became routine, but never ordinary. Recalling Eli's comment about the wisdom of a high regard for nature, Rocklan gave the mountain wildlife respect and learned where and how to look for it. He took many clues from Jack, whose awareness of the life around him was exceptional. The dog lived for now, and that's exactly what Rocklan was doing.

There were times when he was sure that the dog saw its role as his protector, positioning itself between the man and whatever game they came across. Rocklan would laugh when the husky barked at woodchucks and hare, but came to appreciate his nose, which allowed them to avoid startling something dangerous. A loyalty was building between the two, something new to both.

When stopped for the night in the open, Black Jack would normally curl up by himself, warm in his double layer of fur. But in the morning, Rocklan often would find the dog pasted against the blankets in which the man had wrapped himself.

Eventually, Rocklan discharged his mail delivery responsibilities and began the long trip back to Maseah Mountain. But, as so often can happen in the high country, winter had one more late delivery. The temperature dropped swiftly, and the wind picked up with force. He found himself out in the open, exposed and in danger. He was shivering, and the horse and mule were suffering as well.

He was caught in an elevated, broad mountain plain with no shelter. The landscape offered only the occasional grove of fir trees—no rock shelves or places to break the wind's deadly bite. The snow was blowing hard, piling up against the low-hanging branches of the trees, creating white cones in the otherwise stark expanse.

Rocklan dismounted, strapped on snowshoes, and began to lead the horse as best he could. He was unable to see much, and not quite sure where he was going anyway. He was in real trouble. For the first time in his travels, he was at a loss. But he knew he needed to stay warm, and to do that, he needed to get out of the wind. The image of the frostbitten man in London's *To Build a Fire* came to mind. He recalled his visceral reaction to the story when he first read it. What a fool the character was to be caught out in such weather. The thought ended with remembering that the desperate man considered killing his dog to put his frozen hands inside the animal's warm body.

Just as the image fled from Rocklan's mind, he watched Black Jack run to one of the field's snow-covered fir trees. It was a large tree whose swooping branches touched the ground, forming a conical pyramid of snow. *How can he possibly want to chase a rabbit now?* Rocklan wondered. Shortly, the dog returned, sat, and simply looked at him with his pale blue eyes.

It took Rocklan a moment to understand. Then, he led the animals over to the tree. Jack had dug a hole through the branches. Using his snowshoe, Rocklan shoveled away enough snow to get his shoulders through the low pine boughs. The inside was dark, but there was a little daylight yet, high up through the thick network of limbs. He found a four- or five-foot space, lined with a bed of needles. Several branches grew low on the tree inside the natural shelter, so he found his hand axe and crawled into the protected space. By hacking off the boughs close to the trunk, he was able to bend the limbs upward, wedging their butt up and between others higher on the tree. In this way, he was able to create more space while maintaining a roof and walls of branches and snow.

He left the pack on the mule and the saddle on the horse, hoping they would offer at least some warmth. He pushed his bedroll, an extra blanket, and his ground cover into the tree space. Then, he led the two animals to a small grove of firs growing tightly together. He forced the animals down together in between the trees, tied them securely, and covered them as best he could with a tarp. They would either survive, or they wouldn't. He had little choice.

Returning to his rabbit hole in the tree, Rocklan crawled back in, bringing Black Jack with him. Using the ground cover over the pine needles, he built a flooring of sorts, laid the roll down, and pulled the dog to him, covering both of them with the second blanket.

He thought about building a fire, but again recalled London's unfortunate traveler doing the same and bringing the snow from a tree limb down on himself and the fire. So, he concentrated on the warmth of the dog in the blankets, and that way spent a long and painful afternoon and night as the storm raged on.

While most of the time Jack seemed to sleep peacefully, Rocklan lay huddled in a state of half-wakefulness. He thought or dreamed about many things, including the story of Dr. Whiteley finding Eli and his mother under a tree. But he mostly thought about his life and how it had changed so radically. What used to be important to him seemed foreign and absurd now. The Maseah had taught him a new set of rules, and along with it, he had discovered the need for a different set of principles. Money, respect, reputation, and status marked the objectives of his old life. What was important now was quite apart from those things. They seemed temporary and ephemeral. This new life seemed somehow more substantial, tangible.

He thought about himself often these days. It wasn't ego; it was simply self-review. He knew, of course, that this uniquely human talent is both blessing and curse. And he smiled at the thought that Jack might waste a moment thinking about who he was. But Rocklan was after just that—who was he? And what mattered most to him?

He realized now that leaving his old life behind was a futile attempt at escape. It was futile because who he was never altered with a simple change of venue. Leaving the city and coming up here did, however, offer an opportunity to build something new inside of him—a new foundation.

This idea had started some months ago, when he first launched himself into the mountains. But the real self-analysis began when he found the solitude he so desired. During his time in the high range, Rocklan rethought the values he had always taken for granted. Where had they come from? Why were they his for so long? He didn't ever remember thinking about them, much less thinking them through. They were just there, and he had accepted them without question.

Now, curled up with the black dog, listening to the wind trying to find them, he attempted to name what he truly believed in. Whatever was important to him now had come from experiences occurring after leaving the town of Blackbird. It was the Maseah that had schooled him. And the family at Maseah Mountain. And his dogs. These things provided the experience, the new rules; he identified the underlying principles.

He believed in unconditional loyalty, once committed. He believed in being as aware of as much of the world around him as possible. He valued mental toughness, far more than the physical side. And he believed in the power and importance of tribe, of family, and of the love of individuals. These were the things that were now important to him.

As Rocklan sorted through these thoughts, he eventually came around to Susan, once again. She forced the issue because she had become important to him. He loved her. He also saw in her a chance to be a part of a tribe, a family again. Perhaps, deep down, he wanted to make amends for his poor prior attempt as well.

Rocklan's soul-searching wasn't just a mental exercise; he knew he had to act on his thoughts, if they were to be of any value. What good was a set of strong principles if you didn't work at them and make them who you are? So, he decided that's where he would focus—on what was important to him. That meant, with unequal priority, Susan, the Maseah, and his dogs.

When he woke, the wind had stopped and sunlight could be seen high up in the fir. He burrowed out of their refuge into deep snow with the dog right behind him. The day was bright; the storm was long past, and the sky was a dome of blue, stretched over mighty white peaks. He saw the horse and the mule twenty yards away, still tied to the firs, but now standing, waiting for him. Black Jack stood tall, stretched his paws forward, yawned, and then lifted his nose to the air.

"I think you need a new name, my friend," said Rocklan to the black dog. "The Maseah will know you as Noble Jack from now on."

Chapter 13

Coming Home

As Rocklan emerged from the Maseah's more distant reaches and began his descent, the temper of the great range began to quiet. Snowfields turned into occasional patches of white still trapped in shaded crevices and retreating from the tops of hills.

The strengthening sun brought life, and he watched it emerge from dens, burrows, and nests. Grass and an infinite variety of other green shoots were forcing their way up through the stony soil to the sunlight and still-crisp air. Splashes of primary color washed up slopes and down into high valleys as gardens of the yellow and purple crocus, pansies, sweet William, and forget-me-nots made their appearance. Clear, cold streams gurgled past in their hurry to join others to become the snowmelt rivers that fed the mountains' blue reservoirs.

He watched Noble Jack about fifty yards out in front of him. The dog was working back and forth across the trail, tracking a scent he found interesting. Rocklan watched his companion and thought about his dog team. They were a season away, but he was anxious to start working with Jack on the lead. He recalled the animal's former master saying that he'd never run the dog on the front. But Rocklan knew his friend was born to it. Jack would set a bar that the rest of the dogs—and the musher himself—would have to stretch to meet.

He watched the black dog sprint up a short rise and stop. The husky looked back at him once, then turned and became transfixed on something on the other side of the hill. As Rocklan came up to him, Jack barked once to be sure the rider saw the same thing he did.

Rocklan dismounted and reached for the dog, who came to him immediately, whining and agitated.

"It's okay, Jack," the man said. "That's home you see."

The two stood together staring out across Maseah Mountain's green bowl. Under a deep blue sky, the Maseah's great, white-capped crests stood sentry around the rich valley and the life within it. It was a picture that Rocklan would hold in his memory forever. New grass had taken hold in the fields. A small, tightly packed flock of sheep ran this way and that as a working dog moved them out to longer grass. Dun-colored cows grazed next to the Virginia stack rail fence that had to be used in the Maseah's shallow soil. Two horses, mare and foal, raced by the cattle on the other side of the barrier, tossing and shaking manes as they ran, feeling the fresh spring weather. A man with a tether was working a young colt in the corral, and chickens could be seen pecking for corn and insects as they avoided the yearling.

The barn rose from the bowl, its whiteness reflecting the sun, making it seem even larger than Rocklan remembered. Beyond the big structure, smoke curled up from the ranch house chimney and was carried off slowly by the slight May breeze. A woman came out onto the gallery, which had been hung with planters of early flowers and trailers of green. She wiped her hands on her apron, then raised them to her forehead to block the sun as she peered at the two figures standing on the ridge.

Except for the short stay to exchange the sled and dogs for a horse and a mule, Rocklan had been gone nearly four months. He recalled the sense of homecoming that the place engendered, even on his first ride around the ranch. Now, the feeling swamped him. He had come to think of Maseah Mountain not as something he owned, but rather as a part of himself that he was now rejoining. He had only lived here for a few months, true, but since then, many nights under cold stars had been spent thinking about the place and those who lived here. Eli never tried to explain his regard for Maseah Mountain, and now Rocklan understood why. The emotion had to be experienced.

Rocklan rode down into the bowl and followed the road that led to the paddock between the house and barn. There, Maria waited for him with Joseph, Carly

Blue, and a young boy he had never seen. Daniel had stabled the colt and joined them as well.

"Well, the prodigal returns," said Maria, smiling.

"Yes, I'm back for a while now," said Rocklan, shaking Daniel's hand after getting down off the horse. "It's good to see you all."

He climbed the porch steps, clapped Joseph on the back warmly, and stood before Maria.

"Well, are you going to give me a hug?" she asked. He was surprised at her welcome, but more than happy to show that he missed her.

He gave Carly a squeeze as well and asked, "And who is this young man?" Rocklan extended his hand to the boy.

"This is Noah Lodge," the girl said. "He's Patty's replacement. And, at the moment, my student." She turned to the young man. "Noah, this is the owner of Maseah Mountain, Mr. Rocklan."

"Patty's replacement? Your student?" he asked, confused. "It sounds like a few things have changed around here. And please, I think it's about time we dropped the 'Mr. Rocklan.' Don't you? I wish you all would call me John, or anything else you want besides 'Mister.'"

"I thought Susan was the only one allowed to do that," the cook teased him. "And before you ask, she's not here. She's at a conference and visiting friends in Baltimore. We expect her back in a couple of weeks."

Rocklan's disappointment was obvious, so Joseph said, "It looks like you brought home a new friend." The foreman had already reached out to the big black husky and was scratching his deep chest.

"Wow, he's a monster!" said Daniel, who of course knew a good sled dog when he saw one. He too moved to Jack to get a closer look.

"Noble Jack is my new lead dog," explained Rocklan. "But he's pretty raw when it comes to the sled."

Daniel admired the husky, circling and running his hands over the animal's low, powerful haunches. "With this color, he won't get lost in the snow, that's for sure," he laughed.

"I'm anxious to see what he does with the other dogs. He has a history that I'm a little worried about," said Rocklan.

"History?" asked Daniel.

"Yeah, it seems—"

Maria interrupted. "You can talk dogs and sleds all night if you want, but not now. I bet you're tired and hungry. There's some hash on the stove. Come in. We have some catching up to do." She took him by the arm and led him toward the mudroom and the kitchen.

"Wait, wait. I don't want to leave Jack with the other dogs around," said Rocklan. "I think I recognized Matilda out with the sheep, but where's Job and Buster?"

"That's part of the catching up," said Daniel. "Don't worry, Noble Jack and I will get along just fine. He can help me stable the animals. I'll leave your pack on the gallery." With that, the wrangler sat down next to the dog and began to get to know him.

Maria led Rocklan in and sat him at the big kitchen table. She poured Joseph and Rocklan a cup of hard cider and put a plate in front of the new arrival. Carly disappeared with her charge in the direction of the clinic.

Joseph tipped his glass to Rocklan and said, "From the looks of you, you've had quite a spring. Since you're back and alive, it must mean I'm a pretty good teacher." He grinned and took a good swallow.

Rocklan said, "You are my professor, Joseph, and I am your fortunate student."

"That's how I think of it as well," the foreman laughed. He seemed pleased, but the cider might have been a contributor.

"I want to hear about your travels, but we'll have to talk later. Let me tell you about Buster real quick, then I've got to go. Buster and Job were killed by a lion that was raiding the sheep," he started bluntly. "It was the most heroic thing I've ever seen two dogs do."

"Tell me," demanded Rocklan.

"There's not a lot to tell. Job and Buster were with us, tracking the cat. Matilda was busy, delivering pups. Well, the dogs eventually treed the animal late, but they didn't know what they had caught. The mountain lion baited them, then made a terrific leap out of the tree and onto the back of one of our mules. It was dark and chaotic. We didn't know where the lion was. All we could hear was the sound of a mule dying. The next thing we know, the dogs attacked the cat. The noise of the fight drew us to them, and we saw that the lion had again retreated up the tree. Daniel got a good shot in. The beast fell, screaming from its wound, then laid dead at the base of the tree. That's about it in a nutshell."

"Buster's dead?" Rocklan asked, stunned.

"Buster and Job. Job died right there from a tear in this throat. Buster lasted another hour, but he had lost too much blood," Joseph said flatly.

Rocklan was quiet, so the foreman said, "I don't mean to be cold, but up here, you need to maintain perspective. It's all a cycle. What the Maseah takes, it gives back in some other way."

Rocklan remained silent, thinking about his lead dog.

"Well, I've got something I have to do. We'll talk at supper," said the foreman. Then, to Maria, "Are we having mule or mountain lion for dinner tonight?" He looked at Rocklan wryly, then rose and went back to work.

"It was a sad thing, that's for sure. I don't know why Joseph was joking. He loved those dogs," Maria said, shaking her head. "They saved human lives, maybe even Joseph's. If I'm a dog, I have to think that's not a bad way to go, especially if I've had a pretty good dog's life already. We all should be so lucky."

Maria had a point, so Rocklan nodded sadly in understanding and agreement. Then, after a few moments, he changed the subject to Susan.

"She's in Baltimore. Still has friends from her work there. Something about a paper she wrote, too. Patty is with her. Susan's introducing the young Miss Blue around and opening a few doors for her. She'll take entrance exams, and Susan says Patty's likely to be accepted into any school she chooses. Susan is pushing Hopkins, of course, but Patty will make up her own mind."

"Impressive. It's rare that a woman gets into any med school. So, Susan's killing a few birds with one trip," he observed.

"Just like her father," commented Maria.

"Well, you said she'd be gone for a couple of weeks. Just how long is that?" he asked.

"She said she made travel arrangements to get back here on specific dates, just to be sure that she also had a financial reason not to stay too long. If all goes well, she'll be back by the end of June, if not before."

"Good," said Rocklan. "Where's Eli? And what about the boys?"

"The boys are fine. James is here. But he's in trouble with Joseph at the moment," Maria said, rolling her eyes. "But that's another story. Eli and Susan split the duties. He's in Chicago with Ayasah. They took Matthew. He's already been accepted into Loyola. But that boy's really not sure what he wants to do." Again she shook her head, this time with a little worry.

"Matthew's done well, Maria. You know he'll figure it out. You and Joseph have a good, strong, young man there. I can see his potential. And you know he won't be able to stay away from here for very long."

A blush and a smile replaced the cook's fretting. "He will do well," she said quietly, nodding.

"What about Eli? Do you know when's he's back? I've got something I want to talk to him and Susan about. And I need them together." He rose to find Maria's stone jug. He set the cider aside and refilled another mug, then sat back down.

"What's it about?" she pried.

"Now, what kind of man would I be if I talked to you before I spoke to those two? No, I think it best to wait." He was pleased with himself, knowing he had gotten a small payback for all of her poking and prodding of him since his arrival.

"I'll tell you what kind of man you are, raising a subject then dropping it," she said sourly.

Rocklan had worn out his welcome in the kitchen, at least until supper. He wanted to get back to Jack, anyway. So, there was no time like the present to introduce the new lead to the team. He wanted Daniel with him, just in case Noble Jack needed to prove himself with force—a very likely occurrence.

He fished his medical kit out of the pack Daniel had left on the gallery, crossed the road, and went into the barn in search of the wrangler and the black dog. He found them together.

"I just introduced blackie here to Matilda. She's with her pups, and I didn't want any surprises." Daniel laughed. "Your big, bad lead dog seemed very intimidated by the whole scene, not to mention Matilda herself."

"Intimidated? Jack? No way in hell!" Rocklan said in disbelief.

"I can't wait to see him with those bullies out in the kennel, especially Butch. Hoo ha!" Then, seeing Rocklan's face, Daniel said quickly, "Of course, Matilda can be a real bitch sometimes." Then he laughed out loud.

Rocklan laughed too, but was well aware that he already had been the source of humor a couple of times since his arrival back at Maseah Mountain. No matter, he chose to assume it meant they were beginning to accept him—like the hug from Maria.

"Seriously, though," said Daniel, "this could be dangerous. I'm going to take a net; you take this loop. We don't want anyone getting too hurt." He handed Rocklan a pole with a slip loop on one end.

"C'mon, Jack," said Rocklan. "I want you to meet the team."

The two men and the black dog walked through the corral, down the fence line to the kennel. The sled dogs saw them coming and set up their awful noise. They saw the men, of course, as the next opportunity to run. But their volume could only be attributed to their scenting of Noble Jack.

As they neared the compound, sleeping dogs rose and those on their dog-house roofs leapt off. The team milled at the compound's gate, waiting for whatever came through it.

Rocklan held Jack's collar, and he could feel the animal vibrate. His ears and his head were up, eyes on the other huskies. They stopped at the gate to unlock it.

Daniel handed Rocklan a pair of heavy gloves and said, "If it gets nasty, let me use the net on the aggressor. You catch the other one the best you can. If there's a fight, we'll have to watch for flankers. Don't be shy about using your boot if you have to."

He opened the gate, and Noble Jack pushed his way between them and strode out into the compound. He was not aggressive, seemingly, just curious. The team also was curious. But when a sniff turned into a nip of the black dog's haunch, Jack reacted decisively.

Before the men could move, the dog spun, clamped down on the offending teammate's rear leg, and flung him a few feet away. The other dogs immediately closed in. Jack bulled his way through a knot of animals, rolling two of the dogs over in the process. He then leapt atop the nearest doghouse, knocking a barking dog off.

The team was a pack at that moment, surrounding the black dog. Noble Jack held his head low and aggressive between his muscled shoulders. Muzzle up and fangs bared, he started a deep growl as he swung his blazing eyes around the circle. Among the attackers was Butch, Rocklan's powerful wheel dog. With Buster gone, Butch had held sway among the team.

The men moved quickly to the animals, dispersing the pack with commands.

"This isn't going as well as I hoped it would," commented Rocklan.

"What do you mean?" replied Daniel. "This is going perfectly. Your lead needs a chance to assert himself."

At that, Noble Jack launched himself off of the doghouse and at a dog that was particularly agitated. In a brief scuffle, the husky was rolled on his back with a hard bite on his flank from Jack. The dog skittered away to safety. Then Butch made his play. Using his weight, the wheel dog smashed into the big, black dog, sending him sprawling.

Jack was up quickly and immediately on the attack. The two squared off and lunged at each other ferociously, neither finding the advantage they were looking for. Rocklan and Daniel also moved quickly, the wrangler holding the net up in front of Butch, while Rocklan moved Noble Jack back with his pole. The team was giving them room and had quieted a bit.

The men each secured the dogs' collars and held them tight, while issuing stern commands to the other animals. Rocklan began to calm Jack, and Daniel did the same with Butch. The two combatants were then walked around the compound while the men quietly praised them. Eventually, Daniel and Rocklan brought the dogs back together, still holding firmly to their collars. The animals took the measure of each other with their noses, then relaxed. The other dogs did the same, and the introduction was over with minimal damage. Now, Noble Jack could begin to work on the lead. Full acceptance by the team would come from his leadership in the traces.

Maria had prepared a homecoming meal for Rocklan, and everyone at Maseah Mountain joined them. It was the same chaotic affair that most of the ranch's big dinners or celebrations were. He couldn't help but remember his first night here, when he sat at the end of the table like Judas Iscariot at the Last Supper. Now, he was a part of it. And, to his delight, he found that there was an appreciative audience for his stories about his time in the Maseah's back bowls.

James was particularly interested, and couldn't hear enough about Noble Jack and his reputation for fighting.

"Mr. Rocklan, you mean he actually killed two dogs?" asked the Bearclaw teen.

"Well, one I know of. The other, he would have killed, if that musher hadn't brained him," answered Rocklan.

"John, was Noble Jack hurt badly?" asked the young Noah, apparently remembering Rocklan's request to be called John.

Carly was appalled at this, but no one was more appalled than James. How dare this kid call Mr. Rocklan by his first name? Had he ever gone riding with him? Taught him how to ski? It didn't help that James was becoming a little jealous of Noah's time with Carly. The girl, it seemed, had caught his young eye.

"Of course he was hurt. How would you like to get hit in the head with a club?" James asked Noah, delivering an unconscious double entendre.

"James, we can do without the sarcasm," said Joseph.

"But, you said..." began the boy.

"No buts," said his father sternly. Evidently, the two were still having their discussion of earlier in the day.

That drove the agitated boy up from the table. A pointed "excuse me" was offered tersely, and he was through the mudroom door.

Maria looked at Joseph, and he looked back at her sadly.

"He just feels bad because Matthew isn't here," was Carly's assessment.

Later, Rocklan sat alone with a cup of coffee as he watched Joseph and Maria wash and dry dishes.

"Ask him what he thinks," Maria prodded her husband.

"Ask me what?" said Rocklan.

"It's nothing, just family stuff," replied Joseph, trying to avoid the topic.

"It is something, and John's got some experience. Ask him," Maria nudged.

The foreman looked at Rocklan apologetically. "James doesn't want to go to school. Susan says he's the brightest of the lot, but he doesn't want to leave the Maseah. At least, that's what he says."

"He is smart. He writes all of the time. Stories. Plays. He's even started to organize old Dr. Whiteley's notes and memoirs. Says he wants to write a biography of the doctor. Says he wants to write about the mountains." Maria wasn't going to entrust Joseph with the entire conversation, and her husband was just as happy to let her pick it up.

"We have been telling him he can do both—just get his degree first," she continued. "He says he wants to write and he already knows how to do that. It would be a waste of time and money, he thinks."

"He told me that we should let him live his own life," added Joseph.

"He can live his own life," said Maria. "Just after he does what's best for him."

This water was too deep for Rocklan. Without saying it, he tended to agree with the boy. Let him write and explore for a while. What was the harm in it? What was the hurry? He himself had leapt into a life that he hadn't really thought much about when he did it. He had done what others had expected of him. That was a lifetime ago, and he wondered if he would take the same path today, given the choice.

"It's difficult for me to offer an opinion," he said. "I understand the wisdom of your advice, but I also can appreciate James's point."

This was not what Maria wanted to hear, so he continued quickly, "He has to set his own course, and if he knows what he wants now, and it's a reasonable want, then perhaps the sooner the better. It seems to me that there is time to let this kind of thing play out, especially up here."

Neither of the Bearclaws was happy with this thought, but part of that was because they had already considered exactly what Rocklan had said.

CHAPTER 14

PAST IS PRESENT

The spring of 1933 turned into summer, and life at Maseah Mountain settled into its warm weather cycle. The work was ongoing; fields and gardens needed planting, fences needed repair, outbuildings lacked paint, trails had to be cleared, and animals required attention. The men of the ranch spent most of their days outside, making the best of what they knew was a short summer. Maria continued to direct the ranch's domestic life, and Carly seemed to oversee the clinic with little effort and no crises.

In Susan's absence, Rocklan kept a covert eye on the young, aspiring doctor. He found her well-trained and more than capable of handling the summer's normal flow of visitors to the clinic. There was some stitching to do, there were a couple of arms to set, several sprains to wrap, a number of rashes to control, a fever to watch, and other things, but no trauma that would have asked too much of her. There were no resident patients, and even old Billy Whiteshoe decided he wasn't going to die yet, so he returned to his village.

Rocklan was glad for Susan's ability to prepare her charges, because he wasn't ready to return to medicine. In fact, he had no plans to return at all. He would just as soon let his history fade, and so, he never raised his own background and it never seemed to come up. While he knew that both Eli and Susan were aware of his earlier life, they seemed to have kept it to themselves. He was convinced that no one else at Maseah Mountain knew he was a physician, and he was careful to be circumspect during his travels among the villages. He did practice some basic care when it was unavoidable, but he was always sure to explain that Susan Whiteley was the doctor in the Maseah.

By the third week of June, neither Eli nor Susan had returned. And there was no word. Maria reminded Rocklan that the two were not overdue, and they would be along in time. Still, the anticipation of seeing Susan again was excruciating, and made the wait seem endless.

Before he left, Eli made good on his promise to set up the shortwave radio. He built the kit and mounted it in one of the kitchen cabinets. The "magic" he used to power the equipment came from the Maseah—the engineer had gathered the parts and constructed a windmill on a nearby ridge that charged a series of batteries. As long as there was a breeze—which was most of the time—the apparatus worked well. On still days, though, the batteries didn't last very long.

The Shoshone was so pleased with his work that he tied in a second radio kit in the barn's office. Once the equipment was up and working, Eli established two regular links: one into the National Forest Service in Boise for weather and emergency purposes, and the other to the county community services office in Blackbird. Maseah Mountain was now in touch with the rest of the world.

According to some, the best thing about the shortwave was the music, especially the popular music. Others claimed that the news and the serials were the attraction. Whichever it was, the box quickly changed the routine at the ranch.

After supper, evenings now included the news, Roosevelt's Fireside Chats, Eddie Cantor, *Little Orphan Annie*, and *The Lone Ranger*. These last two shows were the favorites of James and Noah, who never missed an episode, if they could help it. James was fascinated with the radio and what he found on it. When he wasn't working or writing, he was Maseah Mountain's de facto expert on the instrument. He had even established friendly relations with contacts in the centers in Boise and Blackbird.

Maria knew how to find "her stations" on the radio, and at almost any time during the day, a listener could hear Ben Bernie's "Let's All Sing Like the Birdies Sing," or any one of the endless hits of Bing Crosby. The cook could do some singing herself. Rocklan heard both a passable "Stormy Weather" and a good take on Gene Autry's "The Last Round-Up."

One time, Rocklan caught her dancing to Ellington's "In The Shade of the Old Apple Tree" as she stirred something on the stove. He wasn't quite sure what got into him, but he took her for a quick spin around the kitchen, showing her a few of the moves that Helen had forced him to learn. It was impulsive and fun, but he mainly succeeded in embarrassing himself. She, on the other hand, was both shocked and delighted. He quickly returned to work in the barn, wondering about the source of his spontaneity.

This was also a time that Rocklan spent walking the trails around the ranch with his dogs. He was itching to go further afield, but he knew that Susan and Eli could appear at any time. So, he stayed close by. Just the same, his walks were a good way to keep the huskies in shape and start to rebuild the sense of team that had changed with Noble Jack's arrival. Rocklan also used an old four-wheeled training cart of Dr. Whiteley's that Joseph had found in the barn's loft. While the thing was tricky to use, it still worked to keep the team fit and ready for snow.

Joseph and James continued to butt heads over the issue of school, neither trying very hard to see the other's point. Most conversations ended in bad feelings and anger. One instance was especially fierce, when a frustrated Joseph commented on the frivolity of the time James spent listening to the radio. This was a particularly unfair observation, given the boy's work on the ranch and the time he spent either with his studies or in writing. His father's opinion set the young man off. Unable to express his feelings articulately, James fled the conversation in exasperation once again.

The next morning, both James and Hawk were gone. Maria was confident that he hadn't gone far, and that he would be back in time for supper. By the time supper had come and gone, the radio shows had concluded, and night had fallen, Joseph and Maria were worried. James knew how to take care of himself, but he was still a boy alone in the Maseah.

After a sleepless night and a morning of indecision, Maria convinced Joseph he should go to look for their son. Both Rocklan and Daniel offered to help in the search, but it was decided that Daniel should stay on the ranch. So, the two men saddled horses and left to pick up James's trail. Rocklan took Noble Jack with them as well.

They found Hawk's hoof prints easily enough; they led up into the mountains. It was logical to assume that the boy would head for Red Cloud's village, so that's where they went. Upon arriving, they were told that indeed James had been there early the day before, but he had borrowed a few supplies for a "camping trip" and left, going deeper into the Maseah.

For the rest of that day, Joseph and Rocklan followed the track that James had taken. But the boy had a lead of a day and a half and was moving rapidly, so they were unable to overtake him. The men and the dog spent the chill summer night in the open, and were back on the trail at first light. They passed through several small valleys and up and over a number of ridges, some offering spectacular views of the high country. At times, the track narrowed, presenting rock walls on one side and sheer drops on the other. The country was, of course, beautiful. But its danger for a solitary traveler was obvious, especially if that traveler was fifteen.

As the second night on the trail approached, Rocklan could see that Joseph was clearly worried. Just as he was going to say something, Jack barked and sprinted ahead and out of sight. The men picked up their horses' gaits and followed at a safe trot. They came upon the husky sniffing the area of a wide, flat space that had opened on the path. When Joseph dismounted, he could see the drying blood that the dog had scented. Jack milled briefly, then again quickly followed his nose further up the trail. Rocklan spurred his horse after his dog, but before long, the rider had to pull up at a grisly scene not far up the trail.

The husky had disturbed several huge turkey buzzards feasting on a carcass that had been worked over first by something large, then by a series of smaller scavengers. Lying among torn-away body parts and the main bulk of the dead animal was Hawk's saddle. There was no sign of the boy.

As Joseph surveyed the area, he said, "They were attacked by something big, likely a bear. The tracks are all here. Wolves have been here, as well. In fact, it looks like Hawk has been feeding a lot of the wild life in the area. Do you see any sign of James?"

Rocklan had been skirting the area, looking for other signs. "No, I don't."

"Then he must back along the trail somewhere. Let's check before we look further ahead," said Joseph.

The two men, leading the horses, slowly retraced their steps back to where Jack first picked up the scent. As they neared the open space in the trail, they noticed the dog on the edge of a precipice, looking down and whining.

Joseph ran to the spot and peered over. He could see James's leg at an odd angle, about fifty feet down on a ledge, protruding from a group of heavy boulders.

"Here he is!" "He's not moving." Joseph was working hard to stay calm, but his voice betrayed his worst fears. "Get the rope, I've got to get down there."

"Joseph, let me go. I think it'll be quicker," said Rocklan, realizing that Joseph's age might create a second problem.

The foreman hesitated, then understood his partner's point. He grabbed a coil of stout rope, gave it to Rocklan to loop around his middle, then secured it to one of the horses. When the younger man said he was ready, Joseph took the bit and created tension on the rope as Rocklan edged over the side.

Rocklan's fear was real, but he wouldn't allow himself to think about the danger as he scraped over the sharp rock, toes scrabbling for purchase as he descended. After what seemed to be an interminable drop, his boots reached one of the boulders on the ledge. He could see that the boy was motionless and wedged. When he was able to reach the ledge itself, he realized how precarious the platform was. There was a good two to three hundred feet of void below him, and Rocklan worried about his added weight.

The former physician found himself back at University Hospital as he carefully inspected James's misshapen body. There was a lot of damage, but thank God the boy was still alive. He was unconscious, yet offering a shallow heartbeat.

"Joseph, he's still with us," Rocklan shouted up to the boy's father. "Can't tell how badly he's hurt yet, but it's not good. He's unconscious. We've got to get him out of here and back down to the ranch as fast as we can."

Neither man may ever be able to explain it fully, but through saddle blankets, rope, cut limbs, and horses, they rigged a crude lift that allowed the boy's body to clear the cliff's edge without causing further damage. What ensued after that was a frantic race down the mountain trail on a travois to the Wolf Clan. There, they picked up a wagon and, without stopping, continued through the night to Maseah Mountain.

James was still with them by the time they arrived at the ranch, but only by a razor-thin margin. Rocklan suspected, in addition to a head injury and a broken arm, the boy had internal bleeding. He was going to have to do something, and he was going to have to do it immediately.

He found, to his surprise and relief that, what Eli had called a "clinic" actually included a well-equipped, albeit dated, pre-op and surgical suite. It wasn't far from his own ideas about "emergency rooms." It came as a shock to both Maria and Carly that Rocklan took command upon their arrival, issuing orders that could only come from someone with extensive medical experience. Soon, with Maria out of the way and Rocklan directing, Carly fell easily into the procedures required by the doctor. Six hours later, they emerged from the clinic, exhausted and worried. They had done all that they could for James for the moment. He had been stabilized, and now it depended upon time, the boy's powers of recovery, and whatever god the Shoshone believed in.

A week after James had been found, he was still drifting in and out of consciousness, although his vital signs had improved greatly. That same week, Susan returned, just as she said she would. Patty and Ayasah were with her.

Matthew had gotten settled in Chicago, then Eli and Ayasah met Susan and Patty in Boise. Eli then left them to take care of some business of his own in Denver. He was expected back in another two weeks.

It was plain that the travelers were glad to be home, but as soon as Susan learned of the accident, she disappeared into the clinic with Patty and Carly. She managed to say hello to Rocklan and offer him a warm smile, but the two had no chance to talk. So, he walked out to the husky compound and was combing burrs out of Noble Jack's fur when she found him there two hours later.

"I didn't get a chance to say hello earlier, and now I also want to thank you for what you did," Susan said. "Carly explained what happened and all of your work. It was as professional a procedure as I've seen. It's good to know you haven't lost your skills."

At another time and place, Rocklan might have been tempted to think, *Of course it was professional—that's who I am.* But now, he simply took pleasure in the compliment. Coming from her, it was especially satisfying.

"I could not have done it without Carly," he said modestly. "You have quite a prodigy there."

"Now, no deflecting the praise, doctor. I could see for myself what you did. Spleens are tricky organs. So are collapsed lungs. Can you tell me what you saw and what you decided along the way? I'd love to compare notes with my own experience."

This was really the first time that they had spoken to each other as equals and friends. He and Susan left the dogs and strolled the ranch without any real direction. Their conversation was technical, and each explored alternatives without intent to criticize or dominate. She asked the difficult questions, and he answered them without defensiveness. When he told her something that was new to her, she was appreciative and connected the information with other data she kept. She, in turn, offered insight and new procedures that she had either read about or picked up in Baltimore. By the time they were finished, they found themselves back at the house.

Rocklan wondered whether he had found the new start with Susan that he had hoped for. He wanted to know, but he said nothing to her. He knew the relationship was fragile. He wasn't backing away, just giving it some time and breathing room. So, he said nothing about his aspirations, handed the patient over to her officially, and returned to the kennel.

As the days lengthened, James became fully alert and began the slow haul of mending, despite being prone to headaches. The summer routine quickly returned to shape life at Maseah Mountain, and the warm sun contributed to both the boy's recovery and everything else that grew in the valley. For the other residents, the combination of long days, hard work, and cool nights made for sound sleeping.

James spent a great deal of time with his father now, finding a comfortable tempo and rebuilding the bond between them that had deteriorated. Joseph and Maria were much more subdued in their thinking about their youngest son, probably because they had come so close to losing him. James, on the other hand, was quickly becoming his old self, chaffing at Susan's prohibition against riding and Daniel's refusal to take him hunting. Just the same, he seemed happy to spend hours with a pen and a black-marble-cover notebook, sitting in Dr. Whiteley's rocker on the porch of the house.

A few days after Ayasah had returned to her family in the Wolf Clan village, two men arrived at Maseah Mountain, asking to talk to Eli and Maria. Their credentials said they were there in an official capacity. One was from the FBI, and the other from the Law Enforcement & Investigations unit of the National Forest Service. They had traveled all the way up to the ranch to investigate some serious allegations made against the late Dr. Whiteley.

The officials were made welcome, and they introduced themselves as Agent Graves and Special Agent Muller. The visitors quickly outlined the reason for their investigation. There had been a formal request to file charges against the doctor for the murder of Anoki Redcloud, they said, pronouncing the last name as one word. The men were quick to clarify, however, that since the doctor was deceased and no body was ever found, charges had not been officially filed—at least, not yet. Regardless, the allegations had to be looked into and reports completed.

The FBI man then went on, in a rather tactless way, to say that there was also interest in understanding "what goes on up here" at Maseah Mountain.

During the conversation, Maria was beet-red, and the federal agent's turn of phrase was all it took for her to explode.

"Just what are these allegations and who's making them? And what are you implying we do here at Maseah Mountain?"

"I'm not implying anything, ma'am," said the government man disingenuously.

Before Maria could continue, Joseph said, "Please don't treat us as fools, sir. Aside from doing your duty when there is an allegation of murder, why are you here? What have you heard goes on up here that requires two officials to investigate?"

"I'm not at liberty to say, at the moment," said the FBI man.

This did not go well with any of the residents, and there was a general clamor of dissatisfaction with the man's highhandedness. Finally, Susan said, "There is no reason for you to take the attitude you are. Perhaps that comes from your experience. But I would suggest that if you want our cooperation, you'd better change your tune. What is it you want to know? We're happy to answer your questions. Just show us a little common courtesy."

The government man didn't quite know what to say; he had started badly. So, Agent Muller said, "Please forgive my partner. He's had little exposure to the mountains, and less experience with the people who live here."

The two officials exchanged dark looks. It was obvious that it had been a long trip for both of them.

The Forest Service man continued, "Red Cloud of the Northern Shoshone Wolf Clan has for some time been writing the governor. He claims that Dr.

Pendleton E. Whiteley was responsible for his son's disappearance, and that he can prove Dr. Whiteley murdered him."

Joseph literally had to push Maria back into her seat. "Maria, I know this is absurd. Just let the men do their job. They'll find out the truth soon enough."

"I am Dr. Whiteley's daughter, Susan. His adopted son, Eli, is in Denver at the moment. This is Red Cloud's sister, Maria."

"Yes, thank you Mrs. Whiteley," said the National Forest agent.

"We would also like to talk to you about the medical clinic you are operating here." The FBI man looked at her accusingly.

"It's Dr. Whiteley, and I'm not married," said Susan, ignoring the fed.

"Yes, of course, my apologies," the National Forest agent said. "You are a physician?"

"I am. My degrees are from the Johns Hopkins University and the Hospital. Would you like to see my credentials? And by the way, that is Dr. John Rocklan," she said, pointing to him standing quietly in the corner of the kitchen. "I believe he practiced at the Massachusetts General Hospital and the University of Maryland Hospital, among other places. You will find him just as capable of providing medical care as I am."

"That may be, Dr. Whiteley, but who authorized the practice of medicine up here?" asked the FBI man, still accusatory.

"The governor of Idaho and the State Medical Board did, Agent Graves. My father had the same authorization, and we both share commendations from the state, as well as from the president of the United States for our work with the Shoshone. The documents are readily available," she answered with no pride or arrogance. "The Board gets monthly reports from us, and all medicines are accounted for and their use documented, as required. Oh, and you're welcome to tour the clinic, if you'd like."

"One would have expected the FBI to have done their homework before coming up here with unfounded suspicions," observed a livid Maria.

"Yes, well. Perhaps," said the Forest Service man with a quick glance at Agent Graves. "Would it be possible to see your papers, just for the record? And we would appreciate a tour of the clinic, thank you."

Susan left to find the appropriate files, and Maria asked, "Before you go through your good cop bad cop routine again, what is it that you want to know about Dr. Whiteley and Red Cloud?"

"We would prefer to question you alone, ma'am," said the FBI agent.

Again, Agent Muller jumped in. "It might go a little quicker if we had some privacy, ma'am. Of course, if you would prefer, your husband is welcome to sit in." This didn't make the FBI man happy, but he said nothing.

"I have a question before I leave," said Rocklan, moving out of the corner. "If the allegations have been made against Dr. Whiteley and the doctor is deceased, who are you planning to charge?"

"We're not planning to charge anyone," said Agent Muller quickly. "We're just conducting an investigation."

Then Agent Graves said, "If a murder has been committed, any number of charges may be filed against those abetting the perpetrator, regardless of whether the killer himself is living or not."

"Have there been allegations against anyone else?" Rocklan asked.

"Not at this time," answered the Forest Service man. "Dr. Rocklan, was it?" "That's right," said Rocklan. He then went out through the mudroom.

Maria cooperated with the officials and answered all of their questions about Red Cloud, Dr. Whiteley, Anoki, and Petah. When she was asked about Anoki's disappearance, her memory of the last time she saw him was hazy, and she could offer them little. Later, in talking to Joseph and Susan, she wasn't sure that she managed to put the question of the doctor's innocence to rest. In fact, her sense was that she only succeeded in establishing a possible motive for Dr. Whiteley to kill Anoki.

Susan offered the officials a room for the night, which they gladly accepted. They were gone early the next morning, however, on their way to talk to Red Cloud himself.

Some days afterward, Rocklan was spending a rainy, chilly day in front of a fire in the library. While he loved the room, he could never enter it without thinking about the will he had tucked away in a volume of Charles Dickens's *Great Expectations*. He still hadn't said anything to Susan, choosing to delay his revelation until Eli's return.

The other memory that he found difficult to purge was his last conversation with Susan in this room. She had spoken her mind, in the process describing him as self-centered, secretive, and needy. Had anything changed since then? Perhaps he could sense a softening in his most recent time with her, but not a lot. As he was musing along these lines, the subject in question walked into the library.

"I thought I might find you in here, today," she said. "It's a good day for reading, isn't it?"

"Yes, it is," he said. "The weather in the Maseah is unpredictable. Who would have expected it to turn cold this time of year?"

"What is it the Boy Scouts say?" she asked, looking at the fire. "Be prepared."

With that she, picked up the copy of one of Meriwether Lewis's Journals that Rocklan was reading. "Getting prepared, are you? Planning more adventures?"

"Oh, I don't know. I'm always thinking about the mountains. I've got a new lead dog, you know."

"Yes, James was telling me. He sounds like quite an animal. Sorry about old Buster. I know you two got close pretty quickly."

"Yeah, well. That was sad. But Buster lived a life he was born to, and he did it for a long time." Rocklan smiled. "May I ask you a question? Now that you've blown my cover, I thought I might as well pick up some of the medical responsibilities in the villages this fall. That is, if it's alright with you."

"Hey, you blew your own cover. That was fine work you did. You saved the boy's life. I'm sure it's all over the Maseah by now."

"It was no more than what you or anyone else would have done," he said with some diffidence.

"I don't know about that, John," she answered. "Do you really want to get back into it? There's not much leading edge or exciting in the villages. There are not many big city emergencies."

"No, but it will allow me to continue to explore the Maseah, and I can help along the way. Besides, as you say, I suspect the word is out on me up there."

"Ah, once again the past has become the present," she said. Then, seeing his confusion, "Just something my father used to say. You are more than welcome to assist me," she said teasing him, at the same time probing his ego. "There's just one condition: you have to continue to be our mailman. That's the deal."

"Done," Rocklan said with a grin.

Susan looked at him for a long moment, then said, "Look, I said some pretty harsh things to you last winter, and I wasn't correct in all that I said. You are not completely who I thought you were. I saw you as dependent, needing a lot of help and resentful over the fact. And the problem was never you. I don't see that trait in you anymore. Your time in the Maseah has created a man who can stand on his own—someone who seems to know what he wants now."

This was the conversation Rocklan wanted to have, and he had a lot he wanted to say. Instead, he sat silently, listening to her, trying to understand what she was telling him.

"I know you may still feel a bit shanghaied by us. But it was just too hard to explain to someone who had not experienced life here. You wouldn't have accepted it if we had tried. You had to experience it for yourself. Now, it seems that you get it—what life is here and what it means to grow. That's what the Shoshone word 'maseah' means, you know."

How could he explain to her how he had changed since arriving at Maseah Mountain? It was difficult, just as she was saying. It was a very personal transition that he had made. He had come a long way, and maybe now he had come far enough.

"Susan, I—"

"John, please let me finish my thought. It's something I've been thinking about for some time. It's true that we misled you, but not much. When Eli said that once you had your feet on the ground, we would move on, he wasn't lying to you. You now have your feet on the ground. So, if that's your desire, then that's what we'll do. It's your choice, of course."

It hit Rocklan that Susan must have been talking to Maria. She knew from the cook that he wanted to speak to her and Eli together. The women must have speculated that the subject was about their leaving Maseah Mountain.

Whatever he was going to say to Susan was gone now. Her mention of staying or going, in light of the will he held, kept him quiet. How could he tell her now? She would think him deceitful. At least when Eli arrived, he could get it all over with at once.

"In my eyes, you have changed, that's clear enough. You have become a part of Maseah Mountain, and maybe even the Maseah itself. Your love for it shows. But I have to tell you that you remain enigmatic and closed. Despite what you did for James and the Bearclaws, despite your offer to work among the Shoshone, I wonder how much you are capable of doing outside of yourself."

This confused Rocklan, and it must have shown. Susan explained, "What I mean is that it's important to know who you are and what you want, but that's only a start. My father taught us that true growth, emotional, spiritual, and otherwise, can only come through others. Once you understand this and make it your life, then you will become a man worth knowing, and one worth knowing well."

He sat there, once again stunned by something she said. And once again, she took it for reticence. As a result, she felt she had said too much, and was a little embarrassed by her own frankness.

"Susan, I'm not sure I fully understand what you just said, but I'd like to have the chance to think about it before I respond. Please believe that I appreciate your comments. They're very important to me, but I just don't know what to say right now. Can you accept that?"

She was immediately relieved by his response. "Yes, I can. Look, if ever you want to talk some more about this, let me know. I was lucky enough to have someone to explain it to me. But, so much of understanding is coming to it yourself, not being told about it."

They parted then, perhaps for the first time without awkwardness.

Chapter 15

Loose Ends

Maseah Mountain marked July 4th, 1933 by flying the flag, picnicking, playing horseshoes, and listening to Souza on the radio. Joseph even fired off a bottle rocket that he had hidden from the boys and saved for the occasion. Maria organized a summer spread on the gallery, and red, white, and blue bunting was hung all around. There were no hotdogs at their picnic, but the cook did grill some very American homemade sausage; there was blueberry pie and ice cream, as well. The residents of the ranch remembered the principles that built the country, were thankful for its beauty, and recognized the courage of its people in tough times. All in all, it had been a rich day and a good way to celebrate not just the birth of the nation, but also the middle of a splendid, warm summer.

Two weeks after the party, the overdue Eli checked in over the shortwave. He was in Boise, on his way home, and bringing building material for plans that he would explain when he arrived. He would be another week or so.

This news gave Rocklan an opportunity to do a little traveling. So, he and Noble Jack again took one of the trails out of the bowl and up into the Maseah. He carried with him the mail and the curiosity of the ranch over what had happened with the FBI and Red Cloud.

The two officials had passed back through Maseah Mountain on their way out of the mountains, but had revealed little of their investigations. They simply said that they would be back in touch. So, Rocklan planned a slow, circuitous route, eventually arriving at the village. Once there, he would speak first to Ayasah for perspective, then to Red Cloud himself.

It was the first summer for him in the high country, and the mountains had transformed themselves yet again. The ranch and its fields could only be described as verdant, but the richness of life in the back bowls of the Maseah was both profuse and energetic. Both plant and animal life flourished, reveling in the temporary respite from the inevitable paucity and want of the winter.

Below the glacially carved ridges of striated granite and down into the U-shaped valleys, Rocklan saw not just elk, but herds of elk. He listened to moose calling mates and red-tailed hawks keening as they floated on the air currents above him. He watched whitetail deer and mule deer grow fat not on just shoots, but whole plants and their flowers. Fields of rabbits and hare came alive as he rode through them. Once, he spotted the golden back of a huge grizzly. The animal was less than a quarter-mile away, on a long slope, digging roots. As the man and dog watched him, the bear's head came up. Then it stood and sniffed the air; soon, it was focused on the distant intruders. The bear eventually lost interest and returned to its task. Another time, Rocklan's binoculars found a creek-side campsite with two tents. Beyond the shelters, he could see three hikers or hunters moving away from him up a steep trail.

About three hours from the Wolf Clan village, Rocklan stopped early to make camp for the night. He enjoyed sleeping outdoors during the summer, and there was no hurry, so, he, Jack, and the horse made a grassy area along a clear stream their temporary home. He hobbled the horse and let it graze at will.

In fetching water and gathering firewood along the stream, he noticed a cutthroat trout resting in a shadowed eddy. Its perfect gold-green was intersected by the species' distinctive orange stripe. It wavered in the water, just waiting for him. He had planned to gnaw on the dried elk he had brought, but fresh fish, turned over a fire, sounded a lot better. He found his collapsible fly rod in his pack and tied on one of Joseph's mayfly nymphs. In short order, Jack was barking at a cutthroat flopping on the bank. Soon, there were two more.

Later, Rocklan lay against his pack in front of the small campfire, listening to a great horned owl and licking his fingers from the meal. He had boned and given Jack two of the fish and a sizable piece of his own, but the dog still sat looking at him, waiting for more.

"That's it, buddy. There is no more," the man said to the dog. Jack turned his head sideways at his master's words, but didn't budge.

"Don't look at me with those spooky eyes of yours. There-Is-No-More," the man said slowly, leaning into his dog's face for emphasis. All this got Rocklan was a lightening-quick lick of his nose.

"Okay. Okay. How about some surf-and-turf?"

Rocklan reached into the pack and produced a sizable piece of dried elk. When he gave it to his companion, the dog took it happily and moved away to chew on it.

Rocklan rebuilt the fire, pulled a blanket over himself, and was soon asleep.

Early the next morning, the travelers were back on the trail. As they climbed, the animals sharing the environment changed. Lofty crags now held mountain goats and bighorn sheep. Eagles soared at impossible heights, and marmots whistled messages across high patches of scrub and scree. Rocklan knew this to be the domain of the cougar, and while he saw occasional tracks of the lion, the shy animal made no appearance.

Riding down off of the ridges and nearing the village, he opened the Chester Reed Pocket Field Guide that he had found in Dr. Whiteley's collection. The profusion of plants and flowers was astounding, but he found that he could only identify a few. So, as he rode in and out of clusters of spruce, fir, lodgepole pine, and larch, in the few miles he covered into the village, he was able to name several plants. He spotted the ubiquitous bitterroot, red paintbrush, and two varieties of mountain heather. There was alpine buttercup, bear grass, fireweed, arrowleaf, and lupin. Others escaped him, producing a resolution to continue to work on his botany.

It was fitting that, as he rode into the enclave, the first person he saw was a little girl holding an armful of buttercups. She finally noticed him out of her reverie, then ran through the hamlet shouting of the guest. Soon, he was welcomed and several friendships renewed. Ayasah was there and invited him into the modest house where she lived with her grandfather and Kimama. The elderly woman was gracious and quickly made arrangements for Rocklan to stay, despite his polite protestations.

He sat with Ayasah in the shade of a crabapple tree on a rear patio that afforded a panorama of the peak the Shoshone called Weda. They shared glasses of cold apple cider.

"This is wonderful back here," said Rocklan, leaning back, shading his eyes and staring up at the crest.

"The Wolf Clan thinks Weda Peak protects them," Ayasah explained. "I never understood that, though, since 'weda' translates in Northern Shoshone to grizzly, not wolf."

"Maybe there's no Wolf Peak," suggested Rocklan wryly.

"I think we are a people of contradictions sometimes," she said. "Did you know that the word 'shoshone' actually means 'in the valley'? Yet, here the Wolf Clan lives happily in the shadow of Grizzly Mountain. Anyway, it makes no difference what the mountain's called; it's still beautiful here."

Rocklan nodded his agreement and she asked, "Are you wandering again? Delivering the mail?"

"A little bit of both," he answered, digging out a thick packet and handing it to her. "But I'm also on a mission to find out what happened up here with the FBI. I have explicit instructions to get all of the details."

The young Shoshone woman rolled her eyes, sighed, and flopped in the chair. "If that's what represents our government these days, I'm staying up here forever."

Ayasah then provided an account of what took place since she left Maseah Mountain. When she returned to the ranch with Susan, she didn't stay long because she had word that Red Cloud was ill. Reaching the village, she found her grandfather, in fact, very sick.

"As old as he is, every little fever becomes potentially dangerous. Luckily, we managed to get the fever down. But it's taken its toll on him. He's been bedridden ever since, and sleeps a great deal of the time. He's inside, asleep right now," she said with a thumb over her shoulder.

"May I take a look at him?" asked Rocklan. Then a little sheepishly, "I guess you've heard—"

"Oh, yes. You're the next coming of old Dr. Whiteley up here," she said with a grin. "How's James doing?"

"He's fine. Still taking it easy, though. No worries, that boy is made of solid stuff."

"Yes, he is," she said. "Do you know why he took off like that?"

"Well, I suppose it's the same reason I wander up here—it helps me to see things I don't normally see."

"I understand that completely," she said. "There's a clarity here that tends to simplify things."

They both sat without speaking for a moment and just peered at the great peak in front of them. Then, Ayasah continued, "Kimama and I would appreciate you looking in on my grandfather when he wakes. You should be able to talk to him then about the cops, as well. Although, you're going to hear the same delusions that he foisted on those flatlanders. It's ridiculous."

"Well, as long as we have a few minutes, may I ask what you know about their visit?"

Ayasah related what took place when the investigators arrived. She described a miraculous one-day recovery by Red Cloud, who sang the praises of his good friend, the governor. He knew, of course, the man would come through for him. The evening before, she had heard him call the state's highest official a "braying ass." She was graphic in her description of the arrogance of Agent Graves, which quickly turned into fawning and wheedling as the agent began to hear the things from Red Cloud that he came for. She was glad for the agent from the National Forest Service, who seemed to listen and ask questions more objectively.

Red Cloud recounted the worn story of Anoki's marital problems in a way that made his son the victim. There was no mention of Petah's beatings, Anoki's drinking, or his refusal to accept his responsibilities. He described Dr. Whiteley as a fornicator, someone who stole his son's wife from him. Petah, of course, was something worse.

When asked about his last conversation with Dr. Whiteley, Red Cloud painted an angry man, full of hate for Anoki. He even remembered the doctor's last words to him: "If you don't stop Anoki, I will."

The Shoshone ignored the question as to why the doctor might be upset with his son. But he was sure Whiteley had channeled that hate into murder, and that the body had been hidden quite well, somewhere in the backcountry.

"'If you don't stop Anoki, I will?'" asked Rocklan.

"If he said that, he obviously would have been talking about Anoki's beating of Petah," she surmised. "She was working with Dr. Whiteley at the time."

Rocklan nodded. "That's all Red Cloud has? No witness? No murder weapon? No trace of Anoki?"

"No, none of that. My grandfather just keeps saying that he saw murder in Dr. Whiteley's eyes that night."

"Well, it doesn't sound like much of a case to me," said Rocklan.

"Me either," said Ayasah. "But that man, Graves, seemed pleased, and the other one would say nothing. Anything could happen when you're dealing with people whose motives you don't understand."

At that point, Kimama appeared and explained that Red Cloud was awake and asking for Rocklan. So, he visited with the elder and heard the story repeated. What was disturbing, however, was that the Shoshone alternately knew Rocklan and then didn't. At least once or twice, he was sure Red Cloud thought he was talking to old Dr. Whiteley.

Eventually, the man ran out of steam. When he did, Rocklan retrieved a black medical bag from his pack and closed the door for privacy as he examined the elder. Aside from a myriad of minor physical issues, there was nothing beyond old age that Rocklan could see. So, he offered advice on the old Shoshone's care to Kimama and Ayasah, then gave them some light analgesics for him. They would send word if he or Susan were needed.

Rocklan stayed the night, then took the long way home to Maseah Mountain. If he timed it correctly, he would arrive a day or so before Eli. He was anxious to get the Shoshone and his sister together. He needed to unburden himself from the secret he had been carrying. He wanted the matter of the will and the ownership of the ranch to be settled and done with. Then, he could get on with whatever he had to do from there.

His thoughts, as he rode the last few miles, were about the will. If he could avoid their contempt of him for not saying something before now, he thought that there might even be a way to work it all out. Maybe. And maybe, he could knock a barrier down between him and Susan in the process.

When he arrived at the ranch, Susan and Maria were not there. A letter from the Idaho State Attorney's office had called Maria to testify before a preliminary hearing on the death of Anoki Redcloud.

Susan had gone with her for support. She had convinced Joseph that she should be the one to accompany Maria, because she had other business in Boise as well.

Eli appeared a day later driving a wagon loaded with construction materials. With him were two young Shoshone men—one a carpenter, the other a stonemason. He introduced them as Michael and Charlie Haloke, two brothers who ran a small construction business in Pocatello.

After supper that evening, Eli sat with Rocklan, Joseph, Daniel, and the two builders. He explained his plans by rolling out on the kitchen table a blueprint for a horseshoe-shaped structure that would serve as a remote backcountry outpost. His idea was to build a halfway station between Maseah Mountain and several of the more distant villages.

"This is something that's sorely needed, and I've been thinking about it for some time," Eli explained. "If you've ever traveled the high country, you know that it's nearly fifty miles of wilderness between the furthest village and here. I managed to convince the National Forest Service that a refuge is needed, and in fact, I'm working on a contract from them. There are certain restrictions, given that we would be building in a protected forest, but nothing I wouldn't do anyway. All of the paperwork has been done and the permits secured. I even have a spot in mind—just below Marmot Pass, about twenty miles northwest of here."

"This is a pretty aggressive structure," observed Joseph. "That wagon you brought looks full, but there's not nearly enough in it to build something like this."

"You're right about that," said Eli. "The wagon has a few framing pieces, some cement and hardware, but it's mainly tools and other things we don't have up here already. There is some available lumber and slate in one of the storage sheds, but it'll have to be carted up to the Pass. The rest, we can cut up there. I know the area has a number of streams that are a ready source of stone for the foundation and chimney. And there is good water available in the spot I've got in mind."

"How long do you think it'll take to build this?" asked Rocklan. "I assume much of the work will have to be done by hand."

"All of the work will have to be done by hand," said Eli with an impish grin. "But timing depends upon whether I can get you to help us, and whether I can get Joseph or Daniel to do some hauling."

There was a general moaning around the table, so Eli launched into the detailed specs of his plans and offered a proposed schedule that would see a rapid completion no later than the end of September. He admitted the aggressiveness of his timeline, but noted the limitations of the fall weather and the desire to have it ready for use by the time winter set in. They would save time, he said, by living on the worksite.

By the time he was finished, his enthusiasm for the project and the appeal of the work was infectious. It was agreed that Eli, Rocklan, and the two Shoshone craftsmen would stay on the building site, while Joseph and Daniel would rotate the hauling of materials from Maseah Mountain.

Rocklan bought in for the chance to learn some practical skills and, of course, the opportunity to spend time in the back country. He realized, however, that the project would delay his ability to get the Whiteley siblings together to discuss the will and ownership of Maseah Mountain. He didn't care for the loose ends, but at least the work was better than treading water at the ranch, waiting for Susan to return.

CHAPTER 16

A WORKING TRUST

The men had been working together at Marmot Pass for a month. But within the first hour there, it was obvious that Rocklan brought little to the crew in the way of skills or experience. That meant he was the digger, hauler, mixer, lifter, and holder. But he liked the work, and found the physical requirements of his tasks a cheap price to pay for the education he received in the process.

The three Shoshone craftsmen were clearly putting their individual stamp on the construction, yet the project was shared. Each man did his job, but each also felt responsibility for the overall project. A working pattern emerged almost from the start. Solo work was often halted by the need for additional muscle or an extra set of eyes or to rethink early specs. When teamwork was required, it was readily available.

Despite his inexperience, Rocklan quickly became part of it all. His labor was necessary and appreciated. What's more, the skilled workmen encouraged him early on to ask questions and to learn what he could. During the first couple of weeks, he had all he could do to keep pace with the demands of the construction. So, he asked little or nothing at all of the other men. Time and energy were his major resources, and they required close management. At the end of most days, when there was time, there was no energy. He was usually asleep not long after the evening meal.

Slowly, he began to see ways to best use his limited resources. These changes created the opportunity to watch and learn. He then began to ask questions as they arose in his observations. Eventually, the stonemason came to refer to Rocklan as his "apprentice," and the carpenter promoted him to the status of "helper." To Rocklan, as educated a man as he was, these were valued badges of honor and acceptance.

Eli also took pains with the novice. The Shoshone included him in all huddles, often explaining a particular problem and even asking his opinion at times. On the side, the engineer taught Rocklan how to read the station's blueprints and specs. That way, the Easterner could see the individual tasks and phases of the project, but more importantly, the vision for the venture as a whole.

At night, Eli would talk in depth about the plans and some of the design features he was building into the structure. These discussions were what interested Rocklan the most. He could see that the engineer was creating balance between opposing ideas within a symmetrical whole. It was this dichotomy that fascinated Rocklan—it seemed to fit what his life in the high country had become.

Eli was driven to build something that would be a part of the Maseah, something that would respect and honor it. The quality of what he was building would certainly pay due homage to the mountains' majesty. But he was also creating a stronghold, a stout refuge from the mighty range's unpredictable temper. Rocklan immediately recognized the philosophy that Joseph Bearclaw tried to explain to him on that first ride around the ranch. This version, however, had Eli's practical stamp on it.

Rocklan could appreciate these ideas, and now understood their value to survival in the mountains—maybe to survival anywhere. But he thought of this local wisdom a bit differently than the Shoshone did. To him, their wisdom translated to: respect the world in which you live, know what's important to you, and use reason to balance between those two principles. He was able to find that balance working on the high country station.

There was something else Rocklan realized. At sundown, most days, sleep came easily, creeping over and covering the sore muscles he had accumulated for that day. But he was never so tired that he couldn't see the contribution made by his digging, hauling, and mixing. He truly was a part of the crew, and they had come to rely upon him. When that happened, he joined a type of union that had eluded him until then. He had felt a part of the team whenever he was with his dogs, of course, but never before with humans.

It felt good, but the point wasn't teamwork. The point was what the teamwork was producing—the Marmot Pass high country station. What was that old saw about the whole being greater than just a summing of its parts? It was being demonstrated for Rocklan daily. His efforts meant nothing without the work of the others, but together, they were building something extraordinary.

The Shoshone didn't think much about synergy, though. They easily slipped into a working trust because it was what they always did. It was who they were. They understood what it could produce. Rocklan now knew, too.

He recalled the independence he found during his travels in the Maseah. He was proud of that, and saw it as personal progress. He recognized now, however, that it only had been the platform for an additional adjustment. There was another emotional step to be made, and that leap was being driven by the work they were doing. He had not fully formulated the idea yet, but it had much to do with the satisfaction of the kinship he felt with these men.

As a routine settled in, the work moved along steadily. In the first month, the foundation had been dug and laid with rough stone dragged from nearby rock shelves. The hearth and chimney was built from smooth stone, gathered from swift, cold streams nearby. Eli had installed a piping system that made use of a natural spring in the cliff that served as the structure's long back wall. The lumber and other materials stored at Maseah Mountain were used with the area's available timber and granite to form the other walls. Support for the roof had been erected, and flooring and framing had begun to rise from the interior. Throughout the process, care was taken to create harmony with the environment; the objective was to blend the building into the face of the cliff.

By the middle of the second month, the crew had completed the roof and the station had taken its final shape. There was still finishing work outside, including building the gallery. But most of the time now was spent under roof, and out of the occasional thundershower.

The project schedule had another couple of weeks of painting, caulking, pointing, glazing, sealing, and trim work before wrap-up when the Maseah offered a harbinger of things to come. It was not particularly unusual to see snow this early in the fall, but the temperature had been dropping steadily, and at the altitude of the high country station, anything could happen. As it turned out, the wet stuff accumulated up to a foot and the weather stayed cold.

A day after the storm, the sky cleared and the Maseah's blue dome returned. Shortly thereafter, the improved weather also brought Daniel and James who, taking advantage of the early snow, arrived by sled with a last load from the ranch. Daniel, heralded by the sound of barking huskies, was grinning as he swung his team smoothly into the construction site. Leading the team was Noble Jack, looking happy and excited. James was tucked into the large sled in front of Daniel. The teen was euphoric in his first real outing since his fall, and delighted to be a part of the men working at the station.

"This is the only way to travel," he said, laughing, his arms behind his head, leaning back.

"Well, look who's finally ready to pull his weight," teased Eli.

Rocklan tousled James's hair as he walked past the boy, spoke to each of the dogs, and kneeled down to Jack to say hello to his friend.

"I've got to tell you, John, that is one lead dog you have there," said Daniel. "We made it in record time, and he doesn't even look winded. The others really respond to him. I thought I'd take him for a spin myself to see what you've been talking about. Now I know. I hope you don't mind."

"Mind? No, no, not at all. I'm glad to see him. I was afraid he was going to get rusty."

"Rusty is not something this animal is ever going to get," said Daniel.

"I guess ole Noble Jack got a taste of a real musher, huh?" said Rocklan, showing a twinge of jealousy while rubbing the big, black dog behind his ears. The dog was ecstatic. Jack wasn't one to mask his feelings, and this reunion with his master once again proved to the dog that good things lie at the end of the trail.

"Now, John, don't worry. He's not going to leave you," laughed Daniel.

It was late in the day when the sled arrived, so the crew knocked off and prepared for the cold of the coming evening. Since the station was built and generally snug, the men ate and slept inside, gathering around the big stone hearth. Daniel had brought fresh lamb chops, small white potatoes, greens, and berry cobbler.

The food, the conversation, and the long day conspired to knock out all but Eli, Daniel, and Rocklan, who was out in the new pen, getting the dogs settled down. The two men sat propped against the hearth's riser and passed a flask. The others lay around them in various padded shapes, curled in blankets near the fire. The firelight played on the faces of the Shoshone and the old cowboy, and it could have been any year in man's history.

They spoke quietly of the ranch, the weather, and the next set of visitors due at Maseah Mountain that winter. They talked about the station, furnishing it, hauling the stoves, and supplying it, both initially and ongoing. All the while, Daniel drew on an old briar pipe, using the precious tobacco that Eli had brought him from his last trip to the flatlands. The pipe's homey aroma weaved its way through and around the warm, pervasive smell of the wood-smoke fire.

Something Eli said reminded Daniel of one of his responsibilities.

"I have some mail for you. Looks official. Came the day we left." Daniel reached into his pack and handed Eli a pile. "Most of that is for Michael and Charlie. From their families. But there's one there from the City of Denver for you."

Eli found the business envelope, tore it open, leaned toward the fireplace, and began to read. Daniel, of course, was curious, but he would never ask directly about the letter's contents. He did, however, note a change in Eli.

"Everything alright?" Daniel asked, concerned.

"No, no," said Eli. "No. I mean, yeah. Everything's fine. It's just some business of mine."

When Daniel said nothing, Eli added, "Looks like I've got to get down to Denver. Rocklan can keep an eye on things here and finish up. He knows the plans and what's left to be done as well as I do."

"What do I know as well as you do?" asked Rocklan, coming into the room.

"Oh, the station," answered Eli. "I've got to leave. I'm needed in Colorado. Something I've got going down there. You, Michael, and Charlie can finish up here, right?"

"Sure," said Rocklan. "Everything alright?"

"Yes, yes, nothing to worry about. I've got something I have to do and I can't talk about it right now. I'll fill you in when I get back," he said. "I'd better be out of here first thing tomorrow. I'll ride the bay."

Then, because Rocklan and Daniel were staring at him, Eli said, "Sorry, I'm not trying to be difficult. I just need to find something out before I can say anything. I'll tell you when I see you in a couple of weeks."

With that, he gathered what he needed to travel, said goodnight, and rolled up in his blanket.

Daniel and Rocklan looked at each other, not knowing what to say. So, they just sat and stared into the fire, blue smoke curling around the wrangler's head. When it was plain from Eli's gentle snoring that he was not going to tell them what was in the letter, Rocklan asked about another matter of interest.

"Did Susan and Maria get back?"

"Not yet," answered Daniel. "But James heard from Susan over the radio. She and Maria had just gotten into Blackbird and would be along in another day or so."

"And now Eli is leaving again," Rocklan thought out loud.

"I'm sorry?" asked the wrangler.

"I've been trying to get the two of them together for weeks." And now it was Rocklan's turn to be secretive.

Daniel waited for more, but it never came. With a grumble about too many secrets around here, he too rolled up in his own blanket. That left Rocklan watching the red and black embers tumble into each other as the orange and yellow flames danced among the logs.

Eli left before daybreak the next morning, as planned. As long as the weather remained cold and the snow held for a sled trip home, Daniel and James decided to stay awhile longer. The wrangler helped Michael and Rocklan build the gallery, and James was suited to do some of the caulking and sealing work that remained.

By the end of the week, with only some painting left to do, the crew began to focus on cleaning up the site. There was a sense of accomplishment and pride among the men, and they were in a fine mood. On one of their last days, Daniel decided to take James hunting. The idea was to return with enough game for a celebratory feast that would signal the end of the project. A bonfire would be built, Charlie would play his harmonica, and Daniel let on that he had also packed Maria's stoneware jug to assist in the liveliness of the party.

James was antsy to get started, but Daniel needed to help Charlie remove some unused stone first. Rocklan was with the dogs and Michael was in the kitchen, putting up shelving. So, the boy occupied himself in the station's workroom, loading the pack that they would take hunting and preparing the shotgun and rifle they would use. Leaving the kit outside the workroom door, under the overhang, James walked out into the paddock, head down, checking the compass he planned to take.

Suddenly, he sensed a large, dark presence that made him look up. When he did, he saw the grizzly. It had been investigating the site, and stopped when it saw James. The animal was an enormous male. It had curved claws, humped shoulders, and a big, concave face. Its size dominated the opening of the station's U, trapping the boy inside the horseshoe shape of the building. At first, the bear was as surprised to see James as the teen was to see the bear. Then, it let out a deafening roar that froze the boy in his tracks. This brought Daniel and Charlie at a run around the building, inadvertently placing the ferocious animal inside the paddock, between themselves and James.

Feeling trapped, the grizzly attacked. James reacted at that point by stumbling away, falling in the process. His fall may have saved his life temporarily, as one huge paw swept over his back. The animal's yellow fangs were wide as he shifted to pounce on the boy.

Just then, Rocklan stepped out of the stable door, distracting the grizzly momentarily. He swung the only thing he had—a galvanized metal feed bucket. It clanged loudly against the massive head of the beast, which reacted by pivoting with unimagined speed and raking its claws across the chest of its attacker.

Rocklan's chest exploded with blood, and he fell back as if a sledgehammer had hit him. The bear was immediately on top of him, biting and tearing at the man. As the others shouted desperately to get the beast's attention, a shotgun blast thundered, then another. James threw down the side-by-side and reached for the rifle, but the bear was now severely wounded and berserk. It was full of pellets and blind with fury, pain and fear.

The grizzly spun away from the inert Rocklan and turned its rage on the boy. Its muscles rippling with frenzied menace, the animal issued a horrible bellow and leapt at James. The weight of the hurtling beast fell on the boy and drove both of them through the door of the workroom. At the same time, the rifle, by pure chance, found the inside of the grizzly's maw and the weapon seemed to discharge itself, sending a round up through the brain of the bear, killing it instantly.

Charlie rushed to the unmoving Rocklan, while Daniel and Michael sprinted to James. As they rolled the eight hundred pound weight off the boy, he was unconscious and covered in blood. Rocklan was also covered in red from multiple gashes and bites, but he was still alive.

The stonemason had enough first aid training to know that Rocklan was dying. But he wasn't dead yet, so the contents of Maria's jug were used to fight infection, and a makeshift pressure pad was used to staunch the gashes across his chest and stomach. Charlie then wrapped the man tightly to hold it. A tourniquet also was applied to stop the flow of blood from a dangerous leg wound along his inner thigh. The scrapes that covered his head, face, and neck were ugly, but didn't seem life threatening, so they were ignored.

"John is in really bad shape. I'm not sure he's going to survive," said a semi-panicked Charlie to the other two men. "We need help."

Daniel was sitting in the doorway, holding James up, who was starting to come around. The boy was frightened, painted in the bear's blood, but not hurt seriously. The wrangler left him with Michael and ran to the stable and dog pen.

"We don't have a choice," he said. "We've got to get him down to the ranch. To Susan. He may not make it, but we have to try."

Daniel and the team were now in their tenth hour of hurdling down the mountain, in and out of valleys and up and over uncountable ridges. They had rested at times, but never for long. The lead dog wouldn't have it. The man had all he could do to balance the runners and stay on the sled. He no longer was giving commands, and Noble Jack had taken over.

He thought about the black engine at the front of the team. He didn't believe that the dog possessed human intelligence or made calculated decisions. What he saw was an animal running on instinct, desire, and loyalty. Jack didn't decide what to do; he simply did what was most important to him at the time, and somehow the dog knew he had to get home.

It was heartening to watch the rest of the team rise to the task behind Noble Jack's leadership. The husky was pushing the limits with this run, Daniel thought. But he found waiting for the dog to falter to be an idle pursuit, because it never came. And it didn't look like it would.

The musher didn't know whether his passenger was dead or alive. It didn't make any difference; they were going to the ranch one way or the other, and they were going as fast as possible. Faster, maybe. All Daniel could think of was lasting until they came up over that final ridge, little else. There wasn't much he could do anyway, aside from checking the tourniquet off and on and making sure the man was bundled tightly. He was not being callous; he was trying to survive.

In fact, he had come to think of Rocklan as family, one of them at Maseah Mountain. He felt a further kinship with the Easterner, because he thought of him as the same kind of refugee that Daniel himself was. They both had found their place—their way out of the flatlands.

The weather was the one advantage the Maseah allowed them. As they descended, the cold was no longer a factor, yet the snow stayed fast enough to carry them. So, they ran at the miles in front of them for hours. As night fell, the Maseah presented its second gift—a moon that lit up the landscape like a muted searchlight. Daniel wasn't sure Noble Jack cared one way or the other about it. His drive showed little difference between day and night.

The wrangler was an expert musher, familiar with the rigors of long runs, but fatigue had begun to take its toll. At one point, he tied himself to the sled as a precaution against falling off. Another time, he caught himself dozing. Finally, he slumped forward over the rail, dead asleep. He lay across Rocklan's unmoving body.

When the house and barn heard the barks of Noble Jack and the team coming off the last ridge and into of the bowl of the ranch, they emptied out into the moonlit road. The sled was coming fast, and Joseph had no time to saddle a horse, so he waited helplessly with Noah and the women. They watched the specter coming at them—a dog team with no driver.

A wild Noble Jack burst into the group, dragging the sled and followed by a team of exhausted animals. Once Joseph was able to stop Jack, the other dogs began to collapse in their traces. Maria and Susan rushed to the sled to discover Daniel unconscious and draped over…what? The women discovered the blood-encrusted face of John Rocklan soon enough, but they thought him dead. Or, if he wasn't, he soon would be.

CHAPTER 17

TRUTH WILL OUT

Susan and Maria had been back for a day or so when the sled carrying Daniel and Rocklan made it home. That same night, Susan took the Easterner into surgery, using transfusions first from Noah, then from Joseph. Rocklan had lost a great deal of blood, and he was very lucky that she was able to find two matches. Once the vital signs were relatively stabilized, the real work began. The intestinal damage was extensive, a lung was punctured, the femoral artery nicked, an arm broken, and there were multiple conical bite marks and tears on his chest, back, and shoulders. All required sutures. It was a long procedure, but Susan and her understudies worked systematically and well. At the end of it, there were still many risks ahead, not the least of which was infection—a danger for which bear claws were notorious. Rocklan became Maseah Mountain's round-the-clock patient as the man struggled with death and everyone else waited.

Somewhere deep in his subconscious, Rocklan began to dream. He was skimming along a snowfield deep in the mountains. Jack was in full rhythm, and the music of the dogs' yipping echoed back from the peaks around him. He could feel the icy wind burning and tearing his eyes. Yet, he called encouragement first to the team, then to the black dog on the lead to keep up their efforts. When he did, Jack turned in his full gallop and gave his master that look of happiness dogs seem to be able to convey. Man and dog were one in their element.

Suddenly, he was among fir trees. As he sped through a stand, their branches lashed him, snatching at his parka and leaving red welts on his arms and face. Once, he was nearly knocked from the sled. Noble Jack turned again, and the dog's earlier joy had become a maniacal obsession. It was no longer pleasure Rocklan saw, but an instinctual fixation that seemed more suicidal passion than choice.

"Where are you going, Jack?" the dreaming man asked his dog. The dog ignored him and merely increased the sled's speed. Then, Rocklan knew that if he didn't stop, Jack would continue until they plunged over a precipice or dropped dead from exhaustion. He was surprised that he had the ability to stop. But he applied the brake, and when he did, he found himself sitting in front of a warm fire under a dry, rocky overhang. He was comfortable, and the dogs were all around him, sleeping peacefully.

He looked up from the depths of the fire to find his wife, Helen, sitting there across from him. They sat in a bubble of light, stolen from the pitch-black night around them. He could see her beautiful face in the firelight, and she was smiling at him, although it was plain that she had been crying. She spoke to him.

"John, you are not who you once were."

"No," he answered simply.

"We could have been so happy."

"Yes. But I couldn't see then, and you could. I'm sorry."

"Don't be sorry," Helen said. "You didn't know."

"I didn't know, but I should have. You tried to tell me."

"That doesn't matter now, John."

"I guess not," he said. The two looked at each other for a long time. Then, he asked, "Lily?"

"Lily has always loved you, John," she answered. Then she was gone, and the sun was rising over the eastern edge of the great pinnacles of the Maseah.

Daniel recovered quickly from his exhaustion. He was hailed as a hero for the historic run. But the wrangler refused the credit, explaining that it was Noble

Jack who deserved it. This was seen as being overly modest, until Daniel got serious.

"If you don't believe me," he said, "just time it. We left the high country station just before eleven and got here when? Two or three in the morning? That's sixteen hours. It's a two-day trip, and I didn't pull the sled myself. Noble Jack and his team did. I slept most of the way," he said with a weak smile.

This explanation did nothing to reduce the esteem the ranch felt for the wrangler's feat. But it did open eyes to the extraordinary lead dog that drove the sled.

Jack needed some recovery time, as well. He was moved from the kennel into one of the barn stalls, where he lay dead to the world for a day. Once awake and fed, he was still lethargic and dispirited, disinterested in everything except a little attention. No one at the ranch had to speculate on the dog's change. It was Noah who suggested that he be led into his master. Susan balked at this at first, but soon gave way to allowing Noble Jack to see, then nuzzle Rocklan's limp hand. Afterwards, Daniel thought it best to return the dog to his mates in the kennel, but quickly saw that Jack had little tolerance for even the slightest of canine approaches. The black husky was soon returned to the stall for the time being.

Within two days, James rode into Maseah Mountain with the Haloki brothers. The station, for all intents, was complete. And while there remained some finishing work, it didn't require the craftsmen, and they were anxious to get home. Before they left, however, the ranch heard again of the harrowing struggle with the grizzly. This time, it was James who was hailed as a hero for his quick action with the shotgun and rifle. This notice of his bravery embarrassed the boy, just as it had Daniel, and he made sure everyone knew that it was Rocklan, wielding a bucket, who had saved his life. While this was true, the mention of the Easterner, teetering on the brink, reminded everyone of the continuing danger and recalled the unpredictability and power of the Maseah.

One evening, Maria sat with Susan in the kitchen after a long, worrisome day that saw Rocklan take a turn for the worse. He had developed a fever, and was struggling mightily. Susan was troubled and considering taking him back into surgery. However, she was weighing his ability to withstand another trying procedure.

Maria, too, was not herself. In fact, the treatment the two women had received down in Boise, and the news they received there, had angered Susan and unsettled Maria severely. The younger woman had noticed a significant change in her friend's demeanor ever since. She was quiet and withdrawn, and they had spoken little on the trip home. This late sharing of a cup of coffee gave Susan the chance she was looking for. She would find out what was going on.

"Joseph told me that we just missed Eli by a couple of days," she started. When Maria simply nodded, Susan continued, "He said Eli told him he had business down in Denver. Didn't say what it was. He must have left here heading southwest, or we would have crossed paths between here and Blackbird."

When Maria offered nothing, Susan decided to go right at it.

"Maria, what's going on? Eli says nothing to me, just leaves to take care of business that he has never mentioned. That's not like him. Do you know something?"

"No, Susan, I don't," said Maria without enthusiasm. "Joseph told me Eli received a letter while he was working up at Marmot Pass."

"What was in the letter? Who was it from?"

Susan knew that Eli was very concerned about the finances of the ranch, and during his travels had been talking to various sources of possible support for the continuance of the clinic and the education of Susan's charges. In these matters, John Rocklan was, of course, a wild card.

"I don't know what was in the letter, and neither does Joseph. He said Eli was evasive about it. All I know is that Daniel said it was from down in Denver."

With a sigh, Susan said, "Well then, at least tell me what's going on with you. You've been as silent as the grave ever since that FBI agent showed us Red Cloud's letter. You don't believe it, do you? They can't do anything to you with the thin case they have. Can they?"

The Idaho State Attorney and the FBI had called Maria down to the capital to interview her once again in light of new evidence. Graves had obtained a damaging letter, given to him by Red Cloud, addressed from Petah to Pendleton Whiteley. It was dated several weeks after Anoki's disappearance. The FBI seemed to think that its contents implicated both Dr. Whiteley and Maria in the death of Anoki. In addition to clearly expressing her feelings for the doctor,

Petah thanked him for his "decisive" help with her husband and prayed that she could put her life with Anoki behind her. She closed by saying that if it weren't for him and Maria the night of the "accident," she would not have known what to do. This was sufficiently suspicious to the FBI that they implied there could be charges filed against Maria for aiding and abetting a murder. Maria had been steadfast in saying that she had no idea what Petah had meant, if in fact the letter was real. The letter was never mailed, and how Red Cloud obtained it was not explained.

"Susan, I told them everything I know. Now, let it go," said an unyielding Maria.

Joseph was walking through the mudroom door when he heard his wife putting Susan off. Maria looked up at him with tears in her eyes. He walked over to her, put his arms around her, and said, "Honey, maybe it's time you talked about this thing. Susan is family and loves you. She may be able to help." It had obviously been something they had talked about.

"Joseph, you know that I can't. I promised I wouldn't."

"Maria, Dr. Whiteley is dead. Petah is dead. Anoki is dead. Eli was a little boy. You and Red Cloud are the only ones left, and if you leave it to him to tell the story, you will get hurt. It's time."

Maria's tears came stronger, but she wiped them away and looked at Susan with pleading.

"Maria, whatever it is you are holding inside has to come out. It's going to destroy you. Listen to Joseph. Who in this world can you trust, if not the two of us?"

The older woman wiped her eyes and her nose, then took Joseph's hand. She looked at Susan and said, "I'm sorry I have kept this a secret all of these years. I hope you will understand why I had to."

At Susan's nod, Maria began. "I know that Dr. Whitely didn't kill Anoki. I know that it was Petah who killed him. It was an accident. He was hitting Eli." That was all she was able to say before she started crying again.

As shocked as Susan was by this revelation, she moved around the table and took up the older woman's shaking hands. Joseph continued to hold her.

"Maria, how do you know this? What happened? Tell me."

"Your mother was a wonderful woman. Despite the fact that she loved your father, she never cheated on Anoki while he was alive. He was brutal to her, especially when he had been drinking. She never showed her love for Dr. Whiteley until long after that monster was gone."

Susan nodded, encouraging Maria to continue.

"Petah came to me one night with Eli. She was hysterical and he was crying. Her face was puffy and bruised, her nose bloody. Once I got her calm enough, she told me that Anoki had been angry about her working with the doctor, despite that it was income sorely needed. He hit her with his fist, and when little Eli started to cry and tug at Anoki, he hit the boy too. He was kicking and screaming at his son when Petah ran into him with all of her weight. It knocked him off balance, since he was so drunk. He stumbled on the carpet, fell, and hit his head on the leg of their iron stove. When he didn't get up, she picked up Eli and ran to me."

"And then what happened?"

"Well, I told Petah to stay at my place. Dr. Whiteley was in the village on one of his normal stops. So, I found him, told him what happened, and together we when to Petah's house. When we got there, Anoki was laying in a pool of blood, just as Petah had said. He wasn't moving. The doctor told me to go back to Petah and stay there. He would take care of Anoki. That's about all I know."

"Well, what happened after that, Maria? What did my father do with the body?"

"Susan, I really don't know. He had his sled, and he was gone for four days. When he returned, he told us that everything was going to be alright. That we just had to keep it among the three of us. Red Cloud would never have understood. So, that's what we promised each other, and that's what we did."

"But after all those years together, none of you talked about it?"

"No. We just put it out of our minds. That is, at least until Red Cloud got it in his head that Dr. Whiteley killed his son. Now this letter appears."

"These things can't be hidden, Maria. They tend to come back to haunt us."

"That seems obvious now, doesn't it?" asked an annoyed Maria, getting a bit of her edge back.

"I'm sorry," said Susan. "It's just that it seems incredible to me that you could forget something like that."

"Oh, it was never forgotten. But life here with Joseph and your family has been wonderful. It has helped to keep it way in the background. I know it seems odd, but that's what happened."

The older woman put her hands to her face, then fell against Joseph's shoulder.

Susan was stunned by the story. Her mother had killed her own husband, Anoki. Her father had disposed of the body. Maria was an accessory after the fact and was vulnerable, depending upon the mind of the Idaho State Attorney and the FBI. Maybe there would be consideration because so much time had passed. The trouble with that, however, was that living a lie for so long made Maria hard to believe.

Susan struggled by herself with her family's decision to condone a death and then cover it up. It was even harder to imagine how they could have lived with it for so long. Was her sense of right and wrong out of place? After all, she wasn't there. What would she have done if her husband had brutalized her? It couldn't be considered murder; Petah was protecting Eli. It was an accident, wasn't it? But even if it was, did that justify their decision to cover it up? There was also the budding love between her mother and father. Was that what really motivated their actions? Did they get what they wanted at the expense of Anoki? At one time, Susan thought she knew the answer to questions like this. But now, perhaps the answers weren't so clear.

That October, Maseah Mountain was not the same. Patty had chosen Hopkins and was in Baltimore at the University, and Matthew was in school in Chicago. James seemed to retract to a large degree into his writing and spent hours closeted in the library, either penning stories of the Maseah or framing a possible future biography of Dr. Pendleton E. Whiteley. The nightly radio shows were forgotten. Daniel continued his steady ways, but seemed unsettled. There had been no snow since that first storm, and he had been unable to get out on the sled. This made both him and the dogs anxious. Long, solitary walks with Noble Jack around the ranch became frequent. Carly rarely left her responsibilities in the clinic, and was as busy as she had ever been between day-to-day care for the Easterner, training of Noah, and the steady flow of patients arriving with minor ailments.

Joseph kept Maseah Mountain running, of course, but Maria's near-depression was also affecting him and the rest of the ranch, as well. Susan had decided that she had done all she could for Rocklan, and was left with one of her least abundant assets—patience. So, she spent a lot of time corresponding with friends and colleagues, thinking about the past, and trying to reconcile the actions of her father. To fill the time, when James was not in the library, she worked on her father's notes and her own, compiling the medical history of the Maseah.

By the end of the month, Eli had not returned, but he had radioed that he was in Idaho and would be home shortly. About that same time, word came from the Wolf Clan that the elder, Red Cloud, had died in his sleep. There were no final words, no grand epitaph; just the quiet passing of an embittered old man. Most of Maseah Mountain traveled to the village for the funeral, but there was little celebration of the old Shoshone's life. It was not that he wasn't respected or his experience revered. Rather, there was a sense that the man's remarkable and adventurous life had wound down in a way that left people at a distance. He would be missed, but not for long.

The following week, Eli brought a lift of spirits and a major snowstorm home with him. He quickly discovered that he had some work to do to catch up. The news of the passing of his grandfather sobered him immediately. But the story of the bear attack and Rocklan's condition he found horrifying. Still, he brought with him something the rest of the ranch needed.

Susan had always felt better when she had Eli around. It surprised her to realize how long it was since they had seen each other. She stood a little straighter as, arm in arm, they watched from the gallery the snow coming in from the north. *We'll all be together for dinner tonight*, she thought.

"Your grandfather died quietly, Eli. He had a very full, honorable life. He was Shoshone."

"Yes, and that's something to say for any man, I guess. He certainly lived his beliefs. That's for sure. I've got to get up to the village soon to pay my respects to Kimama and Ayasah."

"Especially Ayasah." Susan gave him the Whiteley smile.

"Yeah, I think I'm in trouble. I haven't seen her in forever, either."

"You're not in that much trouble," she said, again with the smile.

"Well, that's the first piece of good news I've heard since I got home. Thanks."
Then Eli turned and looked at her. "Tell me the truth about John."

She told him, and at the end of it, she said. "He's at least in and out of it now.
That's step one. We'll see what comes next, when he's more conscious. I'm not
seeing any strong signs of infection, and that's big. But there's still some praying
and finger crossing to be done. I'll get you in to him tomorrow morning, okay?
You don't want to go now. It's late for him, and Carly's doing what she does."

Then to steer him away from a visit to Rocklan that evening, she said, "Well,
it looks like you won't be going anywhere for a day or so." The snow had begun
to fall steadily.

"No, I'm glad of that," he said sincerely.

"Eli, I have something you need to know. But first, what's all this about
business in Denver? You have us all making apocalyptic guesses. Have you
found our funding? Tell me what's going on. What have you been up to?"

"No, I haven't found a way around our financial problems yet. But I do have
something to tell the family. It's good. There is nothing to be worried about.
But I want to tell it to everyone at once. You understand?"

"I most certainly do not understand. What is it? Tell me now." She threatened
him with a look.

The storm was intensifying, and the wind was blowing it at them in earnest,
so he laughed. "I think we'd better go in now."

She grabbed his sleeve, but he said, "Susan, dinner is only an hour away.
You can wait."

He shrugged her off and made a dash for the mudroom door. She stood in
frustration with his resolve to make a dramatic announcement about whatever
he was doing. Missing the chance to get his thoughts and advice on the situation
with Maria and Anoki also annoyed her. Susan stood for a moment with her
arms crossed and stared angrily at the swirling white. Then, she too turned and
went into the house.

Eli escaped Susan by finding James in the library. There, he got the bear
story as only James could tell it. The boy did have a knack. But their conversation
was interrupted by a call to dinner. So, Eli ended with a tip of his hat to the
young man's courage and a suggestion that the teen get his tale down on paper,
because a lot of people would want to read it.

Chapter 18

No Secrets

Maria had let her secret out and felt no better for it. In fact, she felt worse. The Shoshone woman had failed two people she had loved. Once, she was their protector; now, she knew that Susan would never leave it alone.

Maria was also a worried woman, and she had cause to be worried. The threat of the law was real—she had been an accessory, and she lied to the FBI. But it wasn't just that. Maseah Mountain's cook was also uneasy about whatever Eli was engineering. She didn't have any real idea as to where he had been or what he had been up to, but she feared the change it was sure to bring. She knew that Susan and Eli were concerned about the future of the ranch and their ability to keep it going. That meant the life she and Joseph had built might not be the same. Further, the lack of money put Dr. Whiteley's wonderful dream of educating the Shoshone in jeopardy.

And then there was John Rocklan. Maria had watched him change, even helped him through it. She thought of him as one of them now, and if the survival of the ranch was up to him, she was sure that something could be worked out. But now, he was dying.

Eli's coming home picked her up out of these depths. He was just her Eli, but he had always been able to do that. So, Maria rallied, putting her cares behind for a night. Once again, she was on her game in the kitchen, and volunteer help was plentiful and willing. The result was a big, snowbound country dinner at Maseah Mountain that night.

When Susan saw Maria's mood change, she quickly came out of her own temper. The importance of this gathering was obvious to her. The snow and the dinner had brought them all together again, something that was sorely needed.

There had been a cloud over Maseah Mountain, but it was lifting. She would help its ascent for certain, but she wasn't going to let slip the opportunity to get something more than just food out on the table either.

While no one said it, in many ways, the dinner was testimony to their summer's work and the generosity of the Maseah that year. There was a general sense of a job well done, and that brought some contentment. What Maria could bring to a table also brought contentment, and it was timed perfectly. The meal served to mark the time of year that the fall rhythms take over at Maseah Mountain. Anyone who could not feel the change up to that point was now attuned, and the early snowstorm made it final.

It was a fall feast that boasted of the strong growing season and the abundance of game. Full platters and steaming bowls crowded the table and were emptied quickly enough onto Dr. Whiteley's well-worn collection of bone china. At first, there was a lot of polite passing of dishes, but that quickly devolved into apologies for unmannerly reaching. When loaves of hot bread found their way from the oven, the butter and the gravy went quickly, twice. When both versions of the cider made the rounds several times, the noise got louder. And when the huckleberry pie arrived with vanilla ice cream, there was a lot of counterfeit groaning, but no one refused it.

Susan enjoyed herself, of course, and made sure everyone else did as well. As usual, she and Maria were in flight much of the meal, yet neither of them missed a word of the chatter around the table. There was a tone of relief in the family's conversation, even though their cares still lurked. It was as if some unseen curtain had dropped, signaling an intermission in the drama.

Eli talked of Marmot Pass and what was left to be done. James had a new version of the saga of the grizzly. This time, he stood his ground with the rifle as the bear charged him. Joseph enthused over the harvest and what had been put away for the winter. Susan and Daniel talked of the horses the Beaver Clan would bring with them during their stay at Maseah Mountain. Carly mentioned a boy she had met from the clan, who was coming down to the ranch with them. This news clearly got the attention of both James and Noah.

Maria urged seconds and assessed the level of appreciation of her cooking by the volume consumed. Flowing in between all of this were those intimate exchanges within a tight family that were not always gentle, yet were thinly veiled expressions of love and need. It was times like this, when the light of the lamps was soft, when the windblown snow was insistent against the windows, when a bounty was shared, when the company was close, that Maseah Mountain's sense of tribe was at its greatest.

As the dinner wound down, Carly excused herself to check on her patient. Noah followed and, with his eyes on the younger boy's back, James departed for the library. That was the moment Susan chose to tell a joke about FBI Agent Graves that ended in something about his lack of knowledge of asses and elbows. Her wit received a derisive snort or two at most. But she didn't care, because it gave her the entree she wanted.

"Graves is no Shoshone," she said wryly. Then she turned to look at Eli. "Do you know what those feds told us?"

"Susan, before we talk about that, I have something I think everyone should know," interrupted Eli, rocking forward in his chair.

But Susan would have none of that, so she said, "Look, what I'm trying to tell you is important. You have to listen to this now."

Her brother started to protest, but seeing the look in her eyes, he just shrugged and sat back in the chair.

"Eli, Maria and I were called in by the authorities because they said they had new evidence in the death of Anoki. That new evidence was a letter from your mother to Dr. Whiteley. They said it supported Red Cloud's contention that our father murdered Anoki. What's more, it suggested that Maria knew about the murder, may have abetted the doctor in the crime, and has been covering it up for years."

"Susan, I..." began Eli.

"No. There's more, a lot more. Maria told them she didn't know what they were talking about. But that wasn't quite true, was it, Maria?"

"You're right to get this out in the open, Susan. It can't stay hidden now. But let me tell him," the older woman said. She knew this was coming, but Susan's directness put her a little on edge.

The younger woman passed the conversation to Maria with a wave of her hand and looked around the table. Joseph was looking down, but nodding encouragement, and Daniel seemed baffled. Eli sat with his arms crossed on his chest and an odd look on his face. He said nothing.

"Eli, I know that Dr. Whiteley didn't murder your father. I know that because I know your mother, Petah, killed him—accidentally. I was there that night. Anoki was drunk. She pushed him and he fell, hit his head. I was there because your mother had come to me, and I managed to find Dr. Whiteley. The only thing the doctor did was remove Anoki's body."

Maria took Eli's surprise at her words for shock, so she plunged on. "I don't know how Red Cloud got his hands on that letter, but he gave it to Graves. It was Petah's handwriting, for sure; I saw it. The things she said in it were true, but the authorities are taking them the wrong way."

Daniel, who had been sitting quietly and listening, asked, "If it was an accident, why didn't Petah or Dr. Whiteley just go to the sheriff's office?"

"It was an accident, as I said. But Petah still pushed him, and the FBI believes that there was motive for murder in the love that she and the doctor felt for each other. Everyone knew Anoki beat her, and Dr. Whiteley had already warned Red Cloud that he would stop Anoki, if the elder didn't."

Then Susan said, "The problem now is that Maria is vulnerable to charges. At this point, we're waiting for the other shoe to drop."

She looked at Eli, expecting a response, an opinion, a grunt, anything. She got nothing but a thoughtful look and an enigmatic half-smile.

They stared at each other for a long moment. Then Eli said, "I don't know how to react to your story. I think it has some holes in it."

"Story? This is no story!" she squawked. "We're telling you what happened. We're telling you we've got a problem!"

"Well, let me tell you what I've been trying to tell you, and you'll see what I mean," he said. "But honestly, I'm not sure I know what it all means yet myself."

Eli leaned up on the table, looked at Maria, then Susan, and made a confession. "I never told anyone this, but I have spent a fair amount of time over the years asking around about Anoki, son of Red Cloud. I didn't know whether he was dead or alive, until I ran into a car salesman down in Pocatello who is Wolf Clan. He told me that Anoki had come in to try to buy a car. He knew him from the village."

"How could—" began Susan.

"That's right. If this guy is correct, Anoki was alive. That's exactly what I thought," said Eli, making the leap for her. "It wasn't so hard to pick up his trail after that. I simply started cruising drunk tanks, homeless shelters, and social services agencies whenever I stopped in a town. The issue wasn't following the trail; it was the length of the path."

He had them now. "Daniel, my apologies, I was pretty stiff in not saying something to you up at Marmot Pass. That letter was from one of my stops in Denver. Anoki was there, in St. Vincent's hospital, dying. He had been brought in to dry out, but developed pneumonia. They didn't know how long he had left.

"So, I tore off to the city. And I'm glad I did, because he was still alive when I got there. He didn't know who I was at first, of course, and refused to talk to me. But the nuns were more than happy to let me in, not so much because I was a relative, more because I was a chance to free up another bed. There were no vacancies in that place that I could see. Anyway, I sat there for a half-hour telling him who I was and who he was. When he finally got it, he denied it. Then, he started to talk. He told me he was sorry for the things he has done, but he couldn't quite remember what those were. So, I reminded him."

Muttering was heard around the table, but Eli continued, "He said a lot of things that were either wrong or hurtful or both. I never thought of him as my father, so I wasn't particularly wounded, but he seemed to think it was painful for me. He would look at me for a reaction that I never gave him or felt. He told me that Petah nearly killed him and Dr. Whiteley had saved him. Brought him down here to the ranch. All he needed was a few stitches and a lot of aspirin. Then, Anoki told me that Dr. Whiteley paid him to leave the Maseah. He said that he was never going back to the village anyway, and if the fool wanted to pay him, fine. Then, in the same breath, he whined that Dr. Whiteley had 'stiffed' him.

"Anoki told me that he didn't care about my mother or 'the boy,' as he put it. That's when I realized that he thought about his days in the Maseah in the abstract, despite the fact that I was sitting right in front of him. Well, I won't bore you with the details of his story of dissolution, but let's just say that Anoki's life was in continuous descent from the day he walked out of the mountains."

The family sat at the table, unable or unwilling to respond. The occasional gust of blowing snow could be heard in the silence. They now knew what Eli meant when he said he didn't know what it all means.

"Anoki died last week, not in the village twenty years ago. I was there when he went. He just blinked out like a dim point of light. I made arrangements to bring him back to the Wolf Clan for burial. But that's all I care to do."

Susan was the first to rouse. "That certainly means that Maria didn't abet or cover up a murder. There was no murder—there wasn't even an accidental death. Father was only guilty of giving Anoki what he wanted."

"Not quite," said Maria, clearly upset. "Why didn't he tell Petah and me? He lied to us," she asserted with tears in her eyes.

"Wait, Maria," said Joseph, speaking for the first time. "What exactly did the doctor say when he was asked about it? All he ever said to me was that Anoki left the Maseah for good."

"Well, I never really asked him about it directly," she answered. "That is what he would say on the rare occasions when the subject came up. But why didn't he tell us the whole story? Why did he let us think that Petah killed Anoki?"

"I think I can answer a part of that," said Eli. "Anoki told me that the doctor didn't want Petah worried that her husband was coming back. In truth, this man was dying, and he still thought that it was funny that someone would think that he was ever going back to the village."

If that was the reason, Maria was neither convinced nor mollified by it. "But why let her think that she killed someone? Why let me think she did?"

"Those two were as close as it gets," said Joseph. "We really don't know what he told Petah. Judge the doctor if you like, but Petah was never as happy as she was here with him. That goes for you and me, as well."

Susan decided to stay out of Maria's grievance against the doctor. She was much relieved that the case that seemed to be building against the cook was now groundless. She also watched her brother closely to see if Eli's assertions that he cared little for his natural father were real. When he noticed her watching him, he gave her an annoyingly smug smile.

"Okay, Eli," she said contritely. "I should have let you explain. Sorry." Susan was sincere, but her words were only as enthusiastic as an apology could be from a sister to a brother.

Eli and Susan spoke frequently during the few days that they were snowbound. They talked of Anoki, Maria, Petah, and the FBI investigation. It was decided to connect Agent Graves with St. Vincent's and the Denver coroner's office. The expectation was that in due time, they would receive a notice from the Attorney General announcing a withdrawal from the inquiry and the closing of the case. With Anoki turning up alive and all other parties deceased, no one was about to earn additional stripes battling over whether Maria should be charged with obstruction of justice.

The only other concern was Maria herself. But the two determined that she would have to forgive their father in her own time. They knew that Dr. Whiteley rarely did anything without trying to accomplish other objectives. It was Eli who suggested that perhaps his stepfather wanted to keep the authorities—and outsiders in general—away from the Maseah. A tale of love and murder, scented with brutality and dereliction, would do no one any good, and it would dishonor the great range. That was something Dr. Whiteley would have considered.

So, they decided to let this piece of their story fade into history. The life of Anoki was just what Dr. Whiteley had said it was all along—a fall from the grace of the mountains and a life not worthy of the Shoshone.

As soon as Eli could, he took Noble Jack and one of the dogsled teams up to the Wolf Clan village. There, he found Ayasah once again, paid due respect to Kimama, and carried the news of Anoki's death. A week later, he was back at the ranch with Ayasah, announcing plans for a spring wedding, once the snow melted. This news seemed to remove any remaining vestiges of Maseah Mountain's former melancholy.

The remaining concern was for John Rocklan. At one point, Susan gave him little chance to survive his wounds, much less the intendant infection. But the Easterner hung on doggedly, and fought back each time from the repeated fevers that plagued him. She saw his consciousness restore gradually. Then, she saw the return of some of the strength that had been sapped away. Eventually, Rocklan took a firm step back from the edge. He was now conscious, but often hung somewhere between drowsiness and sleep. Susan tried to keep him as comfortable as she could, but with his senses came pain, fear, and the memory of the grizzly's ferocity.

When he first emerged from weeks of oblivion and was able to find a weak voice, it was a different, older Carly that he addressed. He surprised her as she was changing his sheets.

"Carly? Can you tell me? How is James?" were his first words.

"Oh, Mr. Rocklan! You are back with us," she said with some excitement, never really able to call him John. "It's good to hear you talking. James is fine, just fine—thanks to you."

He gave her a wan smile and immediately dozed, falling back into the kaleidoscopic netherworld that had been his for weeks. When he next woke, Susan was there. He had been dreaming of her. He was back in the city, and he was searching for her. She had given him directions. But somehow, while he understood where she was, he just could not find the right street. Even when he woke, knowing it was a dream, the frustration and sense of failure clung to him like a bad odor. Then, she reached out and took his hand.

Over the last several months, even before the attack, Susan had begun to see a different John Rocklan. He had developed self-confidence, certainly, but it went beyond that. He now seemed to be clearer as to what was important to him. But it was even more than that. She started to see him act and say things that reminded her of her father. He was now a different person than when he first came to Maseah Mountain. He was stronger inside, but it was no longer just about him. It was true that he remained secretive in many ways, but she noticed him beginning to think in terms of those around him, and she could see them responding.

The residents of Maseah Mountain asked about him frequently, and eventually began a regular stream of visits to the clinic. Susan knew the patient had become one of Maria's projects by the cook's determination to feed him back to his old self. It was also obvious that both Joseph and Daniel had accepted him, even respected him, due to the bond their shared experiences had created. For James, Rocklan had become something of a hero; in his latest recounting of the incident with the grizzly, the boy called the Easterner "The Water-Pale Warrior," a bad pun for which the young storyteller offered no apologies.

At one point, Susan interrupted Eli enthusing over Noble Jack while recounting for Rocklan various sled trips he had taken that fall. In truth, she was not sure how Eli really felt about the man. She had never asked her brother about John because the friction between the two had been overt. None of that seemed to remain now, but true to who she was, Susan made a mental note to pin Eli down on the subject. It suddenly seemed important to her.

Susan felt good about the Easterner's gradual return to normalcy, maintained by her young team's constant and professional attention. But she watched him recover mainly through some inner fire that he stoked in silence. It was this seclusion, this not knowing exactly what made him tick, that frustrated her the most and forced her to maintain her own reserve with him.

By the time the Beaver Clan arrived at Maseah Mountain for their winter stay, Rocklan was wobbly, but now at least mobile. To his delight, he found Susan frequently during this time, and together they found places to walk and talk of everything and nothing. He began to tell her of his former life, his failure in his first marriage and the loss of his wife and daughter. He spoke little of his feelings about it all, just provided the unvarnished facts without trying to offer explanation or to absolve himself of his responsibility for it. He would always have the scar, just as he would the ones the bear had left.

Susan now understood that she might never fully hear of his past, not because he was hiding something, but because he had left it far behind him and it meant little to whom he was today. She knew this because Rocklan preferred talking about his time in the Maseah. He talked of what it had given him and how he believed it had changed him. He was eloquent in his explanation of his acceptance of the world around him and his place in it. He was boyish in relating the experience of kinship up at the Marmot Pass station, and heartfelt in expressing his love for the people of Maseah Mountain. In this manner, despite not knowing it all, she felt the man open up to her in ways he had never before.

There were two topics left unaddressed, however. She knew he was waiting to talk to Eli and her, and sensed it was about his ownership of the ranch and his future plans for it. But he maintained his silence, stubbornly waiting for the right moment.

He also didn't raise the subject of his feelings for her. Inside, he longed to talk about it and the possibility of the two of them together. But the lack of success of his prior attempts cautioned waiting for her to come to him. So, he did.

One clear, cold day, when the temperature was not so low that it prevented one of their walks, but chilly enough that Susan felt justified in tucking herself in against his arm, he asked if he could talk to her and Eli together. As they climbed the steps to the gallery upon their return, he couldn't help but remember the night they crossed to the barn in a snowstorm, and she had held on to him for support. He stopped short of going into the house and she turned to him.

"Don't you want to go in? I thought you wanted to talk to us?" she asked.

At that moment, he knew he was going to wait no longer. He also knew that there was no need to. She looked up at him and her eyes told him all he needed to know. He took her in his arms and pulled her close. He kissed her in a way that crumbled any reserve. Her intake of breath and ready response immediately dispelled the pain of long months of dreaming. It spoke of what could be, what would be.

They separated, and she offered him a look of real surprise. It was surprise not for the kiss, but for her own reaction to it, for its newness to her, for her recognition that perhaps this was not something she could control with her usual determination. She came back to him, put her arms around his neck, and kissed him again. This time longer.

"That was a long time coming," he said to her. "But I'm glad it did."

"Yes," she said and just looked at him.

"Maybe we can explore this further," he suggested.

"Yes," she said again.

Maybe we can explore this further, after I speak to you and Eli?"

"Yes," she said a third time and took his hand to go inside.

"Wait, Susan, I want to stay out here. I want to talk to you out here," he said, sweeping his hand to the Maseah all around them. "Will you find Eli and bring him outside?"

She said nothing, just looked at him. Then, understanding, she went inside to find her brother.

CHAPTER 19

WHERE THERE'S A WILL

Through the window, Maria watched the three sitting on the gallery and talking intently. She was concerned that John was out in the cold as long as he was, given that he had just returned from the brink to them so recently. But it wasn't just that. She believed she knew what the conversation was about, and found it hard to fight back the urge to be part of it. After all, Maseah Mountain was hers, too.

She fought her normal inclination to interrupt, seeing the earnest look on the faces of both Eli and Susan, who sat on either side of the ranch's owner, leaning in, listening. Maria would just have to wait.

"Momma, what's going on?" asked James, coming up behind her and putting his arm around her.

"I think the future of Maseah Mountain is being decided, honey," said the Shoshone woman, hugging her son.

The conversation had not gone well at first, as Rocklan told Eli and Susan that he had found the will almost a year earlier and had said nothing to them. The realization that Maseah Mountain would stay in the family brought an immediate surge of relief in the Whiteleys, but that was soon followed by a sense of suspicion and a feeling of betrayal by someone they had grown to think of as family. And just as that emotion washed over them, it was followed by the practical concern of how they would be able to keep it, even if they did own it.

The news produced a stony silence from Eli as he processed the information and began to think through its implications. A few months earlier, Susan might have lit into Rocklan with fury. But things had changed between them. She was now willing to give him the benefit of the doubt, give him a chance to explain. So, she sat, disturbed, but listening to him unfold his story.

Rocklan watched their faces closely, trying to read what was not being said. He knew he had to get all of his thoughts out, to try to defend his thinking and to press on quickly to what he had to offer.

"I know I should have told you of the will as soon as I found it, but there were reasons why I didn't. In retrospect, maybe they weren't good reasons. But ultimately, I think I'm glad in a way that I did wait," he told them.

This brought no greater clarity or acceptance, so he hurried on. "I know now that I didn't understand a lot of things then. I didn't realize what this place is or what it means to you and the rest of the Maseah. I couldn't see what my role here was, despite the fact that I was fully committed to it, literally. The only thing I knew was that I wasn't going back to my former life, and losing the ranch seemed to suggest that. As I saw it, I had time to think about what I was going to do. Once I began to sort some things out, to really see what was here, to understand its importance, I began to think differently. At the same time, the opportunity to tell you never seemed right, or things got in the way. In truth, I guess I found excuses not to tell you."

They were being patient with him and his insubstantial explanation.

"There were other reasons, as well. Some of which involved you, Susan."

This caused Eli some confusion, and he sat back with his arms out behind him and just looked at Rocklan.

Susan, on the other hand, leaned toward him and asked, "Me? What do you mean, exactly?"

Rocklan looked at her with a request for a bit more forbearance, then turned to Eli.

"Eli, I'm in love with Susan and have been for some time. Up until recently, those feelings were all one-sided, and my desire to win your sister colored much of my thinking. Said plainly, once I delayed telling you, I feared that the delay would be recognized as deceit. I didn't want to risk that."

"Wasn't it?" Eli asked bluntly.

"Yes, I guess it was," Rocklan answered candidly. "But the harm, as I saw it, was minimal. The bills were getting paid, and life here was going on as it had previously."

"That ignores all of the efforts I've made outside of here to resolve Maseah Mountain's financial issues," said Eli, annoyed.

"Yes, I'm sorry for that. When I knew finally what I was going to do about the will, I tried to avoid some of the pain of my decision to wait by trying to get the two of you together to tell you. As you know, that has not been easy as of late."

"No, it hasn't," Eli admitted.

Susan, somewhat caught off-balance by Rocklan's declaration, sat considering as this exchange occurred. Then, to buy a bit more time to think, she asked a secondary question. "Where did you find the will?"

"The document was stuck between two waxy pages in your father's *Gray's*. I don't think he was intentionally hiding it. I came across it not long after I arrived. Just dumb luck, or fate, really. You'll find it in the copy of *Great Expectations* in the library."

His choice of hiding places produced a small, ironic smile. Then she said, "Did I just hear you say that you loved me?"

"Yes. I love you, Susan. I think you've known that for a while."

She smiled at him and nodded. "I'd like to talk to you some more about that, but I don't think I want my big brother sitting here when we do."

"I won't be," said Eli.

"Look, John," Susan said. "About the will and your keeping it to yourself—as I see it, that is who you were. In fact, it's a perfect example of who you were. Maybe that's all behind you now."

She was giving him an out. This was the response Rocklan was hoping for from her, because it gave him the opportunity to move past his deception.

"Yes, it clearly is behind me, and I'd like to give you an idea of what else I've been thinking. When you get a chance to read what Dr. Whiteley had in mind, you'll see that his plain intent was to leave Maseah Mountain to the two of you equally. But that's not all. In addition to a few conditions of ownership, he has established a trust and made some financial arrangements that should allow you to continue the ranch as it is."

This drew Eli back into the conversation, and Rocklan continued, "I don't know what those arrangements are or how substantial they may be. But I do know that, whatever they are, I'd like to be a part of that, if you would allow me to be. My earlier life has left me more than capable of supporting this place and whatever plans you may have for further educating your students. Perhaps together, we can do even more."

Susan was now grinning, and she held onto his arm and slid closer to him. Eli, however, wanted clarification.

"Are you saying that you'd like to be a part of Maseah Mountain? That you would invest in this place, even though it's not yours?"

"I'm saying something beyond that, Eli. It's my desire that whatever I have would be accepted as belonging to Maseah Mountain, to the family. In fact, more basically, I'm hoping that I could become a part of the family."

At that, Rocklan fell silent. He had said what was in his heart.

In the following days and weeks, Maseah Mountain was once again deep within the grasp of the great range's winter. The Beaver Clan had arrived as planned, and all of the traditional rituals observed. During the welcome dinner, the Whiteleys used the occasion to announce the change in ownership, but it was done in a way that made clear that the ranch was part of the Maseah, and that the Whiteley family was its caretaker. Nothing would change in that regard. It was also made clear that John Rocklan was now a part of the family.

Matthew made it home for winter break just after the Beaver Clan arrived and added to the general spirit of the ranch. This was especially true for James, who clearly had missed his brother. The two could be found together with Daniel and the dogs or, more often than not, on horseback, trading stories of schoolwork, girls, and brushes with grizzlies. Their parents watched both of their boys with great pride, happy to see them together again. Joseph saw a transformation in his oldest son, and was heartened as he listened to Matthew tell his younger brother of the wonders of campus and city life. It was obvious that James heard Matthew with new ears.

Eli and Rocklan worked together and through attorneys that winter to make the legal arrangements necessary to settle Maseah Mountain, clear the trust set up by Dr. Whiteley, and create joint accounts among the two men and Susan. Although it took months to do, all were ultimately satisfied that the ranch was finally in good, permanent hands, despite the depth of the national depression.

Maria never seemed happier, and the entire ranch benefitted from her fine frame of mind. Once again, she danced in the kitchen to the sounds coming from the radio, especially her favorites, "We're In the Money" and Ethel Water's "Stormy Weather." She continued to orchestrate the family's dinners together and made sure they remained a renewal of unspoken bonds. Maseah Mountain was hers again.

Carly, with help from young Noah, earned her final stripes during the Beaver Clan's visit, seemingly spending all waking hours in the clinic. It wasn't too far into the clan's stay that Susan began her initial conversations with the budding medical student about next steps in the girl's education. A certain Baltimore hospital always happened to surface in their talks, so that particular beat went on as well.

Ayasah and Eli found time to formalize the spring wedding plans they had thought about for a year. Hammered out during various midwinter dinners at Maseah Mountain, the ceremony and party would be held at the ranch. The invitation list, while sometimes taking on the usual political and emotional overtones, was eventually settled upon with minimal damage to feelings. It obviously would be the event of the Maseah's social season, if there were such a thing.

The limitation of movement during the winter months gave Rocklan and Susan an opportunity to explore a life together and to make their own plans. While these plans certainly included the possibility of a family of their own, they were never closer than when they talked of their medical lives. Together, they developed ideas to expand preventative care in the villages, more efficient use of the clinic, and the training and certification of physician's assistants among the local clans. They spoke of ways for Susan to organize and publish both her and her father's experiences with the Shoshone, and to create income for Maseah Mountain in the process. With Susan's help, Rocklan began to think again about trauma and new procedures, now influenced by his time in the mountains. They made plans for sharing the spring, summer, and fall rounds in the high country, giving Rocklan time with his dogs and some of the solitude that still held appeal for him, albeit less than it once did. Perhaps to Susan's greatest excitement, they began to dream about expanding the school at the ranch and creating greater opportunities for the Shoshone in the field of medicine. It was a warm, productive, and satisfying time for both of them.

When spring finally arrived, once again it became abundantly clear as to why the native people named their mountain range "Maseah." There was growth everywhere, and in everything.

Epilogue

Rocklan woke in the middle of the night and could tell no difference in the storm's rage. Holding a blanket close around him, he rebuilt the fire in the hearth to a roar, then lit a lantern and made his way into the kitchen. The temperature outside had returned the room to a tomblike cold, despite the fact that the stove was still warm to the touch. This he restarted as well.

He wrapped the blanket around his waist, grabbed the parka from the peg on the wall, and cinched it in a way that held the blanket. He wouldn't be that long. Next, his feet went into his boots and he snatched his gloves from the stove's drying shelf. The lamp showed the windows mostly covered in snow and ice, and he was surprised that the Maseah had dropped that much already.

Moving into the workroom, he really began to feel the cold, and his concern for his dogs took a jump. What was the temperature? He took the interior passage from the room into the adjacent stable. On his way, he thanked Eli once more for his foresight in the design of the station. Avoiding the wind was a blessing.

All was quiet as he came into the stable, but Noble Jack greeted him with a lift of his head from the middle of a large knot of pulsating fur created by the team, who had found each other's flanks in defense of the bitter night. He could see no other heads, since noses were tucked in under tails, legs, scruffs, and other fur-covered body parts. The last thing the dogs needed was the man disturbing them, and he laughed at himself for not knowing better.

He resisted calling Noble Jack to him because the scratching he would have given his lead would have been more for his own comfort than the dog's. Still, it wasn't easy walking away from this animal he loved. But he did, just the same, while thinking about the dog and his father before him. This "Jack" was the second with whom the musher had built an unbreakable working trust. Both this one, and the big dog that sired him, were extraordinary sled dogs, and amazingly similar, right down to their black coats. They were so similar that the two huskies had become one in his mind, giving him seamless years of devotion and strength, miles and miles of unfailing power, and the will to run forever.

How many years had it been now? He challenged his memory. Lately, his time and experiences in the mountains had morphed into one large, comfortable picture. He had forgotten much of the detail, and would never remember any of it, unless a particular time or specific story was brought up around a hearth or campfire. Even then, it seemed that they were talking about something or someone else.

A quick check on his wounded husky in the next stall found the animal still sleeping, buried under the blanket with which the man had covered him earlier. Steady, easy breathing indicated that all was well for the moment, so he left the dog alone.

Back in his own blankets, in front of the big stone fireplace, he re-spun a wool cocoon and listened to the wind. He was warm and comfortable, but still would have preferred to have Susan under the covers with him. His independence was important, but he had discovered its limitations a long time ago. Seeing his dogs' interdependence, even tonight, reminded him of his own preferences these days. So, he fell back asleep thinking of his wife.

Sometime in the morning, a foot had escaped the blankets and cold toes woke him. The wind had dropped significantly, but when he peered through a window that was practically ice-covered, he could see that it was still snowing.

His trip back to the stable found the dogs up, noisy, scrapping with each other, and hungry. Even the husky he had isolated was on its feet and looking for attention. He let them out into the snow, where they took the opportunity to answer nature's call. It wasn't long, however, that the animals were back in the small barn, demanding breakfast. Once fed, they found the hay again, plopped down, and watched the man through their eyebrows, wondering whether they would be called upon to run that day. They would run if asked, of course, but their current preference was obvious.

Closing the stable's outside door, Rocklan called Jack to him, and leaving the others there, the two made their way through to the workshop. The man wanted some company, and the black dog was more than willing to comply. The shop's wood stove was lit and radiating heat, a pot of coffee kept warm atop it. He opened the room's shutters to let some additional light in for the standard overhaul of the sled, something sorely needed after yesterday's long run. He also had to rig the windmill and charge the batteries for the radio that would put him in touch with the Maseah Mountain ranch. They needed to know he was safe, and he needed a weather report.

"John, it's good to hear from you. We were concerned. That was a nasty storm that blew through here yesterday."

It was James Bearclaw, and he had been trying to raise the Marmot Pass station since early that morning.

"Well, James. How's the famous mountain storyteller doing?"

With some gentle irony, Rocklan used the sobriquet with which James's publisher had saddled him.

"All's well here, but we're buried. What about you?"

"Tucked in nicely, thank you. Ran into some wolves yesterday, though. Lost Beau and Frankie to them. Roscoe's a little chewed up, but he'll be okay."

"Man, you shouldn't be alone up there. You know that," said the ranch's wrangler.

James had returned to Maseah Mountain after school and had begun writing in earnest. His talent was quickly recognized, and his following grew just as swiftly. Six books and uncountable stories into his career as an author, the young man had also taken over the ranch duties after Daniel Bilbao's passing just a few years before.

"I've got to do something with my time. And besides, there's a few sick people up here," replied Rocklan.

"You've got plenty of help in the villages these days. Let them do the job you and Susan have trained them for all these years."

Rocklan smiled, thinking of how James had become a man who, in many ways, he still thought of as a teenager. "How's Susan? Is she around?"

"She's here, but in school at the moment."

"Have you heard from Pennie?"

Susan and he had named their son after Pendleton Whitely. The young man had shown promise and interest in medicine, and was a graduate of Susan's library/clinic med school. He then followed in his father's and mother's footsteps, training at Hopkins. Pennie was now building a practice of his own in Maryland, but had recently started to make noises about returning to Maseah Mountain.

"John, I'll fill you in on everyone, but right now, you've got to get out of there. The U.S. Weather Service Bureau says there's a bigger storm right behind this one. So, unless you want to be there for another two weeks, you need to move. What's it doing there now?"

"The wind is down, but it's still snowing. Cold."

"Can you make a run?" James asked. "We can meet you halfway. Make sure we all get home safely."

"I sure don't want to get snowed in up here. I've made some minor repairs on the sled, and I should be good to go. Who would come with you?"

"William is here. A damn good musher. Strong. He and I can meet you at the ten-mile mark."

William was Eli's son, and the family had recently returned to Maseah Mountain after spending some years in Chicago. When Matthew Bearclaw had been taken in the War, during the invasion of Normandy, the entire clan had gathered at the ranch. This served to remind Eli and Ayasah of the peace the place afforded, and the family was eventually drawn back to their roots in the mountains.

"Raise me when you're ready to go, but make it fast," said James.

Rocklan knew that what James suggested made sense. There was no pride or hierarchy to follow in these matters. The Maseah would make sure of that.

"Okay, I'll get back to you shortly. I need to load and batten this place down. Should be about a half-hour. Don't say anything to Joseph. Your father will want to come."

"I know, I know. Not to worry, the old man isn't going anywhere. My mother would roll over in her grave if I let him do the things he thinks he can do."

James also kept a close eye on his father, who continued to act like little had changed in twenty years.

They had started in a steady snowfall, but it had stopped an hour before, and Rocklan had even seen a brief patch of bright, white sky for a while. Not long after, however, the Maseah's dome was once again a heavy gray, promising the storm James had predicted.

The new snow made for slower going, and the trail was invisible to anyone who didn't know it the way Noble Jack and Rocklan did. The team of man and dog gave their situation the respect it deserved, and worked cautiously but steadily down out of the back bowls. To Rocklan, balancing on the rails with the kit stretched out in front of him and listening to the song of the dogs seemed more natural than almost anything else he did in the mountains.

As the wind began to build and the front edge of the new storm hit them, he stopped at the top of a rise and looked out over a broad meadow of snow. Visibility would be scarce in a few minutes, and he wanted to check his bearings and see if he could spot the party coming to join him. He was not far from the ten-mile point.

As he squinted through the weather, he saw two black lines emerging over the far ridge. He waved, and then gave Jack the go-ahead. The dog immediately responded with a new burst of energy and a higher pitch to his yipping. The team followed his lead, falling into their rhythm.

Greetings were brief, and the men quickly turned for home. Since James led on the way out, William and his team took the point, with Rocklan between the younger men. The trail had been broken, so the going was a little easier.

Despite the sting of now blowing snow and dropping temperature, Rocklan realized again how happy he was. He had made it a regular practice over the years to use his time with the dogs to pause in his existence and think about what he had. Time and time again, he returned to the thought of how fortunate he was to have found the Maseah. Whenever that happened, he also made sure to offer humble thanks for having been given the opportunity to live there.

These were Rocklan's thoughts as William stopped atop the final ridge that led down into the Maseah Mountain bowl. The three sleds pulled even with each other, and the men peered through the gauzy curtain of the snowfall to the lines and shapes of the ranch buildings. They could see the lights of home, and the wind offered the occasional whiff of wood smoke.

Goggles, parkas, and masks hid the faces of the travelers, but Rocklan knew his escort felt the same overwhelming emotion that he did. As many times as he had stopped in this very place to lock in the memory of the sight, it was never old and never less powerful. Once again, he was returning to his tribe.

THE END

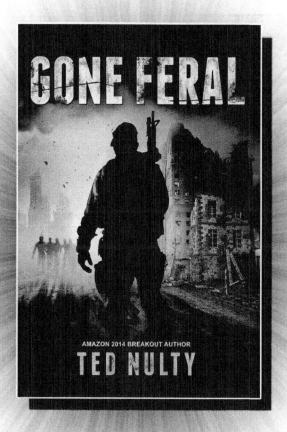

CUTTING-EDGE NAVAL THRILLERS
BY
JEFF EDWARDS

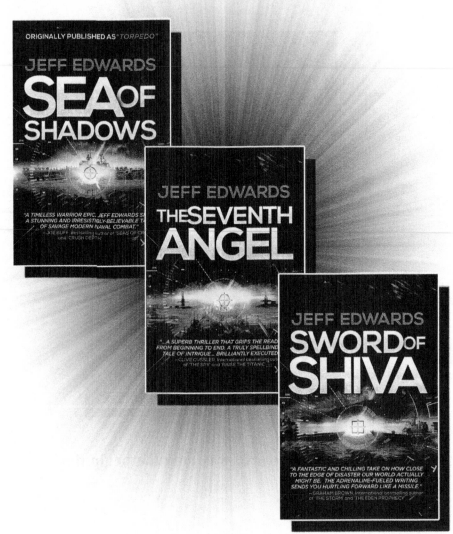

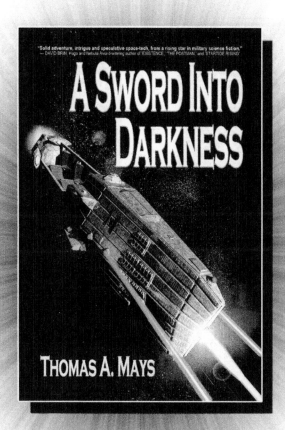

WHITE-HOT SUBMARINE WARFARE
BY
JOHN R. MONTEITH

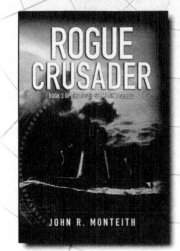

www.braveshipbooks.com

HIGH OCTANE AERIAL COMBAT

KEVIN MILLER

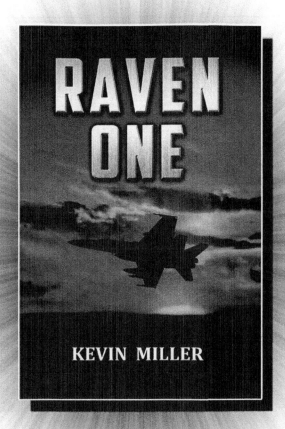

Unarmed over hostile territory...

www.braveshipbooks.com

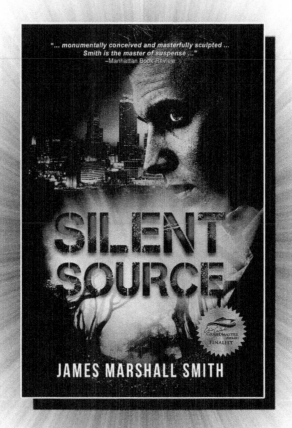